Cold Rain

Also by Craig Smith:

The Whisper of Leaves
The Painted Messiah
The Blood Lance

Cold Rain

CRAIG SMITH

MYRMIDON

Myrmidon Books Ltd
Rotterdam House
116 Quayside
Newcastle upon Tyne
NE1 3DY

www.myrmidonbooks.com

Published by Myrmidon 2010

A catalogue record for this book is available
from the British Library.

ISBN: 978-1-905802-34-0

Typeset in Sabon by Ellipsis Books Limited, Glasgow

Printed and bound in the UK by
CPI Cox & Wyman, Reading, RG1 8EX

1 3 5 7 9 10 8 6 4 2

For Martha, Shirley, Douglas and Maria
no rain too cold...

Also by Craig Smith:

The Whisper of Leaves
The Painted Messiah
The Blood Lance

Cold Rain

Cautiously, the way of a dog meeting another at the junkyard social, 'A novelist?'

'Prof,' I said. 'Writing's an avocation.'

Like the holy of holies, Walt added, 'Published.'

A prof with a published novel that Buddy Elder didn't know? He couldn't imagine it. I could see the calculations sparking in his bloodshot eyes. Maybe I was something from Mathematics or one of the hard sciences writing sci-fi with my left hand or a guy from the school of business taking a turn as Sam Spade. Probably getting rich to boot. People in English hate writers who make money.

'What department are you in?'

'English,' I answered.

'Here?' He was baffled, certain I was lying. I actually lie quite a bit, if only to keep my hand in, but as it happened this was one of those rare moments when truth was exquisitely more rewarding.

I nodded and got a don't-mess-with-me look with just a bit of a grin to cut the edge. Buddy Elder was in English. He had been in English since August. What was I trying to pull? He knew all the writers in the English department. He gave a quick glance in Walt Beery's direction, still green enough to be uncertain of his ground.

'I'm David Albo,' I said. 'I've been on leave this year.'

Buddy Elder threw his head back like a man laughing, but all he did was smile. 'I've got you for Advanced Fiction Writing next fall,' he said.

'Can't wait,' I said with an icy smile I'm sure he had no trouble reading.

I LEFT SHORTLY AFTER THAT. I even got a sweet smile from the dancer with no name. Now that I held Buddy's fate in my hands, I was worth that much. Come autumn I expected I might even get offered a lap dance or two, if she was still in play.

I bought them a round as I was heading out. It is the only way to leave folks without getting the worst of your stories told right off. Outside, the daylight was something of a surprise, as was my sobriety. A good feeling, I decided. Clean. Like being fully alive for the first time in years.

I was not to see either Walt Beery or Buddy Elder again for several months. I did hear a few stories about Walt though. I had my sources. Seems he had begun telling some tasteless homosexual monkey jokes at the faculty club. There was talk of it being the last straw, but talk was all it would ever be. Walt Beery had a good lawyer and pockets deep enough to pay the fees.

I don't recall so much as a fleeting thought about Buddy Elder or his girlfriend. Buddy belonged to that other world I had inhabited in that other lifetime. While my sabbatical continued I wrote each morning and spent my afternoons at Molly's side turning the last rooms of an early nineteenth century plantation-style mansion into a showpiece. I fed and groomed my stepdaughter's two racehorses. I baled hay twice and once a week or so mucked stalls solo like an old hand. I mowed the pasture a few times with a new John Deere tractor. I indulged in a midnight swim with Molly on one occasion with nothing but a full moon covering us, and even told a ghost story to Lucy and a gaggle of her girlfriends who were 'camping out' on our third floor one night in July. Well advanced into adolescence, they had imagined they were far too grown-up to get spooked by anything short of Stephen King, but I told the story as true with the indifference of a man relating an article from the newspaper. In the dark, far from the sounds they knew, I rose up devils those girls had never quite dreamed of. All in good fun, of course.

Lucy told me later they said I was cool, for an old man. I turned thirty-seven that summer, older than Dante when he toured Hell, but only by a couple of years.

Chapter 2

WHEN I WAS STILL A YOUNG MAN an old dog in the academy, dead now, told me the secret to life. No one, he said, forgets caviar. Rise early, work hard, speak no evil, use tax shelters: everyone's got an angle. But caviar made an impression on me. Maybe it's because professors are so long on dignity and so damn short on cash, but serving caviar at parties is worth at least a dozen publications on one's *curriculum vitae*.

That fall I was eligible for promotion. The last hurdle of an academic's career: full professor. I was eight years in the business. Young for the honour, to be sure, but I had been quietly ambitious for a while and had lately come to be well-positioned to get the faculty's nod. Not that the vote was a sure thing. Not for anyone, really. Especially not for one of the younger associates. As a matter of policy, my department rather enjoyed turning people down. The last seven who asked, to be precise. I had tenure of course and was settled comfortably into the broad sea of middle management, which at a university is the rank of associate professor. There were a couple of magazine hits I could drop into a conversation when it was necessary to impress the occasional visiting dignitary in the arts and now a novel. Born in the cold of winter and praised by friends coast-to-coast, *Jinx* wasn't climbing the charts, but it was exactly what I needed for the vote of my peers.

Assuming they didn't forget me.

Molly and I set the party for the first weekend before classes began that fall. I kept the list diverse enough that it didn't look like a departmental meeting of the Olympians, but I made sure everyone with the power of a vote got a written *and* personal invitation. No talk, either, of my promotion. I hadn't even applied for it, had carefully avoided even the most casual discussion of my prospects. That would come later, a few weeks before the actual application, several months after the party. This was just a get-together, black tie optional, to let people know I was glad to be back after a year and two summers of blessed solitude.

The final guest list ran to about eighty people. We started with a nice mix of gypsy scholars and old-line academic aristocrats from across campus, then salted with a smattering of university bureaucrats and our latest batch of teaching assistants, including Buddy Elder. We threw the west pasture open for parking, and set up a keg of beer outside. There were more refined choices within, including copious offerings of champagne and caviar.

After the thing was under way and politics took a backseat to just enjoying myself, I was standing in a circle of young men in the main hall at the bottom of our grand stairway. I was regaling them with one of the anecdotes that had not made the final cut of *Jinx*, when I noticed every eye shift toward the stairs. That could mean only one thing, and being a male, I had to turn and look too. Coming down the polished walnut staircase was the most beautiful woman at the party, my wife Molly. She was not an especially tall woman, but she seemed so because of the confident way she carried herself. Her long hair was the colour of dark honey. Her skin was ruddy from long hours of working in the sun. Her shoulders were high and beautifully developed. As she came off the last step, Molly's blue eyes found me, and she cocked her finger playfully with a come-hither beckoning. I made my excuses affably, my story unfinished, and followed her toward our kitchen, marvelling at how her waist pinched down like a bowtie.

'I need a hand in the pantry, David,' Molly announced in a stage whisper. It was an old game we liked to play at other people's parties, but I was up for it at our own.

We entered a large well-stocked pantry, and Molly shut the door behind us at once. Kissing me seriously, she put my hand under the hem of her black sequined gown, apparently just where she needed it. 'You think anyone would notice if we just disappeared for half-an-hour?'

'Molly,' I said biting her lip playfully, 'everyone notices when a beautiful woman disappears.'

She stroked me mischievously, knowing I would be trapped in the pantry until I calmed down. 'Dean Lintz said he's heard you're a wonderful teacher, David.'

I moved her hand away but could not resist kissing her neck. 'That's shop talk for a lack of scholarship.'

'Morgan read your book.'

Morgan was the vice president for academic affairs. He had a habit of never quite looking my way even if we were the only two people in a room. 'Unbelievable,' I said. 'I didn't know he could read.'

'Everyone likes the house.' Molly slipped her fingers under my cummerbund.

'The house is beautiful. You're a genius with wood.' I kissed her again and, soft touch that I am, let her have her way with me. 'I especially like the pantry.'

When she had me completely excited, she pulled away and began adjusting her dress. 'I think we should put a daybed in here though… for parties.'

'A daybed would be good,' I said, struggling vainly to get things put back in order.

'Randy Winston told me when I got tired of you he'd love to show me what I'm missing.'

I laughed. 'What does he think you're missing?'

'You want me to ask him?'

'Maybe I will.'

'Get another case of champagne, David. We have to take something out.'

'Afraid people will think we're in love?'

'David, we've been married for twelve years. If we're in here fooling around after all that time, the natural assumption is we've been having problems.'

'At the moment I've got a terrible problem.'

She smiled at her handiwork. 'What are we going to do about it?'

'Tonight we're going to finish what we started. For now this ought to do it.' I picked up one of the boxes of champagne and held it before me.

On tiptoes, Molly looked over. 'I don't think so.'

'Tell me something awful.'

'Did I ever tell you about the drunken carpenter who leaned a little too far over his table saw?'

'Awful enough,' I winced. 'You know I hate table saws!'

Molly laughed and opened the door, telling me in a voice loud enough for everyone in the kitchen to hear, 'That should do it for a while.'

I lugged the champagne to a barrel of ice water on our back porch and with the help of one of our servers began slipping new bottles underneath the cold ones. As I was finishing up, Walt Beery came through the back door. Walt wore a smoking jacket and cummer-bund as I had anticipated. To my astonishment he was sober.

'Molly,' he said, giving her a hug, then holding both her hands, 'You look great! If this bum ever forgets how lucky he is—'

'You'll be the first, Walt,' Molly answered, smiling and running her fingers over the ruffles of his shirt. To me and not nearly as playful about it, she added, '...but definitely not the last.'

She went on, leaving us alone. 'That's my wife,' I told Walt. 'Pull your tongue in.'

He turned to me with all the sentiment of a great drunk, 'You *are* a lucky bastard. You know that?'

'I know it,' I answered.

'Do you?' A bit too much passion in this.

'I know it,' I said cautiously.

Walt's eyes tightened now, and something went slack in him. 'You heard about Barbara and me, I guess?'

'Heard what?'

'She kicked me out, David.'

I groaned, struggling for some kind of appropriate answer. Walt's fantasy of freedom had come at last, and I could see it terrified him.

'I'm too old to start over,' he muttered.

'You need a drink.' I said. 'A few beers and things will look better. The TAs are going to show up pretty soon and put a little life in this funeral!'

17

'I'm off the booze.'

'How long?'

'Three days,' he said. 'Three *long* days.' His eyes watered suddenly, so that I had to turn to avoid seeing his tears. 'I had the shakes so bad this morning I almost ...well, you know how it is.'

I didn't, but I nodded. 'Are you doing this on your own?' I asked.

'I can beat it. I have to. I promised myself a week. I make it a week and I go talk to Barbara. Tell her what I'm doing. See if we can get a fresh start.'

'Sounds like it might work.'

'A week doesn't sound like much, does it?'

I shook my head.

'It's like crawling on broken glass. That's the first day. It gets worse after that.'

'It gets better eventually,' I said. 'It gets good, if you want to know the truth.'

'When?'

I thought about one more lie since I was passing them out so glibly, but I didn't have the heart. I simply excused myself.

ACADEMIC PARTIES HAVE A PACE one can only begin to understand after a dozen or so of them. Early there is always a bit of formality. Rank still matters. Masks still fit snugly. Then come the first bits of laughter, nothing too raucous, of course, more like

Jane Austen humour. At this point, the old guard wades in with stories from the Grand Old Days, well-worn lamentations for those of us who were not around when scholarship mattered! Then the associates and assistants take over. A careful crew, these. Paranoia as lifestyle, but with enough booze even the bureaucrats dance. A frosted look, a piece of crass laughter, a slipped confession. The physicist talking lit, the historian discussing the theory of point spreads. Circles and cliques breaking apart, new friendships tested, and finally the inevitable quarrel.

At our party it was the literary merit of the Brownings. Only an English prof could have seen this one coming. Only Walt Beery had the breadth of knowledge to break it apart before someone took a swing. Five minutes later both profs were screaming at Walt. Blessed are the peacemakers.

Late at any such party there is usually a spouse scurrying around alone, too embarrassed to ask about the missing partner. For years I had observed such rituals without ever understanding that the abandoned spouse knows everyone is watching. I had always imagined such displays could only take place under the illusion of not being noticed. It had never dawned on me that such people simply couldn't control themselves.

When Molly and Buddy Elder started talking I didn't like it. I didn't like the look in her eyes, and I definitely didn't like the lazy way he looked at her. When they disappeared, I lost all sense of proportion and with it the last shred of decorum. Even while I scurried around, I had a new appreciation for such dramas, especially the attendant humiliation that comes with it. I knew people were watching me. I knew at least some of them could tell me exactly where my wife had gone and with whom, but I had to walk around like I had misplaced my glass. People pretended not to notice me. I kept a smile pasted to my face. Where did I put that glass anyway? I tried not to imagine the nudges they were giving one another the minute I was into the next room. It wasn't possible. I knew what they were saying. David's turn.

I found Molly at the barn after about ten minutes of running the gauntlet. She was standing a few feet from Buddy Elder in a pale light before one of the horse stalls. From outside the barn it wasn't possible to see them, but once I stepped in, I could stand in a shadow and watch everything. At first it was just talk, then I saw him stepping toward her. I thought he was about to touch her, a finger to her chin maybe, possibly a kiss. Would she let him? I didn't know, and I didn't get to find out because he didn't do what I expected. He put both hands against the stall and looked in through the bars at Jezebel, my stepdaughter's seven-year-old quarter horse mare. A flutter of jealousy and rage shot into my chest feeling like a two-penny nail driven down with a single blow. I thought about waiting them out to see what they were going to do next. It even dawned on me that I should leave, though I dismissed the idea as absurd. I ended up walking all the way into the barn like a man long familiar with a disappearing wife.

'She's not for sale,' I said, and pointed at Lucy's mare.

Buddy gave me a lazy smile that I found a bit arrogant under the circumstances. 'And I was just getting ready to make an offer.'

Molly gave me a look I didn't like, then pushed past me, brushing my shoulder as she went. 'I'd better get back,' she announced quietly. Then to Buddy, 'If you want to come out for a ride sometime, just let me know. I'd love to show you the farm.'

'I might,' he said, smiling. 'If you're sure it wouldn't be a problem.' He glanced in my direction – the problem.

Molly gave me a cool appraisal. 'No problem at all.' No problem she couldn't handle, she meant.

'YOU MIND ME ASKING YOU a personal question, Dave?' Buddy asked, when we were alone.

I minded, but I was also curious. 'What's that?'

'How did you get this place on a teacher's salary?'

I laughed. 'I thought you were going to ask me if I'm a jealous man.'

Buddy and I had walked out of the barn. He leaned

against the grey boards of our old barn, so he was looking up the hill in the direction of our house, the direction Molly had taken. 'I think I know the answer to that.'

'My father was a car salesman,' I said, stooping down and picking up some pebbles. 'The guy they warn you about. Tubs could sell space heaters in hell. Probably is, come to think of it. The old bastard could pitch any car he had to, but he'd only ride home in a Ford. *Any* Ford. A matter of principle, though what exactly the principle was, I never quite understood. Anyway, back in the late seventies Chrysler was on the verge of bankruptcy. The price of the stock was around three dollars and dropping by the hour. Naturally, everyone at the car lot had an opinion. Tubs said he was looking for a comeback. He said the government wouldn't let Chrysler sink. Now you have to understand, he was standing around a bunch of car salespeople who knew his prejudices and back in those days nobody but Lee Iacocca liked a Chrysler, so when he said that, they all laughed. I owe this farm to their laughter, Buddy.' I tossed a few pebbles toward our kennel, emptied out for the occasion of the party, and let Buddy wait for my explanation.

'You see, Tubs could be wrong about a thing. Get him off the car lot, he was as wrong about things as the next man, but one thing Tubs could not abide was another salesperson laughing at him. The minute they did he walked into his office and called his broker and bought five thousand shares. In those days that was about exactly what a new luxury Chrysler would cost, and that's what he said when he came back out, "I just bought my first Chrysler, gentlemen, but thank the good Lord I don't ever have to drive it!"

'This wasn't entirely out of character, you understand. My old man was a plunger, a gambler. Give him a horse, a deck of cards, the right kind of automobile, and Tubs could drop serious money if the inspiration hit him. And over the years, the inspiration hit him fairly regularly. The truth is Tubs lost a lot more than he won. Usually when he made the right decision he would go too light or bail out too early. Good times never ran a full course at our house, let me tell you. The man could screw up the Second Coming, but his one great move after buying Chrysler's stock was to die.' Buddy blinked in surprise and I knew I had him.

'The first few times the stock split even a smart trader would have considered locking in his gains, but my mother didn't know about such things. In fact, she was actually a little nervous about Chrysler sending her the dividend checks. She knew Tubs couldn't stand Chrysler, so the only thing she could figure was they were sending money to the wrong Albo.

'My brothers had no idea any of this was going on. Me? I was just a kid. Thirty years ago I barely knew the difference between a Ford and a Chrysler. She splurged a little on clothes and jewellery, bought a new car now and then, took a trip every year. Got a new house. We figured the old bastard had a ton of life insurance because Mom sure wasn't telling anyone where the money came from. This went on for years, and then one day she asked my oldest brother what was going to happen to Chrysler now that it had been sold to Mercedes. My brother wanted to know why she was worried about something like that.'

I handed Buddy a smile that told him we were at the end of the story. 'She told him how many shares she had of it, and the next day we had a family meeting.'

'You got the farm with your share of the stock?'

'The farm, this quarter horse, that paint gelding, the restoration on the house, Molly's new Ford truck, my stepdaughter's Toyota Highlander, her choice of colleges …the mother lode, Buddy.'

Buddy handed me back a grudging smile. 'Son of a bitch.'

I gave my lottery-winner shrug. 'We were lucky.'

'You should have put that in *Jinx*!'

'You read *Jinx*, did you?'

'I read it this summer. To tell you the truth, the minute I finished it, I wanted to go out and sell cars. Did your dad have names for every one of his closes, like *Jinx*?'

A close is the last step of the sale. It's cash on the

table, a signature on the line. Feast or famine for the salesperson. Tubs had pet names for every close he used: Forbidden Fruit, Love or Money, Take my Advice (because no one ever does), The Bible Close, The Colombo Close. Tubs had a hundred of them. As many as he had faces.

'He did,' I told Buddy. 'At least that's what they tell me. He died before I ever got to work with him.'

'He carry a Bible in his hip pocket like *Jinx*?'

'Son of a bitch wouldn't walk on the lot without it! He might not use it for a week or two, but then he'd meet the right folks and at just the opportune moment Tubs would pull it out like a gun and tell his customers, 'Everyone else carries a price book, but I carry *this* so I won't be tempted to lie!'

Buddy grinned at me sceptically. 'People didn't see through that?'

Buddy Elder had read my book, but he had missed its essence. 'Tubs meant it. That's why it worked. Ever hear of a car salesman that wouldn't tell a lie? That was Tubs. The George Washington of the Wastelands. He could take all your money but he would never tell a lie while he was doing it. That was Tubs: the honest thief – a hell of a lousy epitaph, if you think about it.'

Buddy grew thoughtful. 'I didn't get that from the book.'

'That's good, because I didn't put it in.'

'Maybe you should have. If that's the truth.'

'I wrote another book about that. It's up in a box in my closet.'

Buddy grinned, getting the point. 'The one that's true?'

'Truth,' I answered, 'is a highly overrated virtue.'

Buddy Elder smiled at me as if he had found a kindred soul. 'You think?'

'We better get back to the party,' I said. 'And Buddy, if you're thinking about coming out for a ride some-time… think again. It could be a real problem between you and me.'

'I knew that, Dave.'

I gave him a wink and patted him on the shoulder. 'Just so we understand one another.'

'DID YOU MAKE AN ASS OUT OF yourself?'

Molly and I were standing in the pasture watching Dean Lintz wipe out a stretch of white board fence as he crashed through a shallow ditch. The party was still going, but it was winding down now. Only a few more drunken administrators to kick out and we were home free.

'Nothing too serious,' I answered. 'Did Buddy make a pass?'

She had a private smile. 'Not that you'd notice.'

'I was afraid of that.'

'Where did they find him, anyway?'

I shook my head. 'I have no idea.'

'You ought to write whoever sent him and ask for a dozen more. He's... genuine.'

'What did you two talk about... so intently?'

'Horses... Lucy... restoring old houses. He's run some rooftops. Did you know that?'

'Barb Beery kicked Walt out,' I answered. I was tired of the subject of Buddy Elder, irritated at Molly's unrepentant affection for him.

Molly's face twitched. 'I heard. Quite a few times, actually.'

'You hear why?'

'Fooling around. Last straw. A stripper or something. Very... *Walt*, if you know what I mean?'

'He tells me he quit drinking three days ago. Wants to go talk to her after a week and show her he can change.'

'He can change brands, but that's about all.'

I shook my head, marshalling a defence for my hapless friend. 'He seemed pretty dedicated to the idea.'

'David, a half hour ago I saw him out in the pasture with Randy Winston drinking vodka straight out of the bottle.'

'That's pathetic.'

'I'd say it's desperate. *Pathetic* is tiptoeing to the barn and spying on your wife.'

Chapter 3

LUCY AND HER FRIEND KATHY Jones showed up in Kathy's red Mustang convertible late that evening. The top was down, and Lucy looked a good deal older than seventeen. It had been a good summer for her. She had worked with Molly and me finishing up the house, and had got serious about her competition in barrel racing, sometimes pulling Jezebel to two or three races a week. In the course of the summer she had turned a trim, athletic body into hard ropey muscle. About all that was left of her adolescence was a ponytail. Physically, Lucy had her mother's shoulders and legs and long sinewy back, but her face was round and sweetly intense, as only seventeen can be. Most people said otherwise. They said Lucy looked just like her mother, but it wasn't so. Lucy had a beauty all her own. They looked alike because they shared the same mannerisms, the same stubbornness, the same passions. Lucy needed another decade or so before she could claim the kind of grace and confidence and beauty her mother possessed.

I cannot say I actually looked for Buddy Elder or consciously thought about him when Lucy showed up. I only know he was there, standing in the shadows of the trees that surrounded our house.

'How was the party?' Lucy called out to us.

Molly said it was still going on.

'Any food left?'

'Plenty of caviar,' I told her, very proud of myself for not skimping on the essentials.

Lucy's pretty face screwed up into pure teen. 'Anything good?'

I let her mother answer this and looked back in Buddy's direction, but he was already gone.

Molly and I caught Kathy Jones before she could drive out of the circle and down the hill. I leaned against the door at about eye-level with the girl. Kathy was a new friend and not our favourite. She was pretty and popular and perfectly spoiled. She had dark hair in contrast to Lucy's pale blonde locks, and she was built solidly with round cheeks and round buttocks and firm, thick thighs. She would be a senior in a week or so, like Lucy, but I guessed she was probably three years ahead by experience. That summer Kathy had been among the girls I had terrified with my casual narrative of a perfectly normal middle-aged man who had lived here when the place was cut apart into apartments and who, one night, had killed every soul in the house with an axe. It was a complete fiction, of course, but ever since then Kathy had trouble looking at me without wondering if I might be the next to come under the spell of the old house.

That wasn't the reason for her nervousness tonight, however. Have a nice time? I asked her. Okay. Kathy looked like she wanted to pop the clutch. Find any parties as nice as this one? A few. Perfect evening for a drive with the top down, wasn't it? It was okay.

I thanked her for bringing Lucy home safely and asked how her parents were doing. They were fine. Was she looking forward to school? Not really. Kathy made short work of me, but Molly was a different story. Molly had learned her interrogation technique from the master, her mother Olga McBride. She wanted to know what they had done and *nothing* didn't cut it. Every answer got a lawyerly follow up, all with a smile of course, leaning in close and friendly, just as I had done it.

When Kathy drove off, I looked at Molly and we both said at the same time, 'Grass.'

'YOU SAY SOMETHING,' Molly told me that night as we lay together in bed. We had finished the business we started in the pantry, had worn ourselves out in our happiness, but were still wide awake. 'She won't listen to me about anything,' Molly explained.

'I'll say something,' I answered, 'but I doubt it will do any good.'

'What are you going to tell her? You can't preach. She knows we've both done it.'

'I'll think of something.'

The next afternoon, long before the cleanup was finished, I suggested to Lucy that we take a ride. This was something we usually did once or twice a month, so it was nothing out of the ordinary, and at just that point it made a pleasant break from the work at hand. Like her mother, I had found Lucy's adolescence difficult to handle. Unlike her mother I hadn't resorted to confrontation, interrogation, mental torture techniques or general prohibitions. I could defend myself by claiming the delicate position of a stepfather's status, but the truth was I had grown up under the thumb of a manipulative sweet-talker. Tubs could tell me how good it felt to punch someone's face in, then describe an even finer pleasure: breaking a man's spirit with my words. That was how he handled my first fistfight, age six. When I got a speeding ticket at the age of sixteen there was a story about a kid my age in a wheelchair because he liked to run his cars a little fast. Then, the night I lost my virginity, as if he knew exactly where I had been and with whom, I got the story of a soldier who wasn't careful where he put it and turned up with what could only be described as a welter of cauliflower-like boils on the tip of his manhood.

I liked Molly's parenting far better. It gave a kid a chance. But we are products of others. I could not help myself. I told Lucy stories, and never a better time or place than on one of our rides.

When Lucy met her paternal grandparents for the first time she was six years old. She had known me for about a year, but I wasn't real important, only her mother's new husband. Her father, whom she had never even seen in a photograph, was the centre of her world. So when her grandparents began showing her all kinds of pictures of their son riding all kinds of horses, everything from the childhood pony to the summer of his rodeo, it made a powerful impression. They had sold off their horses after Luke's death, but the next time Molly and I took Lucy out to their place Grandpa Luke had bought a little pony for Lucy to ride whenever she visited. After that, there was no end to it. Lucy turned horse-crazy. We fought it as long as we could but ended up getting her lessons at a local stable. When Lucy turned ten, Molly and I bought her a ten-year-old paint gelding named Ahab. She had been riding seriously for over three years by then and showed no sign of losing interest.

We had shopped for a small animal, but all three of us fell in love with Ahab the moment we saw him. He was enormous, standing over sixteen hands, black mostly but with white lightning streaks on each flank and a few broad splotches of white running up from his belly. He had a white blaze down his long, handsome Roman nose and three high white socks. And Ahab could run. He had an impressive list of first place victories in barrel racing to prove it, so, despite everything, he became Lucy's first horse. Four years later, we bought Jezebel, a gorgeous bay quarter horse with good lineage and pure fire for a personality. Jezebel came off a racetrack, where she had finished first whenever she had managed to get out of the gate. For a couple of seasons, Lucy struggled with her new mare. One weekend everything would be fine. The next she might not even take a saddle. I expect a lot of kids would have given up. Hell, I was ready to give up. But not Lucy. Lucy had what she wanted. Now it was time to learn how to handle it. Molly and I ended up driving her and Jezebel to one riding clinic after another. When that failed to turn things around completely we drove up to a professional and boarded Jezebel and Lucy for two months. From dawn until dusk Lucy rode every kind of animal that came through that barn. By the time Lucy returned home, she was a different girl and all the nonsense with Jezebel was history.

The days were long past when I could give advice to my stepdaughter about anything relating to a horse, but horses still remained our hobby, with Ahab having long ago become my horse.

We took the horses through the pasture at a gallop and waded through the creek five minutes later. From there we raced over a couple wooded hills before coming to the back gate at what used to be an orchard. Our property extended well beyond this gate, another eighty acres in all, but these fields we rented to a farmer who paid us a share of the crop.

At the gate Lucy moved Jezebel around and opened it while she was still in the saddle. This involved moving Jezebel sideways, having her turn from one side of the gate to the other, and then dance sideways again. Ahab was also trained to do this, but the one time I had tried it I embarrassed him so much that afterwards I either let Lucy open the gates or I dismounted and walked through.

Beyond the pasture, we followed the grassy lane that circled a field of corn. We were still a long way from any road, farther still from other houses. We had a small wood giving us some late afternoon shade. There was just enough breeze to keep us cool. It seemed like the perfect time to talk about marijuana, so I gave a whoop in the direction of the blue sky. Jezebel skittered like a race was about to start. Ahab lugged it along like an old hand. Touch his sides, he could still go. Otherwise, he just let folks make noise if that's what they wanted.

'It's good to be sober!' I shouted.

The hard clay at our feet seemed suddenly very interesting to Lucy. 'Is it hard? Quitting?' She met my gaze at the end of her question, curious, nothing more.

I had been sober two years, just before I started writing *Jinx*. I had quit for no other reason than I really liked to drink and I wanted to prove to myself I still had control of my choices, and because Jinx, a stand-in for my old man, didn't drink. Once I was off the stuff a week, I felt ten years younger. So I stayed off. I called it my one-step program, and counted myself lucky I didn't carry demons on my back like most of the heavy drinkers I knew.

'Sometimes,' I said. 'The payback comes when I can look at you and your mother and I don't have to feel I've let you down. Then it's not hard at all.'

'You've never let me down, Dave.'

I could think of a few times when I had sent her out to feed the dogs and horses because I was still in town wrapped up in some important barroom talk, but instead of recounting my own failings, I started in on Walt Beery, our family's poster child for the evils of drink. 'Three days,' I said, 'and to save his life he couldn't make it four.' That was it. That was my talk on addictions great and small. Tubs would have mentioned his friend, poor soul, now locked up in an asylum because of that one joint laced with PCP, but I wasn't the slimiest parent to have walked the earth, so I kept it simple and let Lucy work out the implications on her own. All things considered, I was fairly satisfied with myself, but Molly said later it was lame.

I expect it was, but I doubt anyone could have turned

Lucy from the course she had chosen for herself that fall. She was growing up. She was suddenly something more than cute. She was, without quite comprehending it, a force of nature. Words can do nothing against that.

TWO DAYS LATER MY sabbatical came to its inevitable and tragic end, and I was sitting in a faculty meeting, the first I had attended in over fifteen months. There were new faces and new procedures in place, but it felt like the same-old-same-old to me. A couple of days after that I met a new generation of students ready for the agony I was paid to deliver. The trouble was I wasn't ready.

I had always liked going back to school in the fall, both as a student and as a prof. This time I had trouble adjusting. It had been too long: two summers and one academic year felt like a lifetime. I had developed new routines. I had gotten used to solitude. I liked staying in the country far away from people, especially academics. I had grown accustomed to silence and working the day through without a single crisis. If I wanted to scream profanities the horses never blushed. The dogs wouldn't dream of turning me in for a pat on the butt or a careless remark. Suddenly, all that was gone. Students were there with their expectations. Colleagues needed a shoulder to cry on. People crowded into my life waiting for me to say something glib or intelligent or politically astute, and I discovered to my dismay I didn't want it anymore.

My teaching, like my office desk, had a patina of dust covering it, as well. It would eventually get cleaned up and straightened out, the teaching and my desk, but not without effort and time. By the end of the first week, things were still not right, and I found I was ready for a drink. As I had no one to sponsor me, the only cure was a long talk with Walt Beery. Living the single life now, Walt's biorhythms had begun a subtle transformation. At eleven-thirty he was still suffering from the night before and could not seriously think about a drink for another two or three hours. That was fine. We decided to have an early lunch at the Student Union.

I asked Walt on the way over if he was still off the booze. I could smell the answer coming out of his pores, but I thought things would go better between us if we got the confession out of the way early.

Walt gave a weary sigh, admitting his failure in a neat aphorism: 'I'm not cut out for sobriety, David.'

Over a wilted salad and stale coffee, I said to him, 'Have you talked to Barbara?'

'She called me this morning.' His eyes twinkled at the memory but faded at once, as close to shame as the practising alcoholic gets. 'I was hung over like a son of a bitch, and she knew it.'

I laughed politely. Wives had certain powers denied

other mortals, I told him. Then, 'I take it you've got a place to stay?'

He shrugged, not exactly happy. 'Got a one bedroom at the Greenbrier.' I nodded, familiar with the place. It was expensive, so there would be no students around. That was good. Walt could screw-up all he wanted around young professional women. And he would, I knew that. Living too close to the co-eds, though, was bound to bring on early retirement.

'Have you seen Buddy?'

This was not an especially pleasant topic for Walt, and his eyes avoided mine. His shoulders slumped a bit. 'Not too much. I don't think he was real happy about what happened with his girlfriend.'

'The stripper?' Walt nodded sorrowfully. 'You were messing around with her?' Walt nodded a bit less sorrowfully at this. In fact, I thought I detected a faint, proud smile, a story he meant to take to the old folks' home. 'Well,' I said, 'have you seen *her*?'

A watery smile, 'Onstage a few times.'

'What happened anyway?'

Walt shook his head. 'It was just one of those afternoons. Oh! Before I forget. Barbara wanted me to ask you a favour.'

Barbara and I had never been close. That came with the territory, I suppose. You turn up in enough conversations involving lost afternoons that somehow drift into the early morning hours, and wives have a tendency to make rather comprehensive judgements. 'A favour from me?'

'Roger has written a book. Well, a novel. She wants you to read it, and see if it's any good. And maybe talk to him about it.' As he said this, Walt kept his eyes focused on the table. He knew what he was asking.

Roger was twenty-five, their only son. When I first met him Roger was a senior in high school with applications out to all the best schools in the country. He ended up turning everyone down, claiming he didn't need to be 'institutionalized.' According to Walt and Barbara there was no reason for Roger's strange and unexpected decision, but it did not take me long to realize Roger Beery had been slowing down and pulling back since the beginning of adolescence. The wonder of the science fair, who was taking Latin and Greek at the university as well as a couple of computer programming courses before his voice changed, had found drugs. Very serious drugs, actually, though nobody had noticed, at least nobody had told Walt and Barbara, because Roger comatose was still among the school's best and brightest.

Since his dropout there had been reports of hopeful developments. Roger had decided to join the military. Roger got a decent job at a local factory. Roger had been hired by a local company to update their computer systems. The follow up to whatever the good news never came. Something always got between Roger and success. I had lost track of Roger a couple of years ago because Walt just stopped talking about him. Then one day I saw him working at a downtown parking lot. He pretended not to know me, and that was the end of it. Until now.

'What does Roger want?' I asked.

Walt took a sip of coffee and looked away. 'I don't know, David. We don't talk.'

I thought about complaining. I had kids come to me all the time who wanted me to read something. Some of them were in my classes, just not my creative writing classes. Some of the kids, the ones I didn't know, would circle me in the halls like wolves edging closer to the campfire until they worked up their courage. The poetry, I could always shuffle off to one of our resident poets. Fiction was not so easy, but I usually steered the younger writers to my introductory course in creative writing. On those few occasions when I had been persuaded for one reason or another to read something outside of the classroom I always regretted it. The issue of quality aside, no one wants to hear criticism. People who have not submitted themselves to the rigors of peer criticism, the kind that occurs in a writing workshop, are especially sensitive to it. I did not want to read Roger Beery's novel because I knew he wouldn't be any different. He wanted me to love his story, and nothing else would do, but refusing Walt at this point in his life was difficult. The kid was a genius. How bad could it be?

'Anytime,' I said. 'Just drop it off. I'll take a look at it and give Roger an honest opinion.'

Walt looked relieved. 'I hate to do this to you, David.'

But he was doing it, and that said it all.

A bit uneasy at having passed his family problems into my court, Walt reverted to form. He started talking about Randy Winston, whom he had seen 'slinking' around the TA offices checking out 'the new talent.' This of course meant that Walt had been slinking there as well, but I let that point pass. 'New talent?' I asked.

Walt cupped his hands in front of his chest. '*Talent*!'

I shook my head. 'I don't know you.'

Walt laughed. 'You can't say tits anymore, David, so we call it talent!'

'I suppose bodacious ta-tas is still frowned upon by the powers that be?' Walt had picked up this unfortunate expression a few years ago. For a season it was all he talked about. It was my understanding he had been investigated for using the word in the classroom, but I could be wrong about that. The investigation I'm recalling might have been the joke about the perfect girl. Between rumours and the actual investigations launched against him no one could keep track of Walt Beery's troubles, and I had long ago quit asking for the particulars.

I recall, as I look back on that afternoon, that after I spoke I happened to look around. It was something I usually did before I started talking to Walt, but I was out of practice. One table away, Norma Olson, Jane Trimble, and Marlene Moss were sitting in rigid silence. The mention of bodacious ta-tas will do that, I'm told.

Walt answered me without noticing them or caring that they were there: 'That's real talent, David. You want *real* talent you have to see Johnna Masterson. Johnna's got more talent than I've got hands!' Walt held up both hands for me to consider the proportions.

'She's in my creative writing class,' I answered sullenly, hoping he would see that he was being monitored.

'Winston dated her last year. Well, I guess it's more like he cornered her at a party. All natural is the report.'

I glanced at the women again. They maintained a petrified silence.

'Winston made a pass at Molly at the party,' I said, hoping to divert Walt from any further discussion of talent by the handful.

'Randy's a son of a bitch.'

'Of course, so did you and Buddy Elder, and probably half a dozen other men I don't even know about.'

Walt's grin flickered. 'We're all sons of bitches, David.'

Chapter 4

AS WE HEADED BACK to our respective offices, Walt started laughing. I looked around to make sure no one was within earshot and asked what was so funny. 'Randy Winston was telling me you and Molly bought the farm with Chrysler stock your old man got in the late seventies.'

I smiled with supreme satisfaction. 'I wonder where he heard that.'

'He said Buddy Elder got it straight from you!'

'I knew a great liar once,' I said. 'I sold cars with him for a couple summers. Larry the Liar. I don't think I ever even knew his last name. I remember one time seeing Larry standing by this big-chested Baptist girl at the back bumper of a two-year-old LeSabre. Larry was slinging his arms around and dancing a little, and she had her arms locked around herself, shaking her head at everything Larry told her. Tubs was managing the floor that afternoon and walked over to me and said, "Twenty bucks if you get that lady on a demo drive." Me? I could get her in the car. I could get the devil himself on a demo drive, but I sure didn't think she was going to buy it! But twenty bucks is twenty bucks, so I walked out, started the car, pulled it back and opened the passenger door.'

'That easy?' Walt asked me dubiously.

'For a demo drive, you don't ask. You pull the car out and open the door. As that particular technique didn't involve lying, Larry wasn't very good at it. Now the minute that Baptist girl and her family got into the car, I stepped out and let Larry drive them off. Larry did great demo drives. Tubs had the twenty in hand for me when I got back to the showroom.

'About fifteen minutes later they all came back laughing. Everybody loved Larry. Tubs told me to manage the deal because they were going to buy, and he was right. The thing went perfectly. Larry shut up like he was trained to do. I got their signature. The easiest sale I ever made. They loved the car. They loved us. Everything was perfect. Then right at the end, the family all tucked away in their brand new two-year-old Buick LeSabre, Larry leaned into the car and said in his squeaky little Southern drawl, 'Oh! And I forgot to tell y'all! When y'all bring this in for service, we got a limousine out back with a driver that wears white gloves, and he'll take you anywhere you want to go.'

Walt laughed. 'White gloves?'

'That's exactly what he said. The lady goes, "Hey, that's wonderful, Larry! Why don't the other dealerships do that?" And Larry goes, "I told you, darling, we're special!"'

'The minute they drove off, I asked Larry why he had to go and tell a lie when it didn't even matter! I said it was just asking for trouble down the line. You know what he said? He said, "A little lie just makes 'em feel good, Davey. That's all!"'

Walt considered this for a moment. 'That's why you lied to Buddy? To make him feel good?'

'Actually,' I said, 'I lied because I don't like the son of a bitch.'

SOMETIME THE FOLLOWING WEEK one of my students in Introduction to Literature came up to me after class. She said she wanted to make an appointment to talk with me. I was heading back to my office just then and said I could talk to her right away, if that was good for her. That would be okay, she said. Did she want to walk along with me or meet over there? She said we might as well walk together.

At that point, I had already asked her name. Denise Conway. So as we started across campus I inquired about where she came from. Different places. Was she a freshman? Did it show? She looked like a senior, I said, but most of the advisers encouraged their people to get the one-hundred level courses out of the way early. That seemed to satisfy her and we walked in a comfortable silence for a while. She was a nice enough young woman, I thought, lacking confidence maybe, and, except for a trim, perky build, not especially interested in her appearance. To be fair, a lot of the kids dressed down for class: raggedy sweatshirts, loose jeans, no makeup, hair unwashed and pulled back sloppily. Nothing unusual in this, nor in the fact that a student wanted to connect with me. It was a large class, and older students sometimes needed to feel as though they had some kind of feel for the prof's humanity, such as it was.

'You don't remember me, do you?'

I had no idea what she was talking about and told her as much.

'We met at Caleb's last spring.'

The moment she said this, I locked in on the brown eyes. Buddy Elder's pale, plain stripper girlfriend who had not said a word. 'You're Buddy Elder's friend,' I said.

'You won't hold that against me, will you?' It was a quick, sweet remark, and I laughed. She did as well, and as she did, I decided I liked her. At least she didn't seem like the anaemic little dolt I had imagined. With a smile, she was actually a good deal prettier than The Slipper's usual offerings. At just this point Norma Olson and Marlene Moss came walking toward us. Norma and Marlene were both graduate students. Both of them had been out to the farm for the party. I greeted them casually and noticed them checking out Denise.

'Usually, when men don't recognize me it's because I have my clothes on.'

Not wanting to touch this one, I said, 'You've changed your hair, haven't you?'

She was in fact a peroxide blonde. 'You know what they say. Blondes have more fun. What do you think? Do you like it?'

'It looks good.'

'Buddy says it makes me look like a total prostitute.' I wasn't sure if this was a compliment in the lexicon of Buddy Elder or not, so I let that go and just looked at her for a moment. 'My tips are up forty percent since I did my hair. Can you believe it?'

'You're still working at The Slipper?'

'I have to pay rent.' I had nothing to say to this. 'I'm dreading the day someone from school walks in.'

'You mean besides Walt?'

She smiled as if I had mentioned somebody's old sheepdog. 'I don't really think of Walty as *university*. He's one of my regulars. With you it would be different. I think if you came in to watch me I'd be embarrassed. You're my professor!'

'I expect we'd both be embarrassed.'

'We're not total nude, but there's not much left to the imagination.'

I started to ruminate on the imagination and decided that wasn't a good idea, so I nodded thoughtfully, praying we got off the subject of nude dancing, or semi-nude dancing, as soon as possible.

In my office, Denise got right down to business. She was having a problem with the sexuality in the material. Since we were reading *Oedipus the King*, I was a bit confused. In fact, I had a difficult time not laughing. 'Sexuality?'

'The incest. I just want to throw up when I think about him married to his mother. Like, they had sex, didn't they? And kids?' I had had complaints before about the *Oedipus*, but never expressed with such conviction. My only answer was to say we were almost done with it.

'But I have to write about it on the test, and I don't think I can. Is there something else I can study?'

I decided not to try selling *Oedipus* to her. The standard line would be to tell her it wasn't really about incest. It was about ignorance, all the things we think we know about our lives but actually just take on faith. I decided instead to extricate myself from the problem with humour. The exam would be fairly general and cover a great deal of material. If the subject of incest bothered her for some reason, she could always choose to write about adultery and murder.

Denise locked on the word adultery. 'I don't need to read some story about adultery! I get that every night at work. Most all of the guys who come into The Slipper are married.'

I wasn't quite sure what I should say, so I tried to relate the material to something in her own experience. I said any number of movies dealt with the same themes. 'You go to movies, don't you?' Sometimes, she said, when she had time. 'But I don't like violent movies.'

'What do you like to see?'

'Love stories.'

'That's it?'

She thought about it. Pretty much.

I made a pitch for a diversity of experience. Besides, it was possible to dislike something and still understand it. She didn't have to like everything she read.

Denise left my office that day promising she would try to be more open-minded. It was a fine moment for me, I decided, teaching open-mindedness to an employee of the sex industry.

Chapter 5

I TOLD MOLLY I was having trouble getting back into the routine. I had been away from it too long, I said. Molly hadn't much sympathy. She wanted to know how many other professions offered a nine-hour work-week, counting an hour as fifty minutes and a year as nine months. Put that way, the whole thing seemed less awful, and I reconciled myself to my fate.

It was not a bad fate actually. I was working on some new short stories, rising before dawn to write for an hour or so. Around six-thirty I would usually feed the dogs and horses, then let them out before I drove to town. In my office by nine o'clock most mornings, I had an enviable schedule, flexible in the extreme. I usually finished up around three o'clock, though on Wednesday nights I regularly taught a night class.

That fall there were no emergencies at school, no grants to write, not even an excessive number of committee meetings. Molly and I owned sixteen properties, a total of forty rental units. At any given time, we might be required to clean a place or give it a facelift. We might shop a new property or unload something for the right price. Once a week or so, I could count on meeting her in town for some kind of business: leaky faucets, replacing furnaces, laying tile, meeting with bankers or our lawyer. That fall was no different. There was always something. Afterwards we would have dinner and once even took in a movie.

Weekends we stayed close to the farm or went with Lucy to her races. In September we began roughing out an apartment for Lucy on the third floor. She was looking at a couple different schools, one in Texas, the other in Oklahoma, both offering rodeo as part of their intercollegiate athletic competition, but there would be summer vacations, and, ultimately, Lucy planned to come back and live on the farm, for a while at least. She was even toying with the idea of going professional once she had completed an undergraduate degree in equestrian studies. The other option, the one I had gently put forward, was an advanced degree in veterinary science. We had a good school only a couple of hours away, so the apartment would get plenty of use for quite a few years.

We were in no hurry though. We wanted Lucy downstairs until she turned eighteen. Besides, we had spent five years getting the house in shape. This was the last step, and we took it almost with a sense of leisure.

Sometimes Molly and I would reflect on the inevitable feeling of getting old, even though she had not turned thirty-four and I was still three winters from the dreaded forty. We made a joke of it, but I think it bothered both of us. Lucy was almost gone. We had raised her. We had built our lives from the ground up, and though we were not in the financial league of Walt and Barbara Beery, we had accomplished everything we had set out to achieve. While that created a sense of satisfaction, we both also felt, I think, a nagging sense of *what now*?

Our success had come with a great deal of planning and careful risk assessment. As with most fortunes, however, the bulk of it arrived unexpectedly. In our case it came as a result of the death of Molly's aunt. After years of refusing Doc's attempts to get her to sell Bernard Place, Doc's sister left her share of the farm not to her brother but to Molly. Doc, realizing Molly would be no more cooperative than his sister, deeded his share of the farm over to Molly. At the time Molly and I were scrambling to acquire property, wrangling contracts from distressed sellers and juggling rental income against a formidable array of mortgage and contract payments. Rather than sell off part of the two hundred acres, tantamount to a mortal sin among the landed gentry, Molly used the property value to leverage more favourable bank loans. With the increased cash flow, she then began to work a series of trade-offs and sales until we found ourselves the proud owners of three small apartment buildings and several very decent old homes in town, Victorian treasures we rented out with extreme discretion.

Over the next five years Molly was certainly active, but her greatest energy she devoted to the old mansion Doc McBride had wanted to raze ever since he moved his family off the farm. Now, with even that almost finished, Molly found herself at loose ends. My fate was no better. Though I had been a part of Molly's professional ambitions, the extra hand a good carpenter needs on any given project, my real passion had always been writing. With *Jinx* published I was not certain what I wanted to do next and so was marking time.

If someone had told me that September my world was about to turn upside down within the next couple of weeks, that my job, my marriage, my freedom, and finally even my life were all about to come into jeopardy, I probably would have laughed. My fate, as I understood it, was set in stone. I was going to get old with Molly. Molly might take the leap she longed for and start building houses instead of renovating them, but essentially neither of us expected or planned on much excitement.

The irony is that even then our world had begun to break apart. We just didn't know it.

'IT'S A BIG ONE,' Walt Beery told me one morning not long after I had agreed to look at his son's novel.

The size of the box he set down on my desk told me I had made a mistake. Seeing my expression, Walt laughed cheerfully. '*Zen and the Art of Motorcycle Maintenance* was about this length before it was edited, David!'

I thought about complaining. I didn't have time to read two or three thousand pages, but all I did was smile. The minute he was gone I set the box on my file cabinet and tried to forget it. I was not even tempted to look inside.

It soon became invisible. I knew it was there, of course, just waiting for me, but I learned to avoid looking at it, my good deed to do, my debt of friendship.

Sometimes, when I sat alone in the office, my back to it, I tried to convince myself that I could skim the entire opus in fifteen minutes and be done with it. Then I would look at the tape holding the box together and decide it would take fifteen minutes just to get the thing unpacked. Methodical man that I am, I told myself to open the box and then have a go at actually reading it later. It wasn't a bad idea, but I could never quite summon the energy to cut the tape.

What finally moved me to read it was a run-in with Buddy Elder. He and Johnna Masterson had presented copies of their short stories at the end of the third full meeting of my night class. The following week they were each treated to a sixty-five minute critique from the class. Johnna Masterson went first. She had written a story about a teenage girl's sexual awakening called 'Sexual Positions.' It was the sort of thing that should have come out badly but was, in fact, one of the funniest things I had ever read.

The technique she employed was reminiscence, the older and wiser woman recalling earlier times, whether real or imagined I could only guess. The encounters showed men and boys in a painfully comic light as they came forward to test young 'Joan's' virtue.

It was difficult for the class to evaluate the piece because it was, like Johnna Masterson herself, perfectly put together, and it was the first story we had evaluated, so they had no idea what kind of stuff they were going to see later. A few people blundered into it, as people will, suggesting changes that would either kill or spoil the humour. Others wanted extraneous details explained, like about how the kid who had started necking with Joan got his feet stuck in the sunroof of his father's Lincoln. That was, like, practically impossible! Shouldn't she explain that a little? There was a bit of incredulity at an aborted attempt (ending with CPR) to perform cunnilingus in the deep end of a public pool. There were those who wondered if Johnna might be taking the wrong approach, making fun of some very serious stuff, those who wanted more, those who wanted less.

Poor Johnna took every comment down, nodding

at the worst of it and inevitably doubting her own genius.

I waited for the praise until I got impatient. No one wanted to say it was great stuff, and finally I let them have it. If the story worked, then tell the writer it worked! Finally a couple of people admitted it was pretty funny. At the break I had the urge to make a run for the exit, but I forced myself to return. Buddy's story was next, and I was prepared to enjoy the ensuing slaughter of his inflated ego.

I was disappointed. Suddenly the class decided I wanted them to be nice, so we listened to insipid praise for one of the nastiest short stories I'd ever had the misfortune to read. Technically, it was not a weak story. Buddy Elder had a certain skill. What he lacked was humanity. His story, 'Lap Dance', detailed the lust of a sixty-something prof named Ward obsessed with a stripper named Dee Dee. It was supposed to be a send-up of the old *Blue Angel*, I suppose, but the culminating scene in the front seat of the professor's Volvo was nothing short of cruel, especially as the old man lost his erection the moment the girl consented.

I said very little throughout the love-fest. Toward the end, however, I made a few pointed remarks about the cruelty. Several people jumped to Buddy's defence. It was funny!

'Actually,' I said, 'it was shit.'

Workshops are not supposed to go like this. The prof expresses an opinion but never shoves it down everyone's collective throat. Certainly, criticism never falls to the level of insult. Profs will sometimes use a bit of the old Anglo Saxon to inspire the nostalgic thrill of academic freedom, but never-ever do they assault a student's best effort with such language. The moment I said it, I tried to get some ground back, but it was too late. Just an opinion, I said, no better or worse than anyone else's. Everyone, including Johnna Masterson, looked uncomfortable. Except Buddy. Buddy had the bright flushed cheeks of a young man who has just been slapped with a glove.

After class he walked away without a word, but the following morning he was knocking on my office door. The duel at sunrise. What transpired between us had a certain complexity, befitting, I think, our brief, uneasy history. Buddy affected indifference as he sat down on the other side of my desk. He would have me believe he was just stopping by because we were friends. I played along for a while, because I knew he wanted to talk about his short story, and as it happened I had plenty more to say.

He was giving me a chance to make amends for an unfortunate remark. When I did not take it and offer an apology, Buddy was forced to open up the proceedings. What exactly was wrong with the story? I probably should have sparred lightly around a few innocent matters concerning style. Instead, I came after him with a direct assault. 'I didn't like it.'

He blushed and tried to laugh. That much he understood. He wanted specifics.

My position might seem perfectly understandable, a bit blunt perhaps, but within my rights. People who have worked in education will know how brutal something like that can be. I knew it, and I said it, because I didn't want Buddy Elder in my class.

'It was unnecessarily cruel,' I said.

'You're the only person who saw it that way, Dave. Everyone else laughed.'

I could have answered this in a number of ways, but I chose silence. Silence, I hoped, would cut more deeply than any argument involving adolescent aesthetics.

'Johnna Masterson did practically the same thing. You thought her story was funny.'

'Johnna Masterson has talent.'

I was not thinking about the euphemistic sense of that word, but Buddy Elder, after a semester of drinking with Walt Beery, picked up on it at once. He gave me a conspirator's grin. 'That's pretty much what I figured.'

I did not handle this very well. In fact, I gave Buddy a definition of talent that left him wanting in every respect. In the process, I made some specific comparisons to Masterson's story, but essentially I broke

Buddy's story down without concern for his feelings and perhaps not even for objectivity. I didn't like the way the man had looked at Molly and Lucy. To be honest, I didn't even care for the way he had looked at my horses. This was my revenge. I did not use a single expletive. I tortured him with the tools of my trade. When he tried to interrupt, I poured on the contempt. He asked for my opinion, I said, so he could just sit there and listen!

I cannot recall ever treating a student to such honesty. I gave it without stint. I gave it because I wanted to hurt Mr Buddy Elder in ways that I did not even understand at the moment.

When I had finished with him, Buddy just smiled, though it was a pale, trembling smile at best. 'You don't like me, do you?'

I thought about laughing, because what he said was a masterpiece of understatement, but I did not want to give him even that much satisfaction. What I said was, 'It's not too late to drop the class, Mr Elder.'

A moment later, I sat alone in my office. There were no students waiting to see me, and I found myself wanting a drink. The feeling actually startled me, all the more so when I realized it was nine-thirty in the morning. I stood up and ripped open Roger Beery's literary nightmare as much to kill the impulse to drink as to finish with all unpleasantness at once.

The title was *Virgio 9*, and it was dedicated to Arthur

C. Clarke. On the first page, a starship commander was battling with a starship malfunction of some sort. I skimmed ahead until he landed at Virgio 9. On page 114, about five minutes at my reading, I slowed down for a seven page sex scene between the starship commander and a shapely hermaphroditic clone. Roger got things worked up pretty well with the male-male, male-female anatomies, but a phone call, via a chip implanted in the starship commander's ear, interrupted them, and our hero had to return to ship before completion of his exotic encounter. I noticed some reveries on the captain's preferences once he was safely inside his ship, and somewhat embarrassed by the writer's unconscious ambiguities, I began flipping pages. With eight hundred pages behind me, I checked the last page. I still had two thousand-some pages to go. At the halfway point, I stumbled into a three-way of aliens and tried in vain to discover if there was more same-sex stuff going on. Because they were aliens, I couldn't really figure out what body parts went where, and I hadn't the patience to work through the thing carefully. I skimmed the last seven hundred pages in another five minutes.

As I still had no students at my office door, I called Barbara Beery. I told her I'd finished her son's manuscript and wanted to talk to him about it. For one of the few times in her life, Barbara Beery seemed to enjoy the sound of my voice. She was almost girlish as she asked me to hold on. 'I'll see if Roger is awake.'

Roger came to the phone sounding like a man pulled from a deep sleep. I told him I was ready to talk about his novel. He seemed to expect something over the telephone, but I lie much better when I can see how it's being swallowed and offered to buy lunch if he could get to campus around noon. Noon was obviously inconvenient, but for the sake of art Roger said he would try.

I hadn't seen Roger for a couple of years. When he showed up at the union building, I have to admit I didn't even recognize him. He had gained maybe sixty pounds. A lot of it was just that, poundage, but I could see a lot of it was muscle too. I was guessing steroids and a really bad diet, but pretty much true to my form, I told him he looked great. 'Have you been working out?'

Roger seemed gratified I had noticed. He had been lifting for a couple of years, he said. We talked about that as we ate. I was in no rush to get around to his manuscript. He was pleasant enough about things. I asked about the facility he used, the cost of it, the hours, the kind of clientele they catered to. Then I offered an observation about the degree of satisfaction one gets from a hard workout. I even ventured to suggest that women seem to notice a man when he is getting in shape.

Roger said he had noticed that too, and shared a sly smile with me. I decided he was still in the denial phase. I shouldn't have really cared, I suppose, but I was curious. The whole dropout scene had always seemed a by-product of drug usage, but it was possible his alienation had more complex origins.

When we finally got around to the reason for our meeting, I lifted the massive box from the floor and set it on a chair so that it was between us. I found it instructive to see the way Roger's eyes fixed on the package. Roger had obviously spent years working on this, and I didn't especially care to disappoint him. In order to do that, I praised Roger's attention to detail. I talked about sentence structure, which, in the parts I had read, seemed fairly solid. I talked about imagery, narrative devices, transitions, and the intriguing eroticism that linked the action sequences. Having a doctor's degree in bullshit, I knew how to deliver these observations with credible enthusiasm. To this point, Roger had been nodding. At the mention of eroticism, though, he asked, 'Was the sex too graphic?'

I danced around this topic expertly. It was always a matter of context. Clearly, sometimes an author needed a graphic depiction for a certain effect. Sometimes an encounter was unnecessary. Only a fool would venture into a generalization about something like that. Roger nodded, clearly expecting specifics. When I offered nothing more, he tried to comprehend what I was saying. 'Was it too graphic anywhere in *my* story?'

It was a fair question, and I made a stab at the first sex scene, at least the first I had noticed. It was good, I said, especially ending with the interruption, but did we need the musings of the starship captain after the encounter? 'Do we really need to know he's uncertain about his own orientation?'

Roger looked me as if I might be an alien myself, and I knew I had made a mistake. The starship captain had an issue. All characters have an issue. His was hermaphroditic clones, I suppose. Of course, I wasn't sure, and I didn't dare take off on ambiguity, aliens, clones, or three ways (even if only two bodies are involved). What I wanted was just a little more time with that manuscript so I could bluff my way through this.

As that was impossible, I said it was difficult sometimes distinguishing between issues and challenges. One was a matter of characterization, the other of narrative design. Now I have a great deal to say about these kinds of things, and at that moment I began to spew. Long summers on the car lot had taught me to read suspicion, however, and Roger Beery had it.

A less experienced liar might have been tempted to make a partial admission of the facts, something like, *I didn't read the entire manuscript* or *I skimmed some of it*. But honesty is a slippery slope, and I was having none of it. I did admit I probably lacked experience as a reader of science fiction. As far as the market was concerned, I said, I was absolutely ignorant, so I really couldn't help on that point. Roger began to squirm as I said this, and I got the feeling that he wasn't interested in selling the manuscript. I decided he wanted to know its artistic merit, and I proceeded to talk about writing and art.

No one understood more than I did the loneliness and frustration of such work, I said, the feelings of doubt, the disappointment of rejection, even if it was only the failure to connect with a single reader! I wasn't making progress. Roger had seen through me. I was lying. I hadn't read his novel. I was pulling a con, and he was not going to forgive me. I still didn't back down. I had noticed a misspelled word on page 1,243, if he called me a liar, but I didn't have to get petty. He drifted, I lectured.

Finally we got completely off the subject of writing. I asked about his mother, how she was handling the separation with his dad. Roger told me she was doing fine. He couldn't answer any specific questions, and I managed to rattle off a couple of platitudes about relationships before noticing my watch. The time had gotten away from me, I said. I had to get back to my office. I still had a class to teach that afternoon.

'I haven't even read the assignment yet, I've been so busy!'

We shook hands and parted like friends, but I left the meeting with that sick feeling one gets when one's lies are not properly and politely swallowed. This would get back to his mother. Instead of feeling guilty, I was irritated at myself. I should have told Walt upfront I couldn't do what he asked. Failing that, I should have given the manuscript a couple of hours and then told Roger that was what I had done, two hours, and this is what I think.

Did I regret my failure to act properly? Well, not really. Like most people, my only regret was getting caught.

DENISE WAITED FOR ME after class that afternoon. I was not in a particularly good mood, and the sight of Buddy's girlfriend with that we-need-to-talk look on her pale, lonesome face put me on the defensive. 'Is this about Buddy?'

Denise shook her head morosely.

I relaxed but only slightly. 'You don't like *Medea*?'

She stared at me as if I had written the thing for Euripides. 'I hate it! I hate the Greeks!'

'Let me guess. She killed her own kids.'

'It's sick!'

'You need to speak up in class, Denise. That's the best place to talk about something you don't like. You'd be surprised how many people will back you up if you speak your mind.'

'What's the *Aeneid* about?'

I smiled. 'We're just reading a single passage, the love story between Aeneas and Dido. Not even adultery if you can believe it. Exactly your kind of story. Except... well, she kills herself.'

'Why?'

'Why else? Aeneas leaves her.'

'Men are pigs.'

'All men or just the ones you sleep with?'

Denise looked like I had slapped her, and I apologized. I said I was out-of-line. I didn't mean it. Bad day. She smiled, but it wasn't as forgiving as I would have liked.

FOLLOWING THAT ABYSMAL day of quarrels and miscues, I managed to bury myself in my work. I expected Buddy to drop my class. I even thought Denise Conway might.

To my surprise, Buddy returned to class the following week with a good attitude. He was not especially attentive to me, but he did his work. His comments about the writings of others were competent, even insightful. In fact, he was pretty good at finding both the positive and negative with the occasional plot twist that even left the prof nodding with approval. I had seen this kind of thing before, a student with modest abilities as a writer suddenly emerging as a potentially outstanding teacher of writing.

In my worst fears I was that guy. Under different circumstances I probably would have approached Buddy to let him know I was impressed with his involvement. Even though it was the right thing to do, I just couldn't manage it. I didn't like him. I didn't like the way he treated Walt or for that matter Denise.

And Denise had become important to me in her own right. To my surprise, she took my advice about speaking up in class. She actually began raising her hand on a regular basis. She was blunt, sometimes funny, sometimes the star of the discussion. An issues-kind-of-student, Denise could complain about Dido's lack of professionalism with a straight face. She had a country to run. Sure, she had feelings, but she had responsibilities too! Didn't she think about that? 'I mean the world isn't all guys! There's other things important too!'

Othello got no sympathy. What a dumbass! Hamlet needed to get laid. And what was with Ophelia? What was the real message here? Girls are nothing without guys?

If a teacher is lucky, there's always one student who can jumpstart a flagging discussion or, in my case, a flagging semester. That was Denise Conway for me, and in various ways I let her know I was proud of her.

Whether in response to my encouragement or because of her own unexpected excitement for all things literary Denise liked to drop by my office two or three times a week. She had an idea for one of the required papers and we talked through that. Another time, she wanted to talk about changing jobs. Did I have any ideas? Jobs? As in no more dancing? She was, she said, starting to feel like a piece of meat. I talked about student worker programs. One day, she came in looking exhausted. There had been trouble at the club the night before. The police had come. One of the patrons had gone to the hospital, one to jail. Walt was there. Walt had crawled under his table. I told her Walt wasn't the man for a crisis. No argument there, but the student worker thing was looking better and better. I made a call across campus and got her set up to meet someone.

The next day Denise dropped in to tell me Buddy didn't want her to quit her job at The Slipper. Could I believe that?

I made a point of asking her some hard questions about the relationship and what she thought the future might hold.

'You know,' I said finally, 'when you're into something like you are, a business like that, it feels like you don't have options. People make you believe you can't do something else. But you can do what you decide you want to do, Denise. It might cost. It might even bruise you, but you alone have the power to change your own life, if that's what you want.'

Denise missed the next class. The day following that, I got a call from Leslie Blackwell in Affirmative Action. Could I come across campus and talk to her?

We made an appointment for the following morning.

Chapter 6

AS A RULE I DIDN'T talk much with Molly about what went on at school. It was my way of separating my realities, and she was okay with that. She knew Buddy Elder was taking my class, but not that he and I had squared off in my office. I told her Buddy's stripper girlfriend was taking my Intro to Literature class but that was the extent of it. I certainly didn't tell her I had been summoned to appear at the office of Affirmative Action. It was simply not Molly's world. She had no interest in it.

Affirmative Action operated under the control of the university president as an investigatory agency. Through its work, the president's office monitored every aspect of the university's compliance to federal law regarding civil rights, including sexual discrimination. Are departments hiring a racially and culturally diverse faculty? Are women treated without bias, provided with the same opportunities, paid according to the same scale as men? Affirmative Action's mandate was to investigate, and naturally the office intruded into business that various professors and departments considered their own.

At that stage, however, most of us were used to investigations. Though it was a bit intimidating getting The Call, most of us had learned to pass it off as part of the modern landscape. Having been interviewed a couple of times in cases relating to Walt, I was actually used to it, and I had no reason to believe this would be any different. All the same, I did not know Leslie Blackwell and decided to check her out through the university website the evening before our appointment. I discovered she was an acting director and new to campus that fall, complete with a doctor's degree in law. I recall thinking that might not be a good thing for Walt, and my first impression of Dr Blackwell the following morning confirmed it.

Leslie Blackwell was a beautiful woman, thus had endured more than her fair share of unwelcome advances. Young enough to want to nurture her career, entrenched enough in bureaucratic matters that she had confidence, she would be, I thought, the kind to confront threats of legal action head-on, and take Walt through every hoop, from complaint to early retirement. Poor Walt.

I had it figured almost perfectly. In fact, I only missed the object of Dr Blackwell's new passion in life.

She placed me at the side of her rather imposing desk, smiled prettily and wasted no time informing me that two of my students, Denise Conway and Johnna Masterson, had charged me with sexual harassment. While I tried to fathom what in the world had precipitated a complaint, Dr Blackwell informed me that it was her job to investigate, that she needed to ask me a few questions in an attempt to verify the statements of the two women, and that I should be aware that sexual harassment was a federal crime, punishable by imprisonment in a federal facility.

Leslie Blackwell's queries came with all of the subtlety of a concussion grenade. Did I sometimes use the phrase bodacious ta-tas to describe female breasts? Of course not. Was I in the habit of talking about talent when I meant the woman had large breasts? Not at all. Had Denise Conway ever been in my office? Certainly. Did I talk about how much I liked her hair? I had commented on it once, as I recalled. Had we talked about the possibility of her dancing in the nude while I watched? Once, I believe. Maybe a couple of times.

I found myself crossing my legs and settling my hands squarely in my lap at this point. I expect Leslie Blackwell got that from a lot of men.

Had I ever been to a bar called Caleb's with Denise Conway? Yes. Had we ever discussed the kind of movies she liked to see? Yes. Had I invited Johnna Masterson to my house? Yes. Had I invited other students? Of course. Had I ever told Buddy Elder I thought Johnna Masterson had extraordinary talent? I had. Had Johnna presented to the class a story called 'Sexual Positions?' Yes. Which was about underage sex? Yes. Was oral sex involved? A couple examples of it, as I recalled, neither to completion. Had I told the class it was delightful? No. I said it was funny as hell.

Did I refer to it, Johnna's story, in later classes by title? I had. Had I talked to Walt Beery about Johnna Masterson's breasts? The topic came up. Had the word, and excuse her please for being so blunt, tits come up? Yes, it usually did when I talked with Walt. And bodacious ta-tas? Walt said tits, I said the other. She scribbled excitedly. Hadn't I denied using that word? No. I wasn't in the habit of using it. But sometimes I did use it?

'Use what?'

'The term bodacious ta-tas.' It actually looked like it hurt her to say the word.

'Depends,' I said, doing my best Bill Clinton, 'on how one defines *sometimes*.'

More notes. Had I tried to get Denise Conway to give up her job as a dancer, promising her I would arrange to get her something on campus in Work Study? I said I had made a call to Work Study to help her set up an appointment. Had I ever asked Denise about her relationship with Buddy Elder? Yes. Did I ask if they lived together? Yes. Had I inquired about their living expenses, who paid for what? Yes. Had I ever suggested that Buddy Elder was in trouble in my class? No. Had I asked her if the men she slept with were all pigs? Yes. Had I made jokes to Denise Conway about adultery? Yes. Incest? No. Had I told my class that in the Old Testament adultery applied only to married women, that married men sleeping with unmarried women committed no sin whatsoever? Yes. Had I called it the Golden Age of Patriarchy? Guilty. Had I ever made jokes about homosexual monkeys?

'Chimps.'

'Excuse me?'

'Homosexual chimps,' I said, 'tossing quarters on the shower floor.'

After a moment of murderous contemplation, Dr Blackwell asked me if I thought such humour was appropriate?

'Seemed so at the time.'

When Leslie Blackwell had finished her questions, she capped her ink pen and gave me a cool gotcha smile. 'I should tell you you're entitled to legal representation.'

'I guess you should have told me that before you asked your questions.'

'This is just a preliminary investigation, Mr Albo. If the charges have any validity, I will forward them to the vice president for academic affairs, and he will conduct a formal inquiry.'

'What exactly are the charges?'

Dr Blackwell blinked as if talking to an idiot. 'Sexual harassment.'

'Sexual harassment involves unwanted sexual advances, bargaining sex for a grade, that kind of thing. Are you saying I did that?'

'I'm not saying you did anything at this point. I'm simply looking at the complaints as they were filed.'

'May I see the complaints?'

'The actual complaints are part of my work product at this point.'

'Meaning?'

'Meaning that material is not available to you until I've completed my investigation.'

I WANTED TO KILL Buddy Elder, but the moment I left Leslie Blackwell's office I had more pressing concerns. I called our lawyer and told her what had happened.

'I want to know what the charges are, and they're refusing to provide me with copies of the complaints.'

'Give me the name,' Gail Etheridge answered. I did, and Gail told me she would take care of it.

I thought about going to Walt Beery, if only to gather courage from the voice of experience, but I decided there was an outside chance that Leslie Blackwell would actually keep the investigation confidential, as that was university policy.

The following Monday, four days after my interview, Dean Lintz called me into his office. He shut the door and sat down behind his desk. 'What the hell is going on, Dave?'

'You tell me,' I said.

'Leslie Blackwell in Affirmative Action informs me that two of your students have brought charges against you.'

'What kind of charges?'

'Sexual harassment. Look, don't play the innocent with me. I know you've been told what's going on.'

'Do you have the complaints?'

'Of course not. That's confidential.'

'Then why are we talking?'

'There's some concern that you will attempt to approach some of the witnesses. Dr Blackwell wants you to understand that any attempt to talk to anyone involved in the investigation will result in your immediate suspension.'

'Who are the people involved?'

'She says you have that information. You want to be careful, David. There's a general feeling that Affirmative Action hasn't done a good job for quite a while. That's why they brought Blackwell in. People want to see her take somebody down, and she knows it.'

I gave Dean Lintz a relaxed smile. At least it was meant to be relaxed. 'Wrong man, wrong case.'

'For your sake, I hope you're right. But try to show some restraint. Who tells jokes about gay monkeys in the classroom?'

'So you've seen the complaints?'

Dean Lintz shook his head irritably. 'I told you no. Dr Blackwell wanted to give me some idea of the behaviour you've been up to. It's incredible! And this thing about adultery, that it's okay for married men and single women! You're just asking for it with something like that!'

'Personally, I'm against adultery, but there's a lot of it going on in some of the literature.'

'Well, skip it! You're a married man, David! What are you suggesting when you say things like this?'

'If I skip *Genesis*, *The Iliad*, *Agamemnon*, *Medea*, *Othello* and *Hamlet*, I've lost the course.'

'Don't give me this academic freedom bullshit. You know what I'm talking about.'

'Actually,' I said, 'I don't have a clue.'

WALT BEERY CALLED ME that evening. What was going on? I told him I didn't know. He said he had been called over to Affirmative Action and they wanted to know what he could tell them about *Mister* David Albo. 'Don't worry,' Walt told me, 'I lied like a villain!'

'I can't talk to you, Walt. You're a witness in the case. The dean told me this morning they're going to suspend me if I talk to any of the witnesses in this case.'

'Then you better not talk to anyone. Blackwell has statements from Randy Winston, Norma Olson, Jane Trimble, and Marlene Moss. Oh, and Buddy Elder. Did you screw Denise, you bastard?'

'I've got to go, Walt. I can't talk about this.'

'You did! You sly old dog!' This was the stuff of laughter. I was Walt's new hero. I had bagged a stripper from The Slipper. Instead of protesting my innocence I simply hung up.

Chapter 7

I GOT A CALL ON Wednesday from my lawyer. Gail had received a copy of the complaints Johnna Masterson and Denise Conway had filed with Affirmative Action. She thought we should go through them. I had a few hours before my evening class, so we scheduled a late afternoon meeting.

Gail was in her early to mid-forties, I would guess, but they were hard years. She had gotten a bit heavier since Molly and I had first met her, but not from a lack of activity. Gail ran a small office with a couple of paralegals. She specialized in the routine business of lawyering: wills, real estate, divorce, trusts, and the whole gamut of misdemeanour crime. We had met when Molly had inherited Bernard Place. We liked her and started running all our business through her office. Because of the nature of Molly's profession, there was a considerable amount of routine legal matters, and Gail had become part of our social circle. Gail knew I was a character. She also knew Molly and I were in love.

I found myself sitting on the wrong side of yet another desk, but at least this time I had a partner instead of an opponent on the other side. Gail had photocopied the complaints, each hardly more than half-a-page. I read them and looked up at Gail. 'They had more than this, all kinds of stuff not mentioned here, including some jokes about homosexual chimps.'

'Chimps?'

'Don't ask.'

'Tasteless?'

'Entirely.'

'Well then maybe over cocktails. Look, these are the complaints. She refuses to provide her notes or any witness statements, so what she has she keeps until they determine if they want to draw up formal charges against you. Right now, it's an investigation.'

'What are we going to do about getting these witness statements?'

'My advice, nothing at all.' Gail made a dismissing gesture with her hand, indicating the two complaints. This is what counts, David, and there's nothing here. Johnna Masterson says you were talking to another professor about her breasts. Hate to tell you this, but that's not sexual harassment.'

'It wasn't my definition.'

'Well, if it is, we can jail the whole bunch of you and be done with it.'

'I didn't say these things, Gail.'

'You didn't say bodacious ta-tas?'

'Not in the context she's suggesting.'

'And when you said to,' Gail checked the complaint, 'Buddy Elder that Johnna Masterson had extraordinary talent you didn't mean... bodacious ta-tas?'

'She's got them. There's no doubt about that, but Buddy Elder knew I was talking about her ability as a writer. Talent has that meaning, too, you know.'

'Okay. They have absolutely nothing here. They'll go through the motions of an investigation, and then drop it. Thank you very much. You don't need me again unless they turn stupid, in which case we sue and win and can both retire from the rat race.'

'What about the other complaint?'

'Conway? Conway doesn't even know what she's complaining about. You brought up adultery in class. Is it in the literature?'

'All over the place.'

'And you called someone on campus about getting her some work?'

'She asked. She said she wanted to quit dancing at The Slipper.'

Gail blinked. 'She's an exotic dancer and she's complaining that you complimented her hair?'

'She asked me what I thought of it.'

Gail shook her head. 'This isn't a complaint, David. This is a piece of paper.'

'These things are supposed to be confidential, but

everyone on campus knows I'm being investigated.'

'You've been harmed by that?'

'I was going to apply for promotion this year.'

Gail thought about this. She shook her head. 'Take the hit. Apply next year. It's not worth the ill-will you'll garner by filing suit.'

I said nothing, but Gail could see I was upset.

'How is Molly handling this?'

'I haven't told her about it. Actually, I wasn't planning on bringing it up.'

'Afraid she'll think there has to be something to this, a little hanky-panky?'

'Molly knows better. Look, we don't talk about what goes on at school because she thinks the whole place is a loony bin and the only reason most of us are working there is it's cheaper for the state to pay us a salary than keep us locked up in an asylum. She doesn't want to hear it.'

'Well, it's your business, but I'd say it'd be a good idea to at least fill her in on the complaints. Just to be on the safe side.'

'I'll talk to her tonight.'

'Good. Now, when Blackwell interviewed you, were you relatively honest? Hell of a thing if they drop the charges and bring you up for obstructing an investigation.'

'I was perversely honest, Gail.'

'Enlighten me. What is perversely honest?'

'I answered the questions without attempting to discuss the setting or context of my words.'

'You didn't try to explain anything?'

'She didn't ask. I didn't offer. What the hell? I didn't do anything wrong.'

'Did she record the conversation?'

'No. She took notes.'

'Let's hope she knows what she's doing and she's honest. Otherwise, she'll have you confessing to anything she wants you to.'

Gail looked at her watch. We had been at it for close to thirty minutes. 'Okay. You're in to me for a little over three hundred bucks. Let's leave it at that for now. If they want to talk again, tell them to contact me. Say nothing. Write nothing down for them. If they attempt any kind of disciplinary action, do whatever they say and contact me immediately. I'll have charges filed against them so fast it will make their collective head spin. And don't talk to anyone about this, except Molly. Are we clear on that?'

'Tell me I don't have anything to worry about, Gail.'

'I make it a policy never to lie to my clients, David.'

'But it's bullshit. You think the complaints are bullshit?'

'You're the man with the farm. You know what it's like when you step in that stuff.'

I WENT TO A TAVERN after I left Gail Etheridge. It

had been a favourite in my drinking days, and I convinced myself they had a good menu. In fact, it was a bar for the locals, safe territory. I knew the people there. It had been two years since I had crossed the threshold, but some of them hadn't even changed seats.

The waitress asked me where I had been. 'Been sober,' I said and ordered a tenderloin sandwich, fries and a non-alcoholic beer.

'We don't serve that crap, Dave. It's the real thing or nothing at all.'

'Possible to have a Coke?'

She gave me a smile. 'For you I'll see what I can do. But this sobriety has to go. You're setting a bad example for the people who keep this place in business.'

While I waited for my order, I found myself reviewing my various conversations with Denise Conway. This was hardly the first time. In fact, less than a week into it, I discovered Denise Conway was becoming one of the most important people in my life.

It seemed to me there were two distinct possibilities. The first involved a series of misunderstandings. Eager and insecure, Denise had sought me out as a familiar face. She wanted assurances that she could handle college. Having received those assurances, her insecurities began twisting legitimate praise into something sinister. The complaint she had filed supported this theory. She wasn't quite sure what I had done wrong! Her only real problems with me she had expressed as evidence rather than a complaint.

My second theory involved Buddy Elder. I much preferred this theory, because there was not much I was unwilling to credit to Mr Elder. In this theory Buddy manipulated Denise Conway into filing a complaint. Johnna Masterson's complaint made more sense as well. Buddy had fed his fellow graduate student choice titbits of gossip and then coordinated a double-assault on the source of all evil, David Albo.

Theory number two had only one tiny glitch. It wasn't going to work. As a piece of sabotage the thing had no teeth. I put myself in Buddy Elder's place. Johnna Masterson had been handled nicely. She had been stirred gently and brought to a simmer. At that point I was sure Buddy had introduced her to his girl-friend, letting the two of them compare notes. It was probably even Johnna Masterson's idea to march on Affirmative Action.

Denise, however, could have brought charges of real substance. Private conversations between the two of us could have taken any form. Why hadn't I offered, in her complaint, an A in exchange for sexual favours? Pressure, manipulation, insinuation, all the elements that make up a genuine case of sexual harassment, just weren't there!

There was no intelligent explanation for this failure.

Buddy knew his way around campus. He was hobnob-
bing with professors who had experienced the inner
workings of Affirmative Action as few ever experience
it. Why hadn't he exploited his opportunity? There
was no answer, and so I was led back to theory number
one, a simple misunderstanding. I didn't like it, but it
was the only logical explanation for the charges.

I WAS MILDLY SURPRISED to see Buddy in my class
that night, actually amazed to see Johnna Masterson.
Johnna had filed charges before our last class, but at
the time I had not known that. I tried to remember
how she had behaved, what looks she had given me,
but it was impossible. The week before, I had not been
under siege. I had been at work. I watched my students
only to know if they were tuned in to the business at
hand. This time, I hardly noticed anyone other than
Johnna Masterson and Buddy Elder. Buddy made a
great show of it. He quietly complimented both writers
presenting their work that night. His observations were
legitimate, though not particularly insightful. Johnna
Masterson put on another sort of face. She had come
to class because she did not want to let some pig ruin
her academic year. Knowing I might have my revenge
on her at my leisure and yet refusing to cower, she sat
bravely before me with only a tremor in her voice to
betray her.

At the break, I saw her talking animatedly with

Buddy. Buddy was consoling her. I could almost imagine his speech. She had to hang on. Tonight and maybe next week and then I would be gone!

Or something like that. They imagined their position to be stronger than it actually was. Part of the climate of the university was a bold rhetoric that rejected even the nuances of sexism. Truth was another matter. Because students never got to experience the process directly, they didn't know. The truth was tenured professors remained, even in these modern times, virtually untouchable. One heard about those rare cases of dismissal precisely because they were rare.

Though Johnna Masterson could hardly imagine it, the deepest wound for me was observing what this had done to her. Catching the gossip, as I was sure she had, she imagined some kind of salacious joking about her figure that turned her talent into *TALENT!* I wanted desperately to sit her down and explain it all to her, but I knew I couldn't. Even if I were allowed to talk to her about the case, I could not persuade her. I could only say Walt Beery had said it. Walt had turned her into a joke. Me? Well, I was just sitting there.

Going along with it.

I decided at some point during the second half of class that maybe I was wrong about Buddy Elder on a lot of counts. Maybe my discussion with Walt about the new *talent* had made its way through the grapevine, and Buddy Elder, actually believing I was coming on to Denise, had brought her together with Johnna Masterson because he believed I was misbehaving. Call it theory number three: all complaints legitimate. I had quarrelled with Buddy because I was jealous. I had crossed some kind of line with Denise, taking liberties that if not overtly sexual were nonetheless intrusive and unprofessional. Denise had talked to me about her job, but it wasn't my business where she worked or who paid the rent. And Johnna? Well, she was pretty. Maybe I liked to mention the title of her story because 'Sexual Positions' prompted certain satisfying fantasies involving the two of us. Maybe I had enjoyed my talk with Walt without understanding the dehumanizing dimension of it.

Such is the nature of accusation: first we are surprised, then we are angry. Finally, we believe what our enemies tell us.

I was still coming to terms with my guilt when I talked to Molly that night. I was tired and so I admitted to being partially at fault for some of it. A misunderstanding, I told her. Two misunderstandings, Molly said. Knowing how it must sound I waited for the inevitable questions. Was I having an affair with one or both of them? Thankfully, these did not come. Molly listened with the impatience she reserved for all matters relating to the university and when it was finished she simply asked if she could read the complaints.

I passed them across the table to Molly. She studied each sheet as if to memorize the actions or reconcile them with what I had just told her. I ran through the complaints in my mind again. In that dark silence I did not invest Buddy Elder with fabulous powers. He was just a young man who did not like someone like Johnna Masterson being turned into a joke. If I was capable of that, certainly my intentions with Denise Conway were less than honourable. I was Walt Beery's friend after all.

'This is bullshit!' Molly said.

I looked up from my masochistic reveries greatly encouraged.

'Gail Etheridge says nothing is going to come of it,' I offered.

'What about your promotion?' I shook my head. Molly threw the papers across the table. 'I hate that place! I think you should quit. Tell those bastards to go to hell, David.'

'That's just what they want!'

'Who cares what they want? You're better than this! You don't need their money. *We* don't need it!'

I tried to explain that I had spent over half my life trying to get where I was. It was insane to throw it away because other people had a political agenda. These charges, I said, would come and go. I could apply for promotion next year or the year after. The important thing was to keep a sense of proportion.

We had been here before. Molly listened, but she did not understand why I was so desperate to keep a job I did not especially enjoy. Before she had gone independent, buying and selling houses, she had run rooftops for various contractors. Hard and dangerous work, but the air was clean and complaints were straightforward, delivered to your face. At Johnna Masterson's age, Molly had joined a new crew. This was right after we were married. One fellow on the crew gave her a rough time because she was a woman and because she was beautiful. She answered him straight on. 'You either stop or I'm going to hurt you.'

He was a perfect fool and just laughed at her. She let it go, thinking he would back off with the comments. The next day, though, as she was climbing the ladder, he whistled and whooped, 'Look at that ass, boys. Is that good enough to eat, or what?'

Molly had climbed back down the ladder and walked up to this giant. He got bigger every time she told the story. By the way she came at him he figured he was in for a speech, and he was all set for an amusing, girlish temper tantrum, exactly what he wanted in the first place. Molly's boot caught him behind the knee, and he went down flat on his back. Then she broke three of his ribs.

That was how Molly McBride filed a complaint.

* * *

WE DECIDED, FOOLISHLY, to keep Lucy out of it. I don't know what she imagined in those first weeks. There was tension in the house. Molly was angry. I was depressed, looking by turns either guilty or distracted. Because she was seventeen, Lucy probably thought it was something *she* had done.

My colleagues had the story almost at once of course. I heard the echoes of the jokes I hadn't quite told. Monkey. Bodacious. Talent. I saw Randy Winston talking to two women from the Department of History. They might have been discussing Caesar's assassination, but I felt reasonably sure by their sudden silence the topic was mine.

I saw Denise Conway with Buddy Elder only a few minutes before my night class was scheduled to begin. She had to know I would be there, but she looked frightened and surprised when I walked toward them. Before I could speak, she walked away. Buddy approached me while I was still watching the sway of her hips. I felt my gut tighten, my fists clench.

'Johnna asked me to tell you she couldn't make it to class tonight. She had to go to the infirmary.'

I blinked in confusion. 'Is she all right?'

Buddy Elder met my gaze without ever losing that slight, cynical smile of his. 'I think she's got bleeding ulcers, Dave.'

Wednesday night I included Johnna Masterson's health in my litany of moral failings. Thursday I went online to browse for psychologists. Most of them listed among their specialties depression and work-related stress. I had not slept for a couple of weeks. For the past several days I had been nursing a sharp pain in my chest. I found three good candidates, and decided if I did not feel better Friday I would start making some calls. I was not sure they could really do any good. It seemed to me I was beyond treatment. This was not the usual helplessness of depression, seeing no way out of my troubles. I could not decide what my trouble was. Was I the victim or the one who had victimized others? The true penitent confesses the sin and so begins a journey back to faith and wholeness. In a medical sense, this was supposed to happen between psychologist and patient. But what exactly should I tell a doctor? I *might* have made a mistake? I believe this could be a conspiracy? Perhaps we could cut right to the essentials. I could talk about Tubs: the last honest man.

I had a better idea on the way home. I stopped for a beer. After three the pressure in my chest eased. After another, I could almost laugh. I got in my truck and headed home. I was cured, at least as long as the buzz lasted.

I called Molly along the way, but there was no answer. A wind had kicked up late in the day. The first chill of winter came as the sun dropped under the horizon. Molly's truck was parked close to the house, but Lucy's

Toyota was gone. The horses were in the barn. The dogs were in the kennel for the evening. Like the old drinking days. If I didn't show up, they got taken care of anyway.

There were no lights on inside the house. The back screen door was swinging free when I got to it. I figured Molly was inside, but I did not understand why the lights were off. I was sorry now for the beers that had tasted so good. Two years of sobriety pissed away. I snapped on the porch and kitchen lights and called out Molly's name.

I walked into the main hallway. 'Molly!' I heard branches crackling against the windowpanes. There was no answer, but I knew she was there.

I found her sitting in the dark in the downstairs living room. She was wearing jeans and work boots as if she had just finished working upstairs. I snapped on the lights, laughing at her. 'What are you doing sitting in the dark?'

Molly's face was swollen and red. She had been crying. In her hand she held a .22 Magnum revolver. It was pointed vaguely in my direction. I staggered slightly. I tried to put the various elements together, but nothing made sense. Molly *never* cried. I could not think of a single occasion when I had seen tears. And the gun. Molly had had the thing for years, had it when I first met her, in fact, but she never got it out anymore. I couldn't recall seeing it since we had moved to the farm. Had someone come out to the farm that afternoon? Had something happened to – ?

'Where's Lucy?' I asked, finally putting it together.

'Lucy's all right. She's out for the evening.'

'What happened?'

She fired the gun in my direction. She didn't really aim. The gun was pointing at me, and then it discharged.

I jumped and swore angrily. Fresh tears rolled from her eyes, and I knew the gun had not gone off accidentally. I screamed my next question. What in the hell was the matter?

'You are.' She fired the gun a second time.

I swore again. I danced, though it was a bit late to be dodging bullets. I demanded an explanation. I expect it sounded more like pleading.

She reached for some kind of small notebook and threw it across the room. It landed at my feet. 'Read it!' she hissed. 'Go ahead you piece of – pick it up and read it!'

'No more shots.'

She fired the gun again. I felt the heat of the bullet pass across my face. I stooped down to pick the thing up. It was the kind of notebook Lucy might have used a couple of years ago, if she had kept a diary. I opened it to the first page. Two tiny rings kept the pink sheets of papers together. The handwriting was neat and round. Circles dotted every *i*. The ink was purple, nearly impossible to make out against the pink background in the poorly illuminated room. I adjusted my position for better light. I held the thing at arm's length because I did not have my reading glasses. I saw the words, *Well, this is it! I'm really in college. Me, Denise Conway! It's not so bad really. Scary, but all the freshmen feel the same way, I think.*

I looked up at Molly. She was studying my face with a bitterness I'd never seen directed toward me. 'Read it, David.'

I skimmed down the page and saw my name. *David came into class today looking very chic and professional. It's hard to think of him as my professor after everything he's done to me in the bed of his pickup!*

'Molly,' I said, 'where did you get this?'

'Read it.'

'Did Buddy Elder give this to you?'

'Read it, David.'

I turned the page. I snatched lines out of context, but the context was clear. *When his fingers slipped into me I almost came...*

Next page. *It's different with David. He needs me. He says Molly doesn't satisfy him the way she used to.*

Two pages later. *We made love in his office after class. People were walking by in the halls outside, and we were making love!*

Next page. *David wants me to quit dancing. He*

says he can't stand it that other men touch me or even look at me. He says if I leave he'll support me. What about Molly? He gets funny when I say her name. I don't think he loves her, but she has some kind of hold on him.

Next page. *In his office today David told me he wanted me to suck him off. It was like I was his whore! I told him NO! I meant it too. He said if I didn't he was going to flunk me. It was like a joke but I could tell he liked the power he had over me. I told him to go to hell and walked out. But then I got scared and went back in and I got on my knees for him. It was so degrading, the things he said while I did it. Sometimes I think he loves me, but then sometimes I think he's just using me for easy sex.*

On the next page. *A bouquet of roses. Buddy was furious. I said it was from someone from the club, and he wants to know who. I think it would kill Buddy if he knew about David and me. He looks up to David. He says David is the best teacher he's ever had. It's like we know a different person. I threw the roses away to show him they didn't mean anything to me. Maybe they don't. After class, David cornered me. He wants me to get a job on campus and leave Buddy. What am I going to do?*

'Did Buddy Elder give this to you?'

'I swear to you, David, if you say another word I'll shoot you in the heart.'

Molly stood up. Taking her revolver in both hands she walked toward me. At least the tears had stopped.

'I trusted you. I thought of all the guys in the world – how could you do this to me? How could you sleep with me while you were screwing that whore, David?'

The barrel of the gun was pointed at my face, and I really thought she would pull the trigger if I tried to answer her.

'I want you to leave. I want you out of the house tonight.'

'Molly—'

She fired the gun. I don't know how she missed me. The barrel of the gun was pointed right into my face. 'Don't you dare even say goodbye.'

Chapter 8

I SAT IN MY TRUCK outside the house for several minutes. I was not sure what to do. I knew that if I found Buddy Elder I would very likely kill him. As pleasant as that prospect was I still had a bit of sanity nudging me toward self-restraint. This thing, this lie, could be straightened out given time. But not tonight. Tonight, I just needed to get somewhere and let Molly cool down.

I had forty dollars in my wallet and two credit cards. It was enough to get some food and a twelve-pack of beer and checked into a motel. Once in town, I stopped at a liquor store and at a McDonald's. Fully supplied for the evening, I drove down to the Super 8. That was when I found out my credit card didn't work. I tried my second card, and it too had been cancelled. The girl cut both cards apologetically.

I ate my sandwich in the parking lot and washed it down with a cold beer. I didn't have a worry in the world. I still had friends. Running through the list, though, I discovered something I had not appreciated until that moment: middle age places invisible limits on friendship. There are the friendships of couples. There are friendships at work that survive only there. There are old friends one sees every year or two and there are the friendships one makes in taverns. When I had finished the list of people I could call and reasonably expect an enthusiastic response, I was down to the ghost-writer of my present travails.

To my chagrin, I didn't even know how to get in touch with him. Barbara Beery's voice changed the moment she recognized me. David, both syllables ugly. 'I hate to bother you like this,' I said.

'Then why are you? Walt doesn't live here anymore.'

'The thing is I need to get in touch with Walt this evening. About a thing.'

'What kind of thing?'

'I need to talk to Walt, Barbara. Can you give me his number or not?'

Barbara gave me Walt's cell phone number and his address at the Greenbrier, but only after she asked if I was drinking again. I told her no. Her silence called me a liar. Off the phone, I pounded another beer, watching for cops like a teenager. Then I called Walt.

Walt was roasted, but the enthusiasm was genuine. 'Sure! Whatever you need, David! What the hell happened anyway?'

'Our friend Buddy Elder happened. I'll tell you all about it when I get there.'

Walt's apartment appeared to be reasonably clean, but that was because Walt did not have anything in his front room other than a reading chair and a lamp. The dining room had a folding card table setup with a single chair before it. Walt and Barbara were worth something over five or five-and-a-half million to the best of my calculations, so this was how Walt chose to furnish his apartment. It was hardly the bachelor pad he had always talked about. In the bedroom he had a sleeping bag and pillow stretched out next to a tiny lamp. Beside the lamp about fifty books lay scattered about. I swore sourly to myself and wandered into the kitchen. I found a pan, a pot, and some picnic dishware. In the bathroom I discovered some extra razors but no second towel, nothing faintly resembling a washcloth, and certainly no toothbrush for the unexpected overnight sweetheart. I asked if I could borrow his toothpaste and he shouted that I was welcome to anything in the place.

Finishing the tour, I said, 'I suppose a blanket and extra pillow is too much to hope for?'

Walt smiled. 'You can always go to the twenty-four hour Wal-Mart. I think it's twenty-four hours anyway.'

I shook my head. I was in no mood to go shopping, even if I could pay for what I needed. 'I think I'll just arm wrestle you for the sleeping bag,' I said as I took the only chair in the room and set my twelve pack at my feet. 'You want a beer?'

Walt waved his glass of Scotch at me and leaned back against the wall. 'I'm drinking the good stuff. What happened with Buddy?'

'You know where Buddy Elder and Denise Conway live?' I asked.

'They live on North Ninth somewhere, a couple blocks from The Slipper, I think.'

I took a sip of beer. 'What's the address?'

'I don't know. I was only there one time.'

'He's not in the phone book.'

'He wouldn't be.'

'Have you got his telephone number?'

'No. What's this about, David?'

I took another sip of beer. 'I'm going to kill Buddy Elder. But first I have to find him.'

'When did you start drinking again?'

'This evening. Right after I read Denise Conway's diary. No. Actually, I forgot. I started this afternoon during the third day of my heart attack.'

'Denise keeps a diary?' Walt looked sick.

'Apparently since she started to school this fall. Buddy delivered it to Molly this afternoon. Molly was crying, Walt. I came home and she was in tears.'

'Molly? *Our* Molly?'

'He made her cry, Walt. That's why I'm going to kill him.'

'You're not going to kill anybody.'

I shook my head and reached for another beer. 'This whole thing! I thought it might be a misunderstanding, but after I read this diary I can see it's no misunderstanding. It's a set-up, and Buddy Elder is the guy behind it!'

'What did it say?'

'It's a detailed account of an affair between Denise and me.'

'Was I in it?'

'No.'

'How much of it is true?'

'If I got a blow job I sure as hell forgot about it. If Denise gave you a blow job in your office, Walt, would you forget about it?'

Walt smiled fondly at the notion. 'Not in this lifetime.'

'She wrote about it! Graphically!'

'And you think Buddy is behind it?'

I shouted my answer. Of course he was! What did he think? Sweet vacuous little Denise was going to dream this up? 'Buddy controls her, Walt. He tells her what to do, and she does it.'

'Buddy likes you, David. Hell, if anything, he's pissed off at me!'

'Tell me about that.'

'You mean Denise and me?' Walt shook his head sorrowfully. 'That wasn't exactly my finest hour.'

'I want the details. I want to know what the son of a bitch is all about.'

'That wasn't Buddy's doing. This was Walt royally screwing up.'

I took a sip of beer and waited. I figured Walt was tuned up enough that I would get a full confession this time.'

'We were drinking at Caleb's.' Walt laughed and finished his drink. He went to the kitchen, presumably for a refill, and called back to me, 'Not the first time! I can tell you that!' I heard him loading his glass with ice. A moment later he was back, his glass filled with scotch. As he spoke, he paced before me. 'Buddy wanted to go to The Slipper. It was Denise's day off, and she didn't want to go. I mean, she spends an eight-hour shift there. The last thing she wants is to go in on her day off.' Walt took a healthy sip.

'You're right about Buddy controlling her,' he said, 'but that girl has a temper! We went, but she was in a mood, let me tell you. It didn't help matters any when Buddy started getting lap dances from one of the dancers. I mean one time, okay. Second time he takes the same girl and Denise starts feeling *me* up!' Walt laughed excitedly. 'I couldn't believe it! She just grabs me and starts stroking it right there!'

'When was this?'

'Finals week. Anyway, Buddy is off getting his third lap dance and she says, 'Let's go outside.' Who am I to argue? We get outside, climb in my car, and I swear it, David, she unzips me and we're going at it—'

'What does that mean, *going at it*? What was she doing?'

'A hand job! She's giving me a hand job and Buddy walks outside. She pulls back, kind of scared, and she runs back inside. I'm trying to get my pants together and Buddy comes over to the driver's window, and he wants to know what we're doing out there. Like he can't believe it.'

'What did you say?'

'I told him nothing! I said we were just talking.'

'Did he buy it?'

Walt shook his head, looking down at this drink. 'Things haven't been the same since. We don't get together anymore. I messed up big time.'

'How did Barbara find out?'

'A couple months later. I guess it was a week or so before your party. Someone called her. She didn't say who it was. A woman. That's all I know, but not Denise. She's okay about it. I went in there a couple of times this summer, whenever I didn't see Buddy's car parked outside. Maybe a few more times than that.' He grimaced as he apparently tallied the number of visits, then shrugged it off. 'Denise is like, hey, we got a little carried away. No big deal.'

'What was Buddy's grade, Walt?'

'That's confidential.'

I finished my beer and threw the can at him. 'What was his grade, Walt?'

'He got an A. I gave him… well, he earned it, mostly.'

'Mostly?'

'He missed the final, and his term paper was about Hank Williams.' Walt's face twitched with the memory. 'Hank Williams: Troubadour and Knight Errant.' It was pretty good, actually.'

'Unbelievable.'

'I told them to be creative!'

'I want you to show me where he lives. I want to have a talk with that slimy son of a bitch, and I want to have it now.'

Walt laughed and held his drink up. 'Can't do it tonight, David. I'm drinking tonight!'

I went into the kitchen and got his bottle. Snatching what was left of my twelve pack, I headed for the door. 'You want to drink, you're going to have to come with me.'

Walt complained that it wasn't fair taking hostages.

AS WE DROVE INTO TOWN Walt defended Buddy. Buddy had every right to be pissed off. 'How would you feel,' he asked me, 'if you walked in on Molly and me?'

'Surprised.'

'Yeah, well, so was Buddy. Friends don't do that,' he muttered with just a touch of righteousness.

'Who is Buddy hanging out with these days?' I asked.

'On the faculty? Randy Winston mostly. Buddy is taking a class from Randy this fall in Shakespeare.'

'Where are they drinking?'

Walt shook his head. Walt was still patronizing Caleb's, but Buddy was going elsewhere. 'No idea, but a lot of times he goes into The Slipper at the end of Denise's shift. I never go in there that late.'

On Ninth Street Walt pointed out Buddy's and Denise's apartment. They were no lights on, but I went up on the porch and knocked anyway. Getting no answer, I went back to the truck and drove to The Slipper.

'I can't go in there,' Walt told me. 'I just remembered. They eighty-sixed me a couple of weeks ago.'

'What happened?'

Walt laughed. 'I have no idea!'

'What does Buddy drive?'

Walt didn't know what it was called, but he knew what it looked like and saw it parked on the street as I circled the block. It was an old Mercury Marquis, what Tubs called a rich man's Ford.

'You okay here?' I asked.

Walt freshened up his drink, though the ice was nearly gone. 'Get some ice while you're in there, will you?'

I told him I would.

* * *

Cold Rain

THE GLASS SLIPPER had been around longer than Cinderella, so long in fact that nobody bothered with the *Glass* anymore, even though the sign still showed an anatomically enhanced outline of Cinderella slipping her foot into a slipper with the help of a kneeling prince. I was under the impression the place had changed owners a few times over the years, but I was quite sure nothing else had changed, including most of the dancers.

A girl in a G-string walked across the room while the doorman took a couple of bucks from me. All things considered, the cover seemed a bit steep. Once past the entrance, I checked the room for Denise. She wasn't there, but I spotted Buddy Elder playing pool a split-second before he noticed me. He held his cue stick up threateningly as I walked toward him.

I didn't care for the gesture and grabbed the thing with both hands. I swung him around like a rag-doll, letting him think I wanted to rip it out of his hands. When he was moving pretty fast, I simply released my grip. Buddy tripped over a chair and fell back against the wall. His head smacked prettily into the plaster, and he slid down to a seated position. Two men grabbed me from behind. I wrestled free of their hold because they weren't even in Buddy's league, and I was just about to get back to Buddy when the doorman stormed into me.

The doorman outweighed me by a hundred pounds.

This turned out to be a good thing, because he simply lifted me up and walked me toward the door with my arms pinned at my side. There was no kindness in this, though I had some hope up to the point that he threw me across the sidewalk.

I had enough presence of mind or beer ingested to roll instead of skid, but it didn't do me much good, because he came out after me. He didn't take much of a swing, but his meaty fist got buried in my gut. After that he walked me back to the building, where he slammed me face-first into the wall. He patted me down, then swung me around and took a long look at my face. 'You come back in there again and I'll really hurt you.'

I think the fact that he wasn't even breathing hard bothered me the most. I nodded my head to let him see that I understood. And I did. As soon as I could breathe again, I fully intended to go back to Buddy Elder's apartment and wait for him to show up there. I had done a lot better with Buddy.

I didn't get the chance though. I was still working on breathing when three men came outside. I had the impression Buddy was one of them, but I wasn't sure at first. The Slipper faced a fairly busy street. When they took me away from the building I thought they just might throw me into the traffic. Instead, they took me to the side of the building and back into the shadows. I ended up on the ground without much trouble on their part. The first kick was the worst. It landed just under my ribs and paralyzed me. I heard a voice over me. 'Look at me.' I expect he repeated himself a few times before I could actually focus enough to do as he asked. I looked up. I could see nothing but a mass of shadow where his face should be. 'You come after me again, Dave, and I'm going to have to kill you.' It was Buddy Elder's voice, nicely punctuated with a kick in the face. His friends kicked my thighs and buttocks, a genuine ass kicking.

When I was about the texture of meatloaf I heard Buddy tell them, 'I'll take it from here.' I was half-conscious, but I did not particularly relish the thought of being left alone with Buddy. Buddy squatted next to my face and pushed a cold piece of metal against my jaw. His voice had the sweetness of a lover. 'This here gun is cold, Dave. I could say you pulled it on me, and I was fighting to get it away from you when it went off. There's nothing the cops would do to me either. You want to know why I don't pull the trigger?'

I didn't answer. I recall thinking he wouldn't kill me, but I knew even then that was exactly what he intended to do, in his own good time.

'I said, "Do you want to know why I don't pull the trigger?"'

This was my cue to say something clever or brave. I said, 'Why?' Even wasting that much breath hurt.

'Because I've got plans for you, Dave. You and

me… we're going to have some fun before I'm finished with your ass.'

With that he stood up and pissed on me.

I tried to roll over, but I only managed to give him a better target. I lay there after he left and I felt more profoundly discouraged than at any time in my life. I don't know if I got to my feet two or three minutes later or if I blinked out for a quarter of an hour. I do know that I came out of the alley just as the police pulled up to the kerb. I was pretty well softened up, and after they had patted me down and cuffed me they got me into the back of their car without breaking a sweat.

I saw the doorman talking to them, and when I looked again, apparently having passed out for a few seconds or what seemed like seconds, they were gone. I assume they were inside taking statements. At the time I was so entirely disoriented I tried to reach for the ignition of my truck. The handcuffs promptly brought me back to reality.

The booking process was delayed long enough for me to be stripped of my clothes and given a shower. One of the jailers was a former student of mine, a pretty good writer, actually. He checked my bruises and told me he didn't think anything was broken. I got a clean jail uniform and a cell with four other drunks. They weren't bad sorts, as it turned out, and we ended up telling stories until dawn.

Chapter 9

I HAD BEEN GIVEN THE CHANCE to make a phone call sometime around midnight. I dialled our home number and got the answering machine. Arrested, I said. City jail. Call Gail Etheridge first thing tomorrow morning. As an afterthought I added, '…please.'

The following morning I shuffled in chains through an underground tunnel to the county courthouse, a nineteenth century relic full of various courtrooms and offices. Gail Etheridge met me outside the circuit court. The sight of her reassured me. She didn't really smile. It was more like a smirk. 'Rough night?'

She was talking about my face, which still had an imprint of Buddy Elder's boot. 'I've had worse,' I lied.

'What happened?'

'Denise Conway's boyfriend.'

Gail made a face. I expect she was calculating the effect on my case at the university. When it was my turn, we went up before the bar and sat at a small

111

table. At that point an investigator for the prosecutor gave a reasonably accurate summation of my actions at The Glass Slipper. The judge, an old grey-haired dog in robes, listened to the narrative with some interest, asked for some clarification, specifically on the condition of my intended victim and the amount of property damage. Finally, he turned his attention to me. He was a man in his late fifties with the indelible signs of a man worn out by routine. I was therefore a rather interesting exception to his day. 'Dr Albo,' he said with something akin to a sigh, 'my impression is that last night was a bit out of character for you. Would you say that is the case?' I looked at Gail. Her expression indicated I should answer the judge.

I tried to assure him that it was, but my voice cracked, and it took a couple of tries.

He looked down at his notes. 'Joseph Elder, Buddy, is one of your students?' I said that he was. The judge considered this fact for a moment. 'You have any idea how the two of you can avoid another incident of this nature?'

'I'd be surprised if he didn't drop my class.'

'And if he doesn't?'

'We're not going to have any problems, Your Honour.'

'Make sure you don't, Dr Albo. You come into my court with another incident involving that young man and I'm going to feel like I made a mistake this morning.'

I felt a flutter of hope.

'I don't like to make mistakes. What is more, the voters don't like it when I make mistakes. Are we clear on that?'

'Yes, Your Honour.'

'I'm going to ask you to make two promises to me this morning. First, that you'll stay out of The Glass Slipper for as long as I sit on this bench. Second, that you'll avoid any sort of confrontation with Mr Elder. Can you do that?'

'I can.'

'Can you promise it?'

'I promise, Your Honour.'

'If you break your promise to me, son, if you so much as get in a shouting match with Mr Elder, I will spare no effort in attempting to ruin your life, in the legal sense of the word, of course.'

It occurred to me that I should attempt to explain to the judge that Buddy Elder had apparently decided to ruin my life, in an illegal sense of the word, and that I might not have much choice about how I dealt with the young man, but I very wisely followed my instinct and kept my mouth shut. I had made my promise and meant to keep it. At that moment I could not imagine ever going back to The Slipper or crossing paths with Buddy Elder again. I had the best intentions that morning, jail will do that, but as things turned out I would end up breaking both promises.

'Ms Etheridge, kindly take your client out of my courtroom. All charges are dismissed.'

We had to wait for an escort back to the city jail so I could reclaim my property and return my orange jumpsuit, though I would have liked to keep it for a souvenir. While we waited, I ran through the incident for Gail's benefit, beginning with the diary. I described everything I could recall reading. I omitted only the fact that my wife had very nearly unloaded her revolver before showing me the door.

A fairly good friend who also happened to be getting paid to listen, Gail appeared to accept everything I said. I had the feeling, though, that she didn't really believe me. She was neither stupid nor naive. If a diary existed which described an affair, then no matter what I said she was going to assume there was an affair. Why else would a young woman write twenty or thirty pages in her diary about it? My wife, after all, who knew me better than anyone, believed it. Why shouldn't my lawyer?

'One thing,' Gail said. 'Do you think Leslie Blackwell will get a copy of this diary?'

I shrugged. 'What if she does?'

Gail's expression grew sombre. 'That's the question, isn't it? The affair started last summer?'

'There was no affair.'

'Right.' Gail tried hard not to roll her eyes. 'The alleged affair allegedly started...'

'Last summer. That's the way I understood it anyway.'

'According to her she takes a class with her lover. The live-in boyfriend makes a fuss when he finds out. He wants revenge, and maybe an insurance policy against the two of you getting back together again, so he has her file her bogus complaint of sexual harassment. Is that about how it works out?'

'There are rules against vendetta complaints.'

'If life were only so simple. Unfortunately, the affair, sorry, alleged affair, lends credibility to Johnna Masterson's complaint.'

'I don't follow. What does Johnna Masterson have to do with it? You said yourself her complaint is groundless.'

'Look at it from Leslie Blackwell's point of view, David. You're engaged in an adulterous affair with a student, teaching students that married men who have affairs with unmarried women are not committing adultery, and you're hooting it up with the unindicted co-defendant at the Student Union.'

'Hooting is probably not the word we want to use under the circumstances.'

Gail rewarded me with an impatient smile. 'Johnna Masterson's complaint is that you have created a hostile environment for her. Her complaint cites a single example. On the face of it, Blackwell should never have investigated Masterson's complaint, but Denise Conway's complaint made it impossible for her to ignore it. So she digs around a little, and suddenly she discovers Denise Conway's diary. In other words, Ms. Masterson's complaint now has substance. You're banging students in your office and bargaining blow jobs for grades, even if it's all in good fun. In that light, anything you might have said about Johnna Masterson forms part of a larger pattern of behaviour.'

'All that is assuming I said something in the first place,' I grumbled irritably, 'and that the diary has some legitimacy.'

Gail's expression suggested my objection was irrelevant, but she very kindly agreed with me. 'True or not, David, if Leslie Blackwell finds out about the diary she'll feel obliged to push the case forward to the vice president. Which means we could be in for a hell of a fight.'

I HAD TO SUPPRESS the urge to vomit as I put my clothes on. My leather jacket was ruined. The clothes needed to be washed. Throughout the morning, I had been watching the time, thinking I could make my afternoon class. With an hour remaining, I left the police station and got into a taxi. On the ride to my truck, I called the department and cancelled my class. Unavoidably delayed, I said. I talked to a student worker, so there was no cross-examination. I then called Molly. Her cell phone was off, so I left a message on the home answering machine. I was out of jail, I said, but I needed money and clothing. I added gratuitously that I hadn't slept with 'that woman.' The cabdriver, who neither appeared to notice the peculiar stink of my clothing, nor reacted to the word jail, checked me out in the mirror as I made this final protestation. That gave me a pretty good idea how Molly would receive it.

Walt Beery wasn't in my truck. Nor was his Scotch. He had, however, left the truck without taking the beer. That fact alone was sufficient for me to call Walt a good friend. I went back to Walt's apartment on the off chance he was there. Since I didn't have a key and there was no answer when I phoned him, I decided to go out to the farm. I called ahead, if only to avoid a shootout with Molly. When she didn't answer, I left another message: 'I'm going to the farm to pick up some things. I'll be gone by three o'clock.'

I saw the farm differently when I drove out that afternoon. I had been in the habit of seeing the things we needed to do. Now I saw what I was about to lose. Barnard Place had been in Molly's family since the 1930s. When Doc and Olga abandoned the farm for the comforts of suburbia, settling just off the thirteenth fairway adjacent to the country club, Doc was not the sole owner of the property, nor could he get an elderly sister to agree to sell. So he did the worst thing possible: he broke that beautiful mansion into apartments. When he gave up the apartment building idea, Doc left the house vacant without even bothering to close the place up properly. Pipes froze and burst. The basement flooded. Trees grew up through the eaves. The windows became target practice for kids who wanted to go out and see the haunted house. Shutters dropped off or went missing altogether. Kids began using the downstairs parlour for sex and drug parties, and at least two campfires had been started on the parquet floors.

When Molly's aunt died and Doc deeded his share of the property to Molly, Molly and I were living in town. The thought of moving out to her family farm excited us both. We had picked out a beautiful site for a new house about a quarter of a mile from the mansion. We decided to build Molly's dream house in stages, letting us move into it within six-to-eight months. Everything was set when, as a whim, Molly and I decided to see how bad the mansion was on the inside. By that point, Molly and I had turned around quite a few houses, probably fifteen to twenty major renovations over the years. Some we had sold immediately, some we rented out. We knew a restoration would be far more complicated than the usual facelift and far more expensive too. The moment we walked into the house, it was clear the whole place was beyond salvation. The faded glory that was left only made the ruin more heartrending.

As a building site it had potential. The trouble was tearing it down was going to take time and cost money. I remember laughing at Doc McBride's enthusiasm for drop ceilings and cheap panelling. Everywhere I looked the original wood was cracked, swollen, or warped. Piles of plaster cluttered the floor. Carpets were stained and rotten. I made a joke about fire being the only decent thing for it, except the place was too water-logged to burn.

Molly had a different idea. She told me about it on the drive back to town. She wanted to save the place. She wanted to live here. I laughed at the notion. I said we could never get the cost of even a half-ass restoration back if we decided to sell it. Worse than that, it would take years to make the place liveable.

Molly didn't care. This was the place where she wanted to live. She wanted the mansion to look like it had at the height of its glory, circa 1930, complete with antique luxury plumbing and electrical fixtures. She had lost this house once when she had been too young to have a say in matters. This time she wasn't leaving.

We bought a house trailer and set it up close to the mansion. Summers, weekends, evenings, every spare moment we had we worked on the house. It was nothing for us, all three of us, to have Sunday dinner seated on sawhorses, tasting sawdust or freshly buffed plaster with our sandwiches.

A stray dog showed up one day. Two more got dropped off the next summer. We fixed up a stall for Ahab, then built an arena for Lucy to ride in. Our only recreation was to drive to various horse races every weekend and let Lucy enter the junior division races. A couple more dogs showed up, and I built a kennel. The dogs all had names, Hawthorne, Melville, Emily D. and Emily B. (they showed up together), Emerson, Alcott, and Wharton, but most of them answered to Dog if they answered to anything. A couple of them had a tragic past and never really got comfortable with the concept of family or trust or, for that matter, human beings. The rest of them were okay, but not really cut out for indoor living.

A few people from school came out to the farm in those early days. They put on a good face, but I knew they thought we were crazy. That was pretty much the point of our party. I wanted people to see Molly's vision in its finished form.

I took a couple of minutes when I first got to the farm to see the dogs. During the day, they always ran free as long as Molly was around. If she had to leave the farm, she usually put them in the kennel. So I was probably safe. They were in the kennel. They were happy to see me, most of them anyway. The sceptics, Alcott and Wharton, hung back and growled as they always did. The horses were in the pasture. I called to Ahab, and he ran across the valley and up the hill to see me. It broke my heart to see that kind of enthusiasm, especially when all I could do was clap his shoulder and tell him I wouldn't be around for a while.

THE PLACE WAS EMPTY, and though it had been home less than twenty-four hours ago, I felt like a burglar. I changed clothes, tossing my ruined stuff in the trash. I packed quickly: some schoolwork, toiletries, a roll of cash from my desk drawer, an extra pair of jeans, a change of shoes, a sweater, some shirts, socks and underwear. We had three sleeping bags stored in a second story closet. I got mine out, snagged some towels and a pillow from one of the guestrooms, and headed for the truck. I was trying to decide if I should make another run when our neighbour Billy Wade appeared at the back of the house. Wade stood close to seven feet tall and carried a broodmare's belly over his belt. His face was long and thick, and he had a habit of letting his mouth hang open as if he had just been asked the one question he couldn't answer.

It was my theory that Molly's parents had moved off the farm primarily to avoid their only neighbours, Mrs Wade and her son. On the car lot, we would have called Wade a bogue. A bogue, the *o* pronounced as in bogus, was anyone who came shopping for wheels without cash or credit. Surprising as it may seem, a salesperson could usually count on running into one or two bogues a week. With a bad run of luck six or seven wasn't unheard of. When that occurred we used to call it bogitus. The worst, though, was having a case of the Bogues. With a case of the Bogues every bogue who showed up pushed past every other sales-person on the lot in order to find the individual so afflicted. Even Tubs wasn't immune. I saw him sell five cars one day, the record for that year for a normal sales day. The next morning all five deals got tossed back in his lap with credit turndowns. Milt laughed at Tubs and said it looked like he might be coming down with a case of the Bogues! After that for about a week every bogue in DeKalb came to the lot and asked for Tubs.

According to Molly, Wade was the nicest man in the world. Most bogues are, but I couldn't look at our neighbour without thinking about bogues. As Wade was, in fact, King of the Bogues, in my book anyway, it seemed appropriate that after my night in jail he should wander across the road for a friendly chat. Bogues always find you when you're down.

'You all shooting guns last night?' Wade asked me cheerfully.

'I lost my channel changer, Wade. What I did, when I got tired of one show, I'd just shoot the TV set and call to Molly to bring in another TV.'

Wade gave me a calculating look. He was pretty sure I was lying, but the concept of irony escaped him entirely. 'That could get expensive real fast, Dave!'

'You didn't happen to think someone might have been over here trying to kill us, did you?'

Wade laughed. 'I figure they'd line up for the chance at you, Dave, but they're feared-to-death of Molly!'

We heard Molly's pickup coming up the lane. At the top of the hill, she cut into the circle, instead of driving down to the shed where she and Lucy usually parked. She took a quick look into the cab of my truck to see what I had, then walked over to join us without quite looking at me. 'Hey, Billy!' she said.

Wade looked like a big dog that had just gotten his belly rubbed. 'Hey, Molly!'

'David has moved out, Billy. I don't want him on the farm. He doesn't have any business here. You see him around and I'm not here, I'd appreciate it if you'd call the sheriff.'

'They disconnected my phone, Molly, but I could break his arm if you want.'

'That's fine with me. Just be careful it's not his drinking arm. Poor man, it's all he's got left.'

Wade looked at me like I was one of the horses. 'Which one is his drinking arm, Molly?'

Molly told the giant she was just kidding and dismissed him with a kindness she rarely offered outsiders. She needed to talk to me about something important. She hoped he didn't mind leaving us alone, but she did want to talk to him sometime. There was a lot of work to do, she said, and she could sure use a hand. Wade said he could clean the stalls right now if she wanted. Molly said she had to think about it first. She had a few other things in mind that were maybe more urgent. This was the usual patter with Wade. Since his mother's death two years earlier, I figured Molly was good for spending a couple of hundred dollars a month on make-believe work for our neighbour. Wade wasn't very handy and for all his size he hadn't much ability with a shovel. He could loiter with the best of them, though, and that was usually the job Molly hired him for.

When our neighbour had wandered off, Molly glared at me. 'You drinking again?'

'Might as well.'

A smile snaked across her face as she brushed a long dark golden lock from her forehead. 'How was jail?'

'Comparably speaking, pretty friendly.'

'Who beat you up, David?'

'It wasn't Denise Conway. I'll tell you that much.'

'The judge got a phone call from Doc this morning. In case you're wondering.'

Doc was Bernard McBride, Molly's father. Before I had gotten to know him real well, Doc told me about a teaching position that was opening up at the university. They hadn't even advertised for it yet, but it looked like something I might be interested in. Like the typical Ph.D., freshly minted and hungry for work, I was interested in anything that looked like full-time employment. I made the call to the contact person Doc had provided, and I eventually landed the position. Only later did I realize Doc had put in the fix. Recalling my fury at that particular indignity, Molly was no doubt enjoying this latest bit of favouritism. 'Judge Hollis and Doc used to play bridge together.'

'Anything your father can't fix, Molly?'

'He can't fix us.'

'I didn't have an affair with Denise Conway or anyone else, Molly. This whole thing, these charges against me... it's a setup.'

'You know what? I didn't want to hear it last night, and I don't want to hear it today either.'

'Even if it's the truth?'

'You said this would never happen, David. You gave me your word.'

'It didn't happen.'

'How is your face? It looks like it hurts.'

'It's killing me. What do you expect?'

'It's not half of what you deserve.'

'I'm going to stay with Walt for a few days,' I said to her as she walked away.

'Tell it to someone who gives a damn,' she answered, never looking back.

*   *   *

I DROVE AWAY THINKING about things through Molly's perspective. I knew her that well. I knew her pain, the absolute sense of betrayal, and even though it was all a lie, I felt guilty as hell.

Chapter 10

WHEN SHE WAS fifteen, Molly fell in love with Luke
Sloan. Luke was seventeen. She was the daughter of
a prominent surgeon, the belle of the debutantes. He
was a cowboy, his best days already starting to fade.
Even eighteen years later, Molly didn't like to talk
about the romance. I expect she still cherished that
part of the relationship, though she pretended otherwise.

I know this much. Luke Sloan was a handsome kid.
I had seen enough action photographs of him on a
horse at the Sloan house to know that. From what I
could put together, Luke was a lot like his father, a
good decent man, the sort Tubs used to call salt of
the earth. The difference was Luke had to make some
tough choices when he was seventeen. I had never been
given the whole story in one sitting, but I was under
the impression that Doc and Olga had forbidden Molly
to see Luke. These are the kinds of things families talk

about in shorthand and never quite explicate for the benefit of the in-laws. Molly told me one time they knew she was seeing him and pretended not to notice. Olga says otherwise.

According to Olga, Luke Sloan would have been invisible to a girl like Molly only a couple of years later. That meant of course he hadn't enough money to satisfy the country club set, nor the kind of ambition that would overcome its prejudices. I had seen his type a hundred times over. Lucy raced against them every weekend. I found myself in grudging agreement with Olga McBride: some men are just too attached to the clay. At fifteen those things are romantic. Of course at fifteen we judge people by a different standard. We see cockiness and think it is confidence. We mistake silence for depth.

Whenever I notice the young Romeos and Juliets of modern-day suburbia cluttering the mall or close against the shadows at a high school game, the kids really in love and not just on a date, I wonder if it was like that for Molly and Luke. It's hard for me to imagine Molly at fifteen. By the time I met her she was twenty-one. The six years between constituted a lifetime of experience, more for Molly than for most. She was not a moon-eyed romantic at twenty-one, and I have trouble imagining her without her endearing streak of hard-nosed practicality. The pregnancy, according to Molly, was an accident. She was taking precautions but just forgot her pill one morning. Sometimes forgetting is a decision, too.

Doc and Olga handled it badly, of course. They pre-empted Molly's right to choose, telling her they knew what was best. I've seen Molly play the same game with Lucy, watched the fireworks afterwards. But never with those stakes. Molly saw her duty to her child, just as Olga did. Neither could understand the stubbornness of the other.

The Sloans went along with the McBrides' decision. They told Molly years later they understood from the McBrides Molly wanted an abortion. If they had known she wanted to keep the child they would have done anything to help.

Maybe it's true. Maybe it's only what they believe now. For Molly and to a lesser extent for Luke, I expect, the parents appeared to stand together. Molly would see a doctor. Afterwards, they would go on with their lives as if nothing had happened.

Molly and Luke took off hitchhiking toward Chicago instead. They thought they could get an apartment and Luke could get a job. In the abstract it didn't seem improbable. Luke was a big strapping kid, capable of giving a day's work to anyone. They had a couple of hundred dollars and Doc's .22 Magnum for protection, the only thing Molly took when she left, other than the clothes on her back.

They lived together for a week in a cheap motel

applying for different jobs, then they managed for a couple of nights without a room as they clung desperately to the last few dollars. Then the rain came. Luke stayed with Molly four days more. They huddled together at night under bridges and close to buildings off the beaten track unable to sleep. By day they walked the streets asking for work and panhandling bits of money. One afternoon Molly looked around to say something and Luke wasn't there.

Molly knew where he had gone. He'd been trying to talk her back from the moment it was clear the money wasn't going to last. It wasn't the end of the world, he said. All they had to do was just go along with her folks. They could keep on seeing each other just like before. It didn't matter what her parents said, they could be together and it wouldn't be like this. This, Luke said, wasn't going to work.

And their baby? Molly asked. There would be other babies, he said.

Molly called her parents a few weeks after Lucy was born to tell them they had a granddaughter. When they asked if she was coming home Molly told them she was never coming home. Did she want them to tell Luke? She said she didn't care.

The McBrides told the Sloans they were grandparents, if only to share their grief with someone. Luke's parents told Molly later Luke was happy about it and only sorry he couldn't find her and help out. He wanted that more than anything. That was what they said. The truth was probably something else. A year after Lucy was born Luke drove into a tree. He was drunk. He had been drunk since he had come back home. It went down as an accident, but everyone except the Sloans knew it wasn't that. It was the shame of his betrayal finally catching up.

After Molly and I were married I persuaded her to contact Doc and Olga and the Sloans. For Lucy's sake, I said. Molly already owned three houses and had a good deal of cash in the bank. We had been up to DeKalb a couple of times. If I could put up with Tubs, she could spend the occasional weekend visiting Doc and Olga. She knew from a friend she had called one time that Luke had died. She also knew the Sloans and her own parents had no one else. She wasn't going to have to face Luke or even an I-told-you-so. She could go home knowing she had done the right thing. Lucy was proof of that, and I think she was almost relieved when we finally made contact.

For a long time, Molly wouldn't tell Lucy the whole story. She said simply that things had not worked out. In a world of broken families this was something Lucy could understand. Lucy of course wanted to know everything about her father. Molly could satisfy her to a point, but as she got older she asked more pene-trating questions. Shortly after Lucy's twelfth birthday, Molly told her everything. She made no apologies for

Lucy's father. She said only that he was a kid, seventeen years old. They didn't have any money. They didn't have a place to stay. It was cold and it had been raining for four days in a row. 'Luke went home,' she said, 'because he could. Anyone would have.'

But of course Molly hadn't.

I think Molly had always wanted to believe I wouldn't have either. That was important to her. Molly didn't love by half-measures. She loved with all of her heart and expected the same. When things got really bad, she knew most men would just turn back and go home. But not the man she loved.

That was the deal in Molly's world. No matter how safe things got for her, she still understood love in this way: in a cold rain you were either there or you weren't.

WALT SHOWED UP AT HIS apartment around eight that evening. I met him in the parking lot. He seemed surprised to see me, but helped me bring my gear in. Once inside, he caught a good look at my face. The way his expression changed, the mix of perplexity and concern, was almost touching. 'What happened to you?'

'Didn't you wonder why I didn't come back last night?'

'Last night? What was last night?'

Such are the joys of a good bottle of Scotch. I went through the whole thing again. When I had finished my narrative, executed with a gentle soft-shoe, I got it all a second time. 'You and Molly breaking up?'

Around ten o'clock, I set my sleeping bag in Walt's bedroom and went to sleep. As near as I could tell, he came 'to bed' around one o'clock and was still reading at four.

The next morning Walt suggested I go to the hospital. I couldn't look that bad and not have some kind internal damage, broken bones, ruptured spleen, some damn thing. I asked him where the spleen was and we went off on that for a while.

On Sunday I gave the hospital serious consideration. The bruise in my side was tender and hot. My face looked almost as bad as it felt. Walt's home-remedy medicine helped, though, and by midnight I slept without pain.

I got to the university around eight-fifteen on Monday, quite a bit earlier than usual, and I was feeling very satisfied with myself until I found a note on my office door from Dean Lintz. My presence was required in his office immediately. The nastiness of phrase was no accident. As a tenured professor I decided I could ignore the note, claim I hadn't seen it when he finally caught up with me, and that's what I would have done, except that the lock to my office had been changed.

When I entered his office, Dean Lintz told me Leslie Blackwell in Affirmative Action had called him Friday afternoon. Apparently, I had not only attempted to discuss the investigation with one of the witnesses, I had actually assaulted him. That was not true, I said. I'd been arrested for assault, but the judge dropped the charges. As far as talking, I hadn't spoken so much as a single phrase to Buddy Elder Thursday evening.

Dean Lintz sighed and shook his head sadly. He liked me, he said, but he had no choice. He was going to have to suspend me.

'What about my classes?'

'I've already instructed your chair to find replacements. We'll need your grade book and syllabi, David. As soon as you've taken care of that, I want you off campus. I have no idea if the vice president will want to bring additional disciplinary action against you for this, but I do know it's likely you'll be looking at additional charges once Dr Blackwell has finished her investigation.'

I was confused. 'What kind of charges?'

Dean Lintz grimaced. 'Sexual misconduct. According to Leslie Blackwell you've been having sex with one of your freshmen students in your office. I mean really, David! Couldn't you at least have taken her off campus?'

'Is it against the rules to have sex in our offices?'

'Smoking in your office is against the rules, David! Of course it's against the rules! You know that, as well as I do! Tenure can only protect you so far. This kind of behaviour… it's an embarrassment for the whole university.'

The dean ended our meeting on a more conciliatory note. The suspension was with pay and benefits. I still had options. I was free to appeal any action taken against me. I was entitled to a faculty adviser and of course free to hire an attorney if I thought I needed one. 'The thing is Affirmative Action has let too much of this kind of crap get by for too long. Leslie Blackwell was brought in to change that, and you just happened to be her first. She needs to let everyone know there's a new sheriff in town, David. I tried to warn you!'

I cleared out my desk under the supervision of the department secretary. She was close to tears the whole time. I left most of my books in my office, as I had for my sabbatical. I had every intention of returning.

On the last trip to my truck, I met Buddy Elder in the hallway. He made a show of making room for me. I had a box in my arms. He understood what it meant. Not a word from him, of course, just the same lazy smile and sleepy brown eyes.

I CALLED MOLLY TO tell her I had been suspended and was bringing some stuff from my office out to the farm. 'Sorry to do it,' I said to her answering machine, 'but I can't unload this in Walt's apartment.' I hesitated at the end of my message. I wanted to tell her that Buddy Elder had delivered a copy of the diary to Leslie Blackwell Friday morning, but I realized that would not seem especially diabolical to her. I was banging a stripper in my office. Maybe the university should know about it. After several seconds of dead space on the tape, I said, 'I'd like to see you, Molly.' I finished by saying I loved her.

I don't know anyone who enjoys talking to a machine. Emotional pitches are especially difficult. You make the speech in the belief that you're talking to a person. After you hang up you are haunted by your own words. You imagine you have said too much or that you sounded as mechanical as the machine you have spoken to. I didn't remember the drive out to the farm. I was too busy imagining what I should have said and worrying about the words I had actually delivered. I was rolling along an empty pavement doubting everything, looking at cornfields and patches of woods here and there, and suddenly I was home.

Except it was not home. Not anymore. The horses were in the pasture. The dogs circled my legs howling and growling, a few of them even wagging their tails. Molly leaned out the window from the third floor. But her tone left no doubt: I was not welcome. 'Put everything in your office,' she called. She retreated at once. I guess she could still see me looking up at the place where she had been, because after a moment she appeared again. 'I'm sorry about the suspension, David. I really am.' And that was it. A couple of minutes later I heard the familiar whine of her table saw.

Chapter 11

MY LIFE IS A RATTY piece of string stretching out behind me in silly, dull serpentine twists. There are little knots and tangles, those points in my existence I know I should have marked as sacred time, but to be honest they did not seem worth the effort. I suppose it was my natural stubbornness. People said your first is unforgettable, so I remembered them all dutifully, but I cherished nothing. My first sexual encounter had transpired with the town tramp in the backseat of my old man's Ford Ltd. demo, an awkward and embarrassing piece of business. My first job as a man had been walking out and shaking hands with strangers and trying to convince them to buy one of my cars. My first diploma came at age eighteen, college graduation four years later. I didn't even put a robe on for that. I did not know what I wanted. I did not believe in much of anything. My sole ambition in life, once I understood something about life, was to avoid becoming a man like Tubs.

Everything changed for me on the afternoon I met Molly McBride. Molly was drunk the first time I saw her. It was pouring down rain and she and her crew had landed in the bar I always went to. I remember I almost went home because of the rain that afternoon, but I didn't keep beer in my apartment in those days. It had been a tough day in the academy, or so I persuaded myself, and I drove over, intending to pop in for a quick one and see if anyone was around.

I saw her the moment I walked through the door. She was laughing at something one of the men had said, bringing her glass to her lips at the same time. Because I had stopped for no other reason than to look at her, the glass froze just as her laughter did. I knew she had caught me staring, and so with some embarrassment I turned toward the booth where I usually sat. None of my crowd was there. To avoid looking at her incessantly I dug around in my back-pack for something to read. I heard her calling to me, her voice having just a bit of an edge to it, 'Everything all right over there?' There weren't many people in the bar, so I couldn't ignore her. I waved my hand and smiled at her. Everything was just fine!

One of the men said something. Molly answered him. I couldn't make out what they said, but their laughter was all about me, I had no doubt of that. I ordered a pitcher instead of a glass because I was suddenly a lot thirstier than I had imagined. I tried to look at the text swimming before my eyes, but I was a young man and just across the room was the most radiant blonde beauty I had ever seen. After one especially long look by her, I came up out of my pretended reading and caught her at it. She looked away at once, and I called across the room, 'Everything all right over there?'

Even in the gloomy light of the bar, I could see her smile. One of the men said something, and she laughed, making a gesture with her hand as if to say just a nice fantasy.

And it was. A pretty carpenter on a rainy afternoon. A bored grad student wondering what he was doing with his life. We caught each other's eye. Nothing more. Then Beth Ruby came through the door and trudged over to my booth. She tossed her backpack on the seat and started complaining about the rain.

I looked up from my book. 'I'll give you a hundred dollars from my next pay check,' I said, 'if you'll sit somewhere else.'

Beth Ruby looked at me curiously, then around the room. Beth was nobody's fool. Her eyes settled on Molly. 'Two hundred,' she said.

I told her I didn't have two hundred bucks, but if I had it I'd give it to her. Could she just give me a break? Beth shrugged indifferently and smiled. 'I could, but I'm not going to. Believe me, you *and* your dick will thank me later.'

I gave up the dream. I tossed my book on the table and started talking to Beth about her total lack of sensitivity, her failure to understand that someone could fall in love at first sight. Beth and I had sparred a few rounds in the office and quite a few more over beer. We both figured eventually something was going to happen between us, but we were both too stubborn to make the first move. As a result, we actually had a fairly decent friendship, as that kind of friendship goes.

While I was explaining to Beth that she had ruined my life out of simple greed Molly slipped into our booth. I had not seen her crossing the room, and nearly jumped out of my seat when I saw her across from me. Molly's smile was so pretty that for a moment all I could do was blink.

'Is he a total asshole or just the run-of-the-mill kind?' Molly asked Beth without taking her eyes from my face. I liked her voice. It was strong and confident. I liked the way she was looking at me, too.

'Total and complete, I'm afraid,' Beth answered almost sadly.

I started to defend myself, but Molly wasn't buying the verdict, not entirely anyway. 'Kind of cute though.'

'And doesn't he know it?'

Molly shook her head, still not taking her eyes from me. 'I hate that in a guy.'

'Dumb and pretty.'

Molly laughed. 'Beats dumb and ugly, I guess.'

Molly had practically the same build as now, though she was leaner by a few pounds. That came of being twenty-one and working twelve-to-fifteen-hour days running rooftops. She had short straight blonde hair with neat square bangs. A blush of freckles ran over the ridge of her nose.

'What are you reading?' she asked, taking the book up from the table and examining it for some evidence about my character. '*Black Spring*. What kind of book is that?'

'I don't have a clue,' I said.

'Amen,' Beth echoed.

On any other occasion I might have rewarded Beth's nastiness with a scowl, but I couldn't take my eyes from Molly.

'Why not? You were reading it?'

'I was trying to read it. The truth is I was distracted.'

Beth rolled her eyes and grumbled something about pathetic pickup lines. 'You two together or something?' Molly asked.

Beth said yes. I said no.

'We teach together,' I said, hoping that explained it.

This, as it happened, was terrible. Being a graduate student was okay, but teaching was a suspect activity in Molly's view. 'If you're going to have your nose up in the air, then at least you ought to have some cash in your pocket.'

'Better than no money and no class,' Beth answered testily.

'Not by much,' Molly snapped. I liked it that she wasn't backing down from a pseudo-intellectual.

When she asked me what I taught I said auto mechanics. Beth said I was lying. 'He teaches English, badly.'

Molly looked at each of us trying to decide who was lying. Then she grabbed my hand and flipped it over. 'Auto mechanics! I bet you can't even change a tire!'

'In theory, I can,' I said, 'but usually I just change cars. It's a hell of a lot easier.'

'He's a used car salesman when he's not in school.'

'A professional liar!' Molly laughed at this information, but she didn't seem especially concerned.

'I never lie,' I told her.

Beth scoffed at this. I was famous in the department for my tall tales and constant run of nonsense, but Molly didn't care. She was trying to read me.

'You any good at selling things?'

'I've been at it for five summers,' I said. 'Every month I've worked for the past four, I've been the second-best salesman on the lot.'

'Second-best? Who's the best? That's a guy I want to meet.'

'No you don't. He's an evil son of a bitch with the moral fibre of the cockroach.'

143

'A liar like you?'

I shook my head. 'No, but he can use the truth like a stiletto.'

She let me touch the palm of her hand. The skin was rough, but I couldn't get enough of the feel of her. 'I don't care if something's true or not, as long as it's plumb.'

Beth Ruby said things were getting too thick, and Molly told her no one was stopping her from leaving. After that it was just the two of us.

Molly tells me she liked me the first time she saw me. Of course she was three hours into a smash-up and there was no competition in the bar, but I think it was more than just chance. I think she liked the fact that I worked for a living, even if it was only dirty-white-collar work. For my part, the feeling was mutual. Unlike almost every person I met in those days, Molly knew exactly what she wanted in life and was already pursuing it. She had just had her offer on an old Victorian house accepted, and she was planning on fixing it up and selling it for a profit by spring. And what was she going to do with the profit? I asked.

'Buy two more. I like the work,' she said, 'but I'll like it a lot better once I'm my own boss.'

I did not know Molly had a daughter or that she had been on her own since she was fifteen. It wouldn't have mattered. Nothing but that moment mattered. Molly was different from anyone I had ever known.

She was sexy, smart, straightforward, funny, unencumbered with pretensions, and totally self-reliant.

We left the bar for 'a demo drive' in my pickup around ten o'clock that evening and didn't even get out of the parking lot. In the middle of what was starting to look like the inevitable, the rope I used to disengage the clutch on the truck Tubs had sold me got in Molly's face. She sat up, swinging at the thing and laughing, more curious than irritated. What was a piece of rope doing hanging down from the roof of my cab? Her breasts were glorious and naked, swinging over my lips. The smell of her sex was intoxicating, and I probably should have pitched a story. Anything would have worked, but the truth would take some time. The truth involved some advice a car salesman had given me that I was naturally too proud to heed.

The night was dark. The rain had stopped. My windows were steamed up. Why did I have to tell her about Tubs?

I think to this day I was at a crossroads and didn't realize it. As it happened, I decided to tell her about my old man, The Bandit of the Wastelands. And that was it. That was the thing we had in common. Molly had an old man just like him! Only hers peeled noses for conceited rich people. We were kindred souls, spiritual orphans, alone and angry at the world. The rest did not matter. We were a perfect fit.

We never got back to what we thought we wanted

that night. We ended up at her house and talked until dawn. The truth is we never stopped talking until Buddy Elder entered our lives. And I never again felt like I was wandering around just killing time until I figured out what I wanted.

'FOR THE SAKE OF half-a-hand-job between us,' I said to Walt that evening, 'we've lost our marriages.'

Ever the philologist, Walt answered me: 'Full hand, David, half-the-job.'

'Why would he do that? What does Buddy get by ruining our marriages?'

Walt didn't believe we were innocent victims. I suppose he needed his guilt, but I kept thinking there had to be some way of figuring out what Buddy really wanted. It couldn't be just spite! Not with the elaborate set-up he had used to nail me.

I tried different theories on. I played the amateur psychologist, muttering Freudian platitudes, but nothing quite held together.

Walt listened politely, but he knew the reason Buddy had come after us. He had no doubt. We tried to sleep with his girlfriend, one of us actually had, apparently, and he paid us back with interest. 'He hit us where it hurt.'

'I didn't sleep with his girlfriend, Walt.'

'You wanted to.'

He had me there. Walt studied me in his own peculiar way. He knew I was an inveterate liar. He knew I enjoyed summoning up the ridiculous and offering it as gospel. Still, he was reluctant to call me a liar while I was at low ebb. If I wanted to pretend it was only a fantasy that was fine with him. Fantasy, reality, it didn't matter. Buddy Elder had not authored our misfortunes. We had.

My friend, my lawyer, my wife: they all asked themselves why Denise Conway would write about an affair that did not actually occur. When there was no logical explanation they could only conclude I was lying, as I was known to do from time to time. It occurred to me that their response was exactly what Buddy Elder had anticipated. He had even arranged matters so that Denise's complaint against me made no sense until the diary exposed her real motive. No one doubted it because Denise had not even wanted to admit the affair when she had filed her complaint.

Had he staggered his attack on me knowing the evidence would have greater effect if it came after the investigation had gathered some momentum? Was the son of a bitch that smart?

Around midnight it hit me, not the reason, the reason still did not make sense, but the method. The method Buddy Elder had employed came from reading *Jinx*. He had confirmed that the first story was a lie by introducing a second story. Because the second story discredited the first, nobody doubted *its* veracity. I had summarized the principle as Larry the Liar's mantra: *Never tell a lie. Always tell two.*

TUBS HAD NEVER SUBSCRIBED to Larry the Liar's method, though he recognized that a great many people thought you had to lie to persuade people to do something. He knew the method worked, but he didn't believe it worked as well as his own. Tubs said truth was its own reward. As a child, like all children, I had imagined he meant the reward would come in the form of feeling good about myself if I said only the truth. I didn't understand that Tubs cut and measured by the dollars and cents of a deal. He meant reward in its most literal and immediate sense.

I finally learned what he meant when I went to work with him. The summer I was out of high school, Tubs made me get what he called 'a real job' with the city. It was mowing and grounds keeping and landscape work, long days of sunshine, heavy lifting, and a whole lot of sweat. And it didn't pay very well. The next summer, Tubs said I could do anything I wanted. I said I wanted to sell cars with him. He just smiled, like he was proud of me, and muttered, 'Too lazy to work, too nervous to steal. You must be my son after all, Davey!'

He set one condition for my employment. He said he didn't care what I did off hours, but when I was on the lot or working a deal, even at midnight over a beer, I was never to lie. Absolutely never. I made the promise and I kept it as long as I wandered around in the wastelands, but I sure didn't think it sounded like fun.

And it wasn't. For two weeks I kept bouncing into people and losing them. I talked and I shook hands and I smiled a lot. I was a hell of a nice guy and so honest people even complimented me on it, but they never bought anything. They bought from Tubs. They bought from Larry the Liar. They never bought from me. Then one night, before I had landed even a bad deal, trudging off the lot with the rest of the sales-people and thinking landscaping wasn't such a bad summer job after all, Tubs called me back. He pointed toward the back lot and said, 'There!' I looked, but I couldn't see anything. 'A man and woman,' he said and he had the reverent intensity of a fisherman about to get a strike. 'They think we're closed.' I couldn't see them, but I knew Tubs was a fisher of men, and he knew when the Big Ones came to feed. 'Davey,' he said, and took my shoulder in his big hand like a coach about to send a player in, 'I want you to go up to them and tell them we're closed for the evening. Give them your business card and tell them to come back tomorrow and you'll take care of them. And if you say it like a total prick and walk away without another word, I'll give you ten bucks.'

I was tired and frustrated. It was easy to be rude.

I figured Tubs knew them, and just wanted to piss them off. I didn't care. It was more fun than being nice. I heard the woman rumbling behind me as I walked away. She had never! And the man yelled loud enough for me to hear, 'You just lost yourself a sale, young man!'

Tubs ran into them on the way to his car, the perfect accidental meeting. They were so mad they had to tell someone about the rude young salesman they had just encountered. Tubs wanted to know who it was. When they gave him my business card Tubs admitted a hard truth, because he could not tell a lie. The impertinent young salesman was his son, and he was mighty sorry he had brought me up so poorly.

When Tubs gave me the ten dollar bill the next morning, he handed me back my business card, too. It was torn into four pieces. He had had both husband and wife rip it once, just to show me what they thought of my salesmanship. He had promised them he would give the thing back to me, and he was, he told me with the straightest of faces, a man who kept his promises. Of course, after the ceremony of the card ripping, it was only natural that the folks had seen just the car they couldn't live without. And wouldn't it teach me a lesson I'd never forget if they bought the thing right on the spot!

It was a lesson I never forgot all right.

My brothers hated Tubs because he was such a righteous old fart who couldn't tell a lie, but I was the baby. I went out summer after summer to be close to the old man and learn his great wisdom. I even practiced his brand of truth on the lot. I never lied out there, but it was the only virtue I respected. I couldn't wait to put the tie on and be there with him, to beat him just one time, one month! That was all I wanted, and he taught me how to do it, too, though I never quite pulled it off. I was always second to the old man, and Larry the Liar was somewhere back in the pack, imagining we just told a better story. Tubs showed me that at the bottom of it all the rich and the poor all come down to the same thing: when they want something they get small and greedy and full of fear. You get people to want a thing, and there is no folly they won't commit in the cause of their desire. Their greatest fear, their only fear really, is that you're lying. You tell them only the truth and convince them that you never lie, no matter what the personal cost, and they will jump into fire to have what they lust for. That was the secret of Tubs's greatness.

As the summers passed, I lost the passion that comes with the kill. My soul got farther and farther from the wastelands the more I read the poets. The poets and storytellers of this world lied for the beauty of a good story, lied for the sake of a higher truth, and when I finished reading their tall tales I had a better feeling about what it was to be a human being.

Of course, I also knew that even the greatest of them all would just be another sucker on the car lot. John Keats rises from the dead and lands his skinny ass in DeKalb, Illinois. Poet or not, you've got to have a car in DeKalb, so he sneaks up at the back of the lot at closing time to avoid the salespeople, and Tubs is there waiting for him like God.

'...a wordsmith are you, Johnny? My son's a poet. It's a beautiful life and we need more like you to sing its praises. Now, tell me, and be honest with me, what kind of a car does a poet drive?'

Young Johnny Keats grabs for the antique purse he's tied to his belt, but it's too late. The strings are already cut.

Chapter 12

I MET MOLLY AT A CAFE about a week after my suspension. The talk was money and the best way out of some rather complicated property holdings, if it came to divorce. That was my position. As far as Molly was concerned divorce was the only reasonable response to my infidelity.

We added things up, subtracted mortgages, and talked through the most intelligent ways to dissolve our holdings. The problem was the farm. It was Molly's but she had leveraged a number of loans with it. If my income suddenly stopped, as it was very likely to, we could be caught short. The option was to dip into our retirement accounts or sell off enough at fire sale rates that we could limp along with the other properties until we got our price on the apartment houses. The best way to handle it really came down to my prospects at the university.

I told Molly I had filed an appeal to my suspension.

That was immediately rejected by the VP, based on what he called 'accumulating evidence of inappropriate behaviour.' I had pushed another appeal forward, but it amounted to nothing more than symbolic defiance. I was getting paid. I had been replaced. No one was going to bring me back into the classroom again until the following semester.

The real issue was the main investigation against me, the charges filed by Denise Conway and Johnna Masterson. The VP had scheduled a hearing to review Affirmative Action's recommendation for disciplinary action. Comprised of faculty from across campus, the committee would review the evidence and make its recommendation. The VP would then forward this along with his own opinion to the president. While I would have the opportunity to appeal the VP's finding and even the president's decision, my best chance, short of court, was at the initial hearing.

How did that look? Molly asked. I ran through a few of the names on the committee. Molly understood what I was saying. I was looking at a stacked deck.

Settling both arms on the table, I told my wife, 'Gail thinks the best approach is to admit wrongdoing. Given the circumstances, I'd probably get away with nothing more than a letter of censure.'

Molly's eyes flashed. She was suddenly very interested. 'What are the circumstances?'

'They have a copy of Denise Conway's diary,' I said.

'According to it, the affair started before she was a student of mine. Gail thinks if I grovel, really do it up right, talk about the problems in our marriage—'

'We didn't have problems in our marriage, David.'

'And I didn't have an affair. We're talking about strategy.'

'I don't believe you.'

'I know you don't. What I'm saying is if I tell the committee we were having problems and that I started an affair last summer this entire investigation becomes something they can understand. Plus, it ceases to be part of a pattern of behaviour. I get counselling and I'm back in the classroom in January.'

'What kind of problems are you going to tell them we had?'

'I don't know. *Problems*. It doesn't matter. If I don't admit to doing something wrong and give them a convincing reason for it, Gail thinks the committee will be, in her words, "less than sympathetic".'

'Meaning?'

'Meaning the suspension will continue without pay.'

'Do what your lawyer tells you, David.'

'It's a lie, Molly. Everything in that diary.'

Molly shook her head, tears brimming. 'Don't do this to me. I don't want to hear it.' She tossed her napkin on her plate and reached for her purse. 'This was a bad idea.' She stood up and stared down at me with nearly the same ferocity as the night she had pointed her .22 at me. 'If we had been having troubles, *problems*, I could understand what you did. I wouldn't like it, I might still leave you, but it would be different! I wouldn't feel so stupid! I wouldn't stay up nights asking myself why you thought you needed her!'

Up to this point, other than sorrow, my emotions had been in check. I did not consciously decide to let go. I just snapped. She wasn't the only one losing sleep and asking why, I said.

Molly bristled the moment I raised my voice. 'Goodbye, David.'

With that, she turned and walked away with absolutely nothing between us resolved. I did not try to stop her. There was no point really.

AFTER THE FIRST FEW DAYS of isolation, I had been able to call Lucy. With her mother's permission, she had met me for dinner a couple of times. I had gone out to her school to watch a football game with her. We talked about the fall races, the people who had asked about me, and all the usual stuff that comes with belonging to a tightly knit group, such as the people she raced against every weekend.

Lucy was her mother's daughter, but she was trying not to play favourites. She knew by now I had been charged with sexual harassment by two women and that I was allegedly having an affair with one of them.

She also knew I was denying it. Molly had not given her the details. Lucy had not asked me about any of it. My guilt was too generally accepted, I suppose.

Her real fear was that I would lie to her as she assumed I was already lying to her mother and the people at school. As long as we didn't talk about it, I wasn't lying to her. Avoidance was her mother's game. My methods were more complex and certainly more devious. Blame it on the blood. I did not think it wise to proclaim my innocence to Lucy directly. It hadn't worked with Molly or Walt or my lawyer. I had no reason to think it would work with Lucy. That did not mean I had nothing to say.

'Have you ever wondered,' I said during our third dinner together, 'why I never asked you if you smoke marijuana?'

We were in a public restaurant, safely tucked away from other people. Lucy had none of the easy exits available to her at the farm, such as something urgent to do in the barn. We were halfway through our meal, an unseemly time to depart for the restroom. But she did her best. 'Because you know I don't.'

I did not remark on this statement. There was nothing untruthful about it, as such. She believed that I believed she had nothing to do with drugs, alcohol, or sex. She was seventeen, sure, but not one of those girls trying to be twenty-two. There had been three boys out to the farm to take her on a formal date, a total of eight or nine times: hayrides, parties, dances, a movie, a football game. She was pretty, but she was headstrong and smart and had no patience for compromise. I had no doubt she had been kissed, kissed plenty, maybe, but there was something so forthright about her that I never doubted her choices. When Lucy fell in love Molly and I would know it. Until then, we were free to delude ourselves with nineteenth century notions of chastity and goodness, if that made us feel better. And why not? Lucy *was* a good girl, whatever that means in the new millennium. Her reward for that was our silence. Even when it became clear she was getting high we didn't say anything. We just watched and waited and hoped she was careful. Because she was seventeen, Lucy misunderstood our silence. She imagined we were stupid.

'Not at all,' I answered. 'I don't ask you about it because I'm afraid of your answer.'

'You don't have to worry about me, Dave.'

Still no lie. 'I don't worry, because I won't ask.' Lucy did not quite understand this. She imagined after she thought about it that I was telling her life as an ostrich has its advantages. I let her work through things to that point before I continued. 'You see, my greatest fear isn't grass. It's that you would lie to me about it if I asked you. *That* would hurt.'

I am an evil man. I know how to manipulate a situation. Tubs taught me all too well. Lucy is an innocent. She cannot imagine I have anticipated her next two moves and already have the roadblocks set, that soon she will be lying to me and hating herself for it.

'I'm not smoking grass.'

Technically, because she did not understand grammar, Lucy thought this was true. She was not smoking it *at this moment*. I tried not to react. Even among loved ones my observations about grammar were not well received.

I had put her here by my wickedness, and now it was time to twist the blade a little.

'I'm not asking you!'

'But I'm telling you.'

'What are you telling me?'

She retreated to silence. One of the first lessons I got in the wastelands was when you asked a question you needed to wait for an answer. I once watched Tubs sit for thirty minutes in front of an older couple. After five seconds the average salesperson will nervously blunder into the silence and ruin a perfectly good closing question. I had seen good salespeople hold out for thirty seconds. I never saw anyone but Tubs Albo last five minutes, but on that day Tubs waited five minutes and nobody spoke, so he just kept waiting. *Do you want it?* That was Tubs's favourite question, and until he heard an answer he would not talk again. Thirty minutes later they were still thinking about it! And not a soul in that dealership was foolish enough to blunder into that closing booth and let them off the hook. Finally, seeing that Tubs would wait all day, the old man said, 'Maybe. If the price was right.' Five minutes later he owned a car. They were, Tubs explained in the post-mortem, the kind of people who liked to keep a car for seventeen years. Trouble was they had met a *real* salesman!

What are you telling me? I asked my stepdaughter, and then I waited.

Now Lucy was cornered by her own words as I had intended, and I was not about to let her off. She tried to eat, but when she saw that I was waiting for an answer, she set her fork down. Three minutes. The waitress came toward us. I held my hand out imperiously, 'We're fine,' I snapped, and she faded. I kept my eyes on Lucy. *What are you telling me?* I would not repeat the words, nor would I change my expression. I waited to see if she would lie again, something she couldn't wriggle out of with a faulty understanding of the present continuous.

'I've been around it. Kids do it. Everyone does it.'

This amounted to as much of a confession as she was willing to make: a syllogism for her step-papa. *Everyone does it. I am part of the class of everyone. Therefore: I do it, too.* That was the logic. The emotion was something else: *I see it, but I don't partake. I'd never do something like that! Now put your head back in the sand!*

But I am a stupid man. I do not understand syllogisms or emotional appeals. I waited for her to answer the question. No one should have such a stepfather.

'Sometimes,' she said finally. 'Not much. If you don't... you feel like—'

She stopped, expecting the lecture. I didn't give it. After providing me with more than enough time to preach on the folly of peer pressure, Lucy had to finish her thought. 'You're mad.'

I shook my head. 'Not at all.'

'I thought you would be really pissed off. You more than Mom.'

'I'm concerned. On the other hand, I'm pretty much concerned all the time about you, even when you're doing everything right.'

'Did you ever smoke grass?'

'Sure. The other kids made me. I mean I hated it, but to be popular... you know how it is.'

Lucy had found an ally and laughed at my confession. She could even forgive me for mocking her.

'You're not going to tell Mom?'

Point of the entire conversation: 'I don't keep anything from your mother, Lucy.'

Lucy's eyes frosted over, 'Right.'

'Is there something you want to ask me?'

'What's the point? You'll just lie to me.'

'That's worse than adultery, isn't it? The worst thing I could do?'

161

Lucy was not confident about the answer to this.

'Tell me something,' I said. 'If I told you I had an affair last summer would you think any less of me?'

Lucy considered this solemnly. She wanted to be honest and she was eager for me to be honest, because, whether she realized it or not, my telling a lie to her was worse than anything else. We didn't play that game, not about the important things. When I lied to Lucy she knew it was a lie. Even Ahab and Jezebel knew it!

'No,' she said, 'not if you were honest with me.'

I smiled at her. 'That's because you already believe it. You think I had an affair, so you've already adjusted your opinion.'

Lucy worked through this as if calculating the possibility for the first time. 'It isn't true?'

I smiled. 'It's a frightening thing to ask that, isn't it?'

She got angry because I had finally gotten her to ask the question and now I wouldn't answer it.

'Is it true or not, Dave?'

'I'm going to give you some time to tell your mother what's going on with the grass. If you don't, she and I are going to have a little talk.'

'She'll ground me.'

I kicked one shoulder up, dismissing the consequences. 'Would you rather lie to her?'

'I'm not lying!'

'Silence is the biggest lie of all, kid.'

I called for the waitress. I made a fuss over the fact that I had been rude. I said we had been having a heart-to-heart. I gave her a wink. You know how those can be? She understood. She had a couple of daughters herself! Lucy corrected her. Stepdaughter. The waitress didn't miss a beat. She had a couple of them too.

I said we would like to have the check. Anything wrong? I smiled. Nothing at all.

In the car I told Lucy I'd like a Baskin-Robbins. 'How about you?'

She thought that sounded good. We were about halfway across town when she said, 'You never answered my question, Dave.'

'You're right. That's because it's not your place to ask it. It has nothing to do with the two of us.'

Long silence and then, 'You did.'

'What if I didn't?'

'I don't understand. Did you sleep with that woman or not?'

'I don't want you to take sides, Lucy. What's going on isn't about your trusting me or believing your mother. It's not about *you*. Believe me, you can be happy about one thing no matter how it ends between your mother and me. You're not a part of the fight and you're not a part of the solution. I came into your life twelve years ago. I'll be there as long as you'll have me. I hope that means forever.'

Over ice cream, Lucy asked, 'What do you think Mom will do about the grass?'

'Depends on which of us tells her about it.'

'You're going to tell her if I don't?'

'I sure am.'

She looked at me craftily. 'Because you never keep anything from her?'

'Never,' I said.

This time she didn't answer wise.

Chapter 13

LIKE A GOOD TRIAL lawyer, Gail fought three battles simultaneously. One involved complaints about procedural errors. The second argued definition of terms. The last objected to findings of fact.

While I resisted an essentially technical defence, I took special satisfaction in one of Gail's letters of protest. Having scoured the university handbook, she wrote the university lawyer to inform him that while smoking was prohibited in faculty offices there was nothing in the handbook, either explicit or implicit, prohibiting sexual intercourse.

Gail explained that by highlighting issues concerning the university's failure to follow its own procedures and by insisting they observe definitions as written in their own handbook, we were essentially demonstrating the wisdom of finding a solution other than firing me. The only trouble with this approach was the vice president's committee would not really care how the thing played out in court. The committee's concern would be focused on my actions. If we could make those understandable, even if we admitted wrongdoing, my chances of the whole thing going away would be excellent. Moreover, the appellate process would still be in place. In other words, I gave nothing up, but I had an excellent chance of finding closure for the case in committee.

'What they want is a victory against sexism. In and of itself, that is more important to the committee than whether you are guilty of either sexual harassment or misconduct. They don't care if a court brings judgement against the university for failing to follow its own rules. It's not their money. The president might because he'll have to find a way to pay you for a wrongful discharge, but the people sitting on your committee are idealists. They're tired of male professors using the student body as their own private harem. These proceedings might be confidential in theory, but nobody believes it. The people on that committee want to send a message to every male professor on campus. That's important to remember. They don't want to fire you, David. They want to make a point.'

We had come to the critical moment. It was time for me to decide. Confess or tell the truth.

GAIL HAD CAREFULLY kept the issue of my innocence in the subjunctive mood. Her letters on my behalf admitted nothing, nor did they explicitly deny guilt.

Every salesperson I ever knew who was worth his salt had been in a situation like this. You negotiate to a certain point, then hand the victory to your customer. Even Tubs routinely employed this method of salesmanship. It's written in all of the manuals: let the customers feel as though they have won a battle or two and you will always win the war.

This was all Gail wanted. If I let the committee members watch me grovel and weep, if I went down on my knees and begged for mercy, they would have no reason to forward a particularly harsh recommendation.

On the car lot, the easiest way to hand your customer a victory was to admit you lied. It assured buyers their view of the world was correct. While it cost the salesperson a bit of lost pride, the commission was usually sufficient to take the sting away. The classic case involved the salesperson delivering a final price. If that did not work, and it usually didn't, the salesperson's credibility was shot but not the deal. The solution was to bring in a new face. Management overrules the salesperson: the customer gets a victory and drives the car home.

Tubs was the only salesman I had ever met who would not stand for it. As a matter of principle, he never drew a line in the sand with a final price. He was too clever to get himself trapped by his own words. His words were his weapons. He didn't hand them over to the customer to use against him! And he never relied upon a single method to close a deal. His only go-to-close was in fact his go-to-hell-close, and he trotted it out whenever he got good and pissed off. He called it his A Gun in my Face Close.

I saw it once, early in my sojourn in hell, but it was a thing of beauty, a memory as bittersweet as any I had of the old bastard.

'I screwed up,' I said, before I told Tubs anything else.

Tubs looked up at me. He had been examining his customer list, divining whom he should call at just that moment. Tubs was not a man to tell you a screwup could be turned into an opportunity. He believed, on the contrary, every screw-up could be turned into *his* opportunity, so he smiled at me in his kindly, paternal way, already counting his fifty percent on my commission. 'What happened, Davey?'

'I told this guy on the phone the Mustang convertible is sixty-four hundred, and it's seventy-four.'

'Tell him you made a mistake.'

'I did. He doesn't believe me.'

Tubs held onto his smile, but it turned icy. He leaned back in his chair. Placidly, he folded his hands over his big belly. 'Is he still here?' I nodded. 'What does he want to give?'

'Five thousand.'

'Have you got him sitting down?'

'We've been at it for an hour. He won't budge. He's sure I'm lying.'

Tubs blinked. 'Let me see what you have.'

I opened my hands. 'Verbal offers. Milt told me to T.O. to you.' A T.O. was a Turn Over, the act of bringing in another salesperson and thus splitting a commission. A good salesperson usually understood when it was time. Most people loved it when they got to make a T.O. to Tubs Albo. If they had a buyer and hadn't gotten themselves stuck on a number, Tubs could get a signature and make a salesperson more money with half a commission than a full commission working solo.

'Can Milt go sixty-four?'

'I don't know. I didn't even know about the car until this guy called.'

'You mention a number yet?'

'Just the seventy-four hundred. I've been trying to get him off five.'

Milt came into Tubs's private office. He was a tall, roughed up looking man, maybe thirty-two or thirty-three years old. Milt was born ready for a fight, but he had a talent for giving back what he got, and he always treated Tubs with velvet gloves. Ask any manager in the world, when a guy sells twenty to twenty-five cars a month, he can do anything he wants. He's the king, and Tubs was all of that. 'Tubs, I got the invoice on that son-of-a-bitch-Mustang we bought last night.' Milt's voice was rotten with cigarettes. He shook a slip of paper at the two of us. 'This cowboy doesn't believe David screwed up on the price, and he's not budging. Where did you get that price, David?'

'Larry told me,' I said.

'Larry! And you believed that lopsided set of duck nuts?'

'I hadn't seen it,' I said. 'I had the guy on the phone, and I had to trust Larry.'

'Next time trust that he's lying!' Milt turned his attention to Tubs, his voice going soft again: 'We're going to lose this guy if we're not careful, Tubs. I can't afford to go sixty-four, and five is, well, he's just pushing David around to see what we can do.' The way Milt said he couldn't afford to go sixty-four suggested to me that if pushed that was a good number. Tubs could automatically add five hundred dollars to such a figure for an excellent commission, even after splitting it. I knew, too, that if I could figure this out, Tubs understood it completely. The numbers were locked in. We had to move the guy, and anything around sixty-four was good, above that, golden.

'Does the guy want the car?' Tubs asked. Tubs always liked to know that before he'd go make a pitch. Amazingly, not many salespeople bothered asking that question. But Milt knew people. Milt had gasoline in his blood. He smiled with big yellow horse teeth. 'Tubs, the guy is creaming his jeans, but he's getting mad. Now, look, I want you to take this invoice to him and show him just what I paid for it last night.'

'I don't need an invoice.'

Milt got just a little excited, considering he was speaking to the Zen Master of the Wastelands: 'He's a hard-headed cowboy, Tubs. He wants the car. He just doesn't want us to screw him.'

Tubs rose, a man called to his sacred duty. 'I'll screw the son of a bitch, and he'll like it. Introduce me, Davey.'

Tubs shook hands and sat down where I had been sitting. The two of them were laughing almost immediately. I'd worn the man down with my young man's grim determination, and Mr Dietrich was glad just to have a man his age to talk to. 'Now Mr Dietrich, Dan, can I ask you a question?' Still pleasant, but Tubs's smile had screwed down a little tighter, and Dietrich could see we were about ready to give him the car. He nodded. I could smell eager coming off the man. 'Do you want the car?'

Mr Dietrich waited almost sixty seconds to see if Tubs would trample over his own question, but Tubs just held his gaze and waited for the answer. Finally, Dietrich reared back in his chair and blew hot air. Last inning, he couldn't play too coy, but he wasn't going to throw away everything he'd won, either. 'Maybe. But I don't want it for sixty-four! I told your son, I'll go five!'

'He told you the price was seventy-four.'

'On the phone, it was sixty-four! I get down here, and you all raise it on me.'

Tubs's smile was gone. 'The moment you got here, David straightened you out. He told you he'd made a mistake, didn't he?'

'That's what he said.' Mr Dietrich was good-natured about lying salespeople. He was an old man. He had scalped plenty of liars.

'He said it because it's true,' Tubs had gone just a little red in the face, the way a preacher will when he gets to his favourite verse.

'Even if it was true—'

'Whoa, now, wait just a minute, please.' Tubs held one hand out to command a full stop. His other hand still held a Cross ink pen over a blank contract. Sometimes it was his lucky pen that no one ever touched except to sign a deal. Today, it was just one of two choices: sign or swing, friend, one or the other. 'I'm going to tell you something, and I'm going to tell it to you once. My boy's an Albo, and Albos don't lie, not out here, they don't! David here will shoot straight even if it costs him. I taught him that. If anyone catches him lying, I'll buy the deal and give the car to the person he's lied to! Then he'll pay me back every penny if it takes him the rest of his life!'

'I'm sure—'

Tubs broke over Dietrich's condescension without waiting for him to set it in stone. 'The price on my car is seventy-four hundred dollars, and I don't care if you put a gun in my face, it's not going for a penny less.'

'That's just bullshit.'

'You think?' Tubs nearly came over the desk. The two men stared at one another like they were about to fight, then in total dismissal of the man, Tubs walked away. 'Come on, Davey.'

As I followed, I heard Mr Dietrich crow, 'You'll have that car marked down to sixty-nine by tomorrow!'

Tubs didn't react. I had thought he would. It had taken us some effort, but Dietrich had finally accepted that seventy-four was our list price. The fact that he had mentioned sixty-nine meant he was ready to close. All we needed to do was settle on something in the mid-six-thousand range and Dietrich had a car. And more importantly, Tubs and I had a commission.

Tubs was having none of it though. He put his back to that man and didn't slow down. In his private office, he sat down at his desk again and resumed looking at his list. I stood next to him quietly. Milt came into Tubs's office a minute or so later. 'What happened?'

'A Gun in my Face Close.'

Milt reeled back the way a kid will when someone farts. 'Not the Gun in my Face Close, Tubs!' Tubs lifted his eyebrows, a definite yes in his vocabulary. Milt groaned. He knew a buyer when he saw one. 'What was your number?'

'Seventy-four.'

'Full pop? Not full pop, Tubs!' Milt was screaming now, albeit in whisper mode. No sense letting the customer know the troops were divided. Tubs's eyebrows flickered. Full pop and not a penny less. Milt kicked a file cabinet. 'Nobody pays full price at a car lot, Tubs!'

Tubs was calm. He had gotten full pop before and he would again, but he understood Milt's position. Milt wanted a sale, not a long shot. 'My man will, or he won't get his Mustang.'

Milt invented sexual positions for the saints of three different religions. He seethed. He sighed. He prayed for someone to shoot him and put him out of his misery. Then he looked at me. 'How high will he go, David? Best guess.'

I looked at Tubs. Tubs nodded. 'He said something about sixty-nine. He'll go sixty-nine, I think, or real close to it.' I was stretching it, vainly hoping I could move my father down five hundred dollars. I wanted the sale as much as Milt.

Milt spread his hands happily. 'Sixty-nine is good, Tubs. I can live with it. He can live with it. Can you live with sixty-nine, Tubs?' Tubs shook his head. He was sitting tight on seventy-four. 'Everybody likes sixty-nine, Tubs!'

'He called Davey a liar, Milt. I won't have that.'

'How about I send Davey back. It's out of your hands. You have nothing to say about it, right?' Milt looked at me. 'Go back and tell Mr what's-his-name he bought a car if he'll go sixty-nine.'

'Davey.'

I knew the tone, and I froze.

Milt rushed to my defence with a touch of desperation. 'It's not you, Tubs. He called Davey a liar. Not you.'

'You can send Davey out if you want, Milt. You're the manager. You can do anything you want. You do it, though, and I'll be selling Buicks before the sun goes down.'

Milt kicked the empty air. 'This close never works, Tubs! Let me go in and buy the deal for sixty-nine. I'll pay a commission for seventy-four. That's good, isn't it?'

'I don't care if I sell that car or not. I put my word on it, and that's that.'

Milt cussed blue smoke in a murderous rage, but he left the office. There was no dealing with Tubs when he got to the issue of his sacred word. I heard Milt on the loudspeaker a few minutes later. He started calling out the specials of the day. He read an interminable list, and then he came to the Mustang. His voice rasped in an awful car salesman's seduction, cylinders, litres, and miles per gallon, '...seventy-four hundred dollars. A steal at that price, folks.' He named a couple more cars and shut up. He paced on the makeshift tower and smoked. He smoked two cigarettes at once.

Mr Dietrich sat for thirty minutes at my desk, absolutely alone. Nobody approached him. Nobody got within fifty feet of that desk. Finally, Mr Dietrich came to Tubs's office. He leaned through the doorway, actually. He wasn't coming all the way in. It was a gesture that announced clearly he was about to make a last offer. 'I'll go sixty-nine, against my better judgement.'

Tubs didn't even contemplate it. 'Mr Dietrich,' he said, 'You need a gun in my face and another five hundred dollars.'

Dietrich was a horse trader from way back, but he laughed. He laughed hard. It was over. He didn't have a gun, he said, but he thought he could find another five hundred dollars for a car that nice. 'Assuming, that is, you all pick up my sales tax.' Tubs smiled and said he could do that, he surely could.

Later, Mr Dietrich told me, 'You got a ways to go, David, before you're as good as your old man.' He thought about it fondly for a minute. 'Gun in my face and another five hundred dollars!' Mr Dietrich shook his head and laughed again. 'I never heard that one before!'

Chapter 14

I WROTE THREE DIFFERENT confessions for Gail to pass on to the committee. I tore each up in turn. Finally, I found the defence I could live with and scribbled it out: 'I am innocent of all wrongdoing.'

The next day I took it into Gail Etheridge's office. 'You want to type this out or just hand it over like this?'

Gail's face showed no reaction. She simply stared at me. 'I take it we are prepared for the consequences?'

'I have a verbal statement as well.'

'Great! Let's see it.'

'It's a verbal statement, Gail. I don't have anything written down.'

Gail looked at my one sentence defence sceptically. 'Can you give me a rough idea of what you intend to say?'

I played the English professor. 'I can,' I said, 'but I think I'll wait until the defence and let you hear it then.'

'I don't like this, David.'

'I like it, and that's what counts.'

She urged me toward 'a more comprehensive statement' but I told her it didn't get any more comprehensive than innocent of all wrongdoing.

We met the VP's committee a couple of days later. Gail made one last pitch as we went in. She thought it might be best if I didn't say anything at all. She would speak to the issue of a complete lack of proof, the lawyer's preferred method of pleading innocent.

By then I had steeled my resolve and shook my head like Tubs. 'It's my execution,' I said. 'I want to tell them I didn't do this.'

The meeting did not feel like a trial. In fact, the vice president for academic affairs, Lou Morgan, assured me repeatedly, while not quite looking at me, that I was not on trial, nor were we in a court of law. The committee had examined the evidence, he said, and they had gathered here today to discuss it. I was free to call witnesses on my behalf, but this was not a forum for cross-examination. Furthermore, he said, the administration rejected our request to interview the two women who had originally filed the complaints against me. Their statements had been investigated and verified. There was no point in involving them in what was essentially now a disciplinary action.

As things developed the meeting involved a good deal of back and forth between the vice president and various members of the committee. One prof, who I remember had consumed a great deal of caviar at my party, wondered if it was appropriate that Leslie Blackwell was on the committee. She had collected the evidence. Shouldn't it be for others to judge it? The vice president made it clear that Dr Blackwell was sitting on the committee as a non-voting member. Gail Etheridge asked for clarification. Was Dr Blackwell to provide guidance? Certainly. Guidance and clarification of law? Of course. Clarification of the evidence as well? That seemed only logical. Gail wrote this down for a future complaint, muttering to me as she did, 'Imagine a trial in which the prosecutor sat with the jury during deliberations.' I nodded thoughtfully. We had already discussed due process. Any break in procedure causing fundamental unfairness in the process would be open season when and if we brought suit against the university.

Curiously, there were no witnesses for the university. This meant the evidence Dr Blackwell presented was the complete case. None of it could be contradicted by oral statements made directly to the committee, nor refuted by cross-examination. Blackwell's notes about her interview with me had me confessing to calling the breasts of Johnna Masterson bodacious ta-tas. When Gail Etheridge complained that I had said no such thing the vice president informed Gail that Dr Blackwell was not on trial. Gail swallowed her exasperation and tried to explain that the evidence itself was incorrect. Her client, she said, admitted to using the term without explaining the context of that usage. Dr Blackwell had either wilfully or unconsciously manipulated an honest response into an admission. A committee member asked in what context bodacious ta-tas would be acceptable.

Gail was ready for that one, 'In the context you just used it,' she said and scored nicely for our side. Another committee member asked if Gail meant to say Dr Albo had been discussing the expression and not a certain feature of the female anatomy. Gail explained that Dr Blackwell had failed to investigate that issue. Without the ability to cross-examine, she said, every piece of evidence put forward was subject to the investigator's whim, and this was a perfect illustration of whimsy. A second committee member pushed the issue. Was Dr Albo asserting that he used the phrase 'in a technical sense?'

Gail finished the discussion with perfect deadpan: 'I wasn't aware that bodacious ta-tas had a technical sense, professor.'

Before the affronted professor could respond, the vice president suggested we move on. The committee could discuss that possibility in private.

It was a grim procedure for the very reason that it lacked judicial procedure. Material was not presented, then challenged. The case lay before the committee as a finished product, rather like a dead fish on the verge of rot. Hearsay and gossip passed for facts because the rules of evidence did not apply. Perish the thought that professors pretend at being lawyers. The committee members could speak whenever they chose to, thus directed the course of the hearing. As a result, there was a great deal of concern about the issue of faculty members performing sexual intercourse in their offices. Rather to their astonishment they discovered the handbook did not address this issue. Instead of discussing the implications of that in my case, one of the committee members concluded, and they all nodded solemnly, the handbook should be rewritten. At about this point, Gail breathed pure rage, whispering to me, 'These people are morons, David.'

I whispered back, 'Welcome to my world.'

For nearly an hour, no one doubted the veracity of any of the charges or the credibility of any of the evidence. The chief concern was if such behaviour constituted sexual harassment. A private conversation with another professor, a professor helping a student leave the sex industry and take a Work Study job so she could continue school... it was not exactly time to bring in the feds. Dr Blackwell pointed out a passage in the diary of Denise Conway in which I threatened to fail Denise if she did not perform fellatio. A joke, Gail answered. Was it? Denise had admitted as much in the same passage. 'Perhaps,' Blackwell retorted,

'Denise was trying to convince herself Mr Albo was joking.'

'It's *Doctor* Albo,' Gail answered with a gratifying touch of outrage. Gail then went on to explain the difference between a complaint and the evidence supporting a complaint. 'The committee is not free to rewrite the complaint of a student, much as certain non-voting members might desire it.'

Blackwell responded as Gail expected, introducing the concept of a hostile atmosphere. Having anticipated her opponent Gail now attempted to cross-examine Dr Blackwell as to the definition of atmosphere. She got as far as asking if a single remark in a private conversation with another professor constituted atmosphere when the vice president reminded her that this was not a trial. People could decide for themselves what constituted hostility toward women. We all knew what a hostile atmosphere was when we saw it, didn't we?

Shortly after this my moment arrived. I held up my statement and then placed it on the desk before me. Dean Lintz, who sat on the committee, had to play fetch. He actually stopped on the way back to the table where the VP's committee sat. Turning toward me with a look of astonishment, he said, 'This is your statement?'

Dean Lintz had not seen such a compact statement since the days his high school English teacher made him read a haiku. I stayed seated and told him that I also wanted to say something. As I had not made copies, my single sentence made its way down the line of the committee members, gathering a look of reproach at every stop. They were quite certain no man is completely innocent, and concluded therefore I must be mocking them.

The vice president told me to proceed, cautioning me to be brief. Dean Lintz could not resist. He said verbal statements, according to the handbook, were supposed to be summations of the written statements. If that was the case, he expected a *very* brief statement. There were a couple of smiles among the committee members, but most of them maintained the grim demeanour of the Salem patriarchs in their heyday.

I remained seated behind a little table, if only to conceal the accused. 'It seems to me,' I said in a conversational tone, 'no one, least of all Dr Blackwell, has bothered to investigate the veracity of the diary of Denise Conway. The sole concern of this investigation has been whether the behaviour itself warrants disciplinary action. My position, however, is that I am innocent of all wrongdoing. Denise Conway's diary is a fabrication first to last.' I gave them a moment to consider this assertion. 'If you believe me, then her complaints lose all credibility. Had the committee allowed us to call Ms Conway as a witness or to cross-examine her about her statements to Dr Blackwell, I believe we could have exposed her diary for what it is: an absolute lie. Since the committee chooses to turn this into a case of he said / she said, I can only tell you it is not true.

'As this leaves you at something of an impasse on what turns out to be the critical issue of this investigation and as this is potentially a very serious matter, the possible dismissal of a tenured professor on the basis of an unsubstantiated accusation, I believe the solution is for Dr Blackwell to arrange a follow-up interview in which she asks a single question of Ms Conway: am I circumcised or not?'

'I think,' the vice president announced officiously, 'that will be enough, Dr Albo.'

'I'm not quite finished, sir.'

'I believe you are.'

'It's a fair question,' I said as calmly as I could. 'According to her diary, Ms Conway got a close enough look. If anyone can answer the question besides my wife, she can!'

'If you are determined to make a mockery of this proceeding—'

'If you have no interest in the truth, you're the one making a mockery of it!' I shouted.

Having no gavel, the vice president slapped the table with the palm of his hand. 'This meeting is adjourned!'

I stood up at this and pointed my finger at the man. 'The evidence against me is a lie,' I roared. 'And I don't care if you put a gun in my face, I'll still tell you it's a lie!'

Feeling as though the ghost of Tubs Albo had stepped into my shoes, I turned and walked directly to the nearest door. I never once looked back.

Gail Etheridge met me outside several minutes later and treated me to a grudging smile. 'You're beautiful, David. You really are.'

'You think they'll ask her?'

Gail shook her head and lit a cigarette. 'Not a snowball's chance in hell, but I guarantee you this, you'll be the talk of campus by sunset.'

Chapter 15

'IS HE OR ISN'T HE?' WALT shouted when he came back to the apartment that night. He was tuned up. I was already roasted. We turned it into a hell of a night. On Saturday Walt invited a select crew of debauched professors from across campus, male and female, to join us. Foregoing the usual stages, Walt's Go to Hell Party, thrown in my honour, was a raunchy affair from the start. Before the night was out, I believe everyone tried to take me into the bathroom for a little look-see, strictly in the cause of truth, of course. I'm not sure how I answered the various inquiries and solicitations, but I had the feeling, shortly before I passed out, I might well face fresh charges come Monday morning.

Barbara came by the apartment at nine o'clock the following morning interrupting a particularly nasty hangover. Walt, so inured to the feeling he hardly noticed, blushed like a schoolboy and started trying to pick the place up. As it turned out I was the reason Barbara was there. Neither Walt nor I had his cell phone turned on, and Molly had asked Barbara if she could drive by and tell me to call Molly's cell phone. At my look she explained. 'Something happened to the dogs.'

I found my phone under a pile of pizza boxes and called Molly a few seconds later. 'What's the matter? What happened?'

'Someone poisoned the dogs, David.'

By the time I got to the farm the animal control unit had packed all seven carcasses into the back of its panelled truck, and Molly was signing something so they could take off. 'You've got the animals?' I asked. The driver could see I was as upset as Molly. He answered apologetically. The sheriff's people wanted them to examine the animals. They wanted to know what kind of poison was used.

I shook my head. I said I wanted to bury the animals on the farm. 'It's our business,' I said. 'They're just dogs. We'll take care of it. I don't care what kind of poison it was, and neither does she.' The man looked at Molly, then spoke to the deputy investigating the case. Finally, he got the bodies out.

They were stiff with rigor and came out of the panelled truck like so many logs. Only the eyes and the fur and the remnant animal smell of them recalled anything of their sad lives. I carried all seven, one at a time, off the hill and down to an area in the pasture where we had buried different animals over the years. We had two cats that had died on us, Pollock and Picasso, and a hamster named Susie. There were two stray dogs already in the earth. They had got hit before we could adopt them: Gilgamesh and Ulysses. I buried the murdered dogs deep in the earth in seven separate holes. Molly left me alone until I had finished. I was tamping down the last, Melville's grave, when she came out to join me. She smiled at my work, which we both knew was partly for Lucy's benefit and partly for my own.

'Lucy hasn't come out of her room since she found them this morning.'

'She found them?' I had been hoping it had been otherwise.

Molly nodded.

'She got home around midnight. She says she didn't hear the dogs, but she didn't think anything about it.'

I understood how she could miss it. The racket they made, *had* made, was so familiar you didn't really hear it. It was the silence you noticed. But I understood why Lucy had missed it.

'So they were dead by midnight? Weren't you around?'

'I heard them barking. I thought it was the wind upsetting them.' Molly began shaking her head as tears formed on the rim of her eyes. 'They were just mutts! They weren't hurting anyone!'

189

I didn't bothering responding. I was thinking about Buddy holding his gun against my face, the words he spoke. '*You and me… we're going to have some fun before I'm finished with your ass.*'

BEFORE I LEFT, Molly showed me the work she had done on Lucy's apartment. Over coffee she told me someone had made an offer on one of our rentals. When we had finished with business there was nothing left to say, so I went upstairs and knocked on Lucy's bedroom door.

She was on the phone and took a minute before she let me in. When she did I told her I had identified each grave, but I wanted her to paint the names on the stones, the way we had done it with the others. That was when she started crying. She cried just like her mother, wiping the tears away, half in embarrassment, half in fury.

I asked her about the night before. She had been at a party. Home at midnight? Pretty much about then, she said. There was no mystery to chase down, except the motive, and Lucy couldn't help me with that. 'Have you talked to your mother about the grass, kid?' I studied her face. This was standard operating procedure. Silence drilled her conscience.

'I'm careful, Dave. I mean I don't do it all the time like some kids. And I don't like lose control.'

'You need to come clean with your mother. Knowing

her, she's probably just waiting for you to show her you're honest with her.'

'What if she grounds me?'

I shrugged indifferently. I'd love to be grounded. I'd take any excuse to move back in with the two of you. 'Does it matter that much? I mean... are you seeing someone?'

'No.'

Between lying salespeople and lying customers eager to promise me anything if I would just let them go home and think about it, I had developed an excellent feel for liars. The standard assumption in the industry was summarized in the acronym APAL: All People Are Liars. The trouble with such universal cynicism is sometimes people will let the truth slip out when they're not careful. You need to know how to separate the gold from the brass. The look-you-in-the-eyes effect was the general method for most amateur liars. With Lucy, who was not a very good liar, the eyes darted first and then they stayed frozen on me. If she was seeing somebody it was all right. She was seventeen. At seventeen that's what you do. But she was lying to me about it. Or not sure herself.

'But you might want to?'

She smiled. 'Maybe.'

'You see him last night?'

'It was a party. He was there.'

'And he smokes grass?'

'He's not a pothead, Dave. He's a nice guy.'

'We're all nice guys, Lucy. That's how we get to be with nice girls. What's his name? How old is he? What kind of grade point average does he have? Does he know I have a couple of shotguns in my office and I'm not afraid to use them?'

Lucy sneered. 'I'm not even going out with him!'

'Yet.'

She smiled prettily, a girl with a lot of hope. 'He's just a guy, Dave. Give me a break.'

'Talk to your mother. Tell her about the pot.'

As I was leaving she called to me. 'Are the horses going to be all right, do you think?'

I looked at the doorjamb and thought about it: Jezebel with a tendon cut, Ahab's neck slit open. 'I don't know, Lucy. If they wanted to hurt the horses I guess they could have last night.'

'Why would somebody kill the dogs? If they wanted to hurt us why not the horses?'

That was when it came to me: Buddy Elder had gone after our alarm system.

BEFORE I LEFT I TOLD MOLLY to keep her revolver close. 'Whoever hurt the dogs,' I said, 'might be back for you.' I said the best thing would be for me to move back in, if she would let me. To my surprise Molly said she'd think about it.

I got back to town at dusk. I went directly to the

house on Ninth Street where Denise Conway and Buddy Elder lived. A girl answered the door. She was overweight but the right age and disposition to be one of Denise's friends from work. Her kid came up behind her as we talked and stared at me curiously. 'Denise Conway live here?' I asked.

The girl shook her head. 'Not no more.'

'Actually, I was looking for Buddy Elder. You know where I can find him?'

'He moved out too. They broke up.'

I tried to get some information from her, but she had been warned. She wanted my name. She wanted to know what my business was. I told her my name was Ralph W. Emerson. I wanted to talk to Buddy about some dead poets. She thought that was strange. I had her write down my cell phone number and told her to tell Buddy to give me a call, if he had the guts.

I was almost back to Walt's apartment when my phone trilled. 'The W. stand for Waldo, does it, Ralph?' Buddy asked.

'Where are you living these days, Buddy?'

'Denise and I broke up, thanks to you, Dave. I got a new place. Just trying to get my head together, start over. You know how it is, I expect.'

'I'd like to come by and talk to you about a few things.'

Buddy gave me his address. I turned my truck around and went back into town. The lights were off in the house, and I was not sure Buddy actually lived there until I knocked at the door. From the darkened house I heard Buddy's voice. 'Door's unlocked, Dave.'

I opened the door and looked into the darkness. 'You hiding?' I asked.

'A long time ago a cop told me if I ever shot a man breaking into my house I better make sure he falls completely inside. Half-in and half-out isn't good enough. You want to come on inside?'

'Are you going to shoot me?'

Buddy laughed cheerfully. 'If you come inside I am!'

He walked to the door. Barefoot, wearing jeans and a T-shirt, he held a nickel-plated .38 revolver. I was guessing it was the same gun he had pulled on me outside The Slipper. As before, he pointed it at me with keen pleasure.

'Where were you last night, Buddy?'

'Why do you want to know?'

'Someone killed our dogs.'

'Your dogs? All of them?' I didn't answer. He shook his head, his eyes locking on mine without the pretence of sincerity. 'That's just a shame, Dave. A real shame.'

I pointed at his gun. 'That's not going to save you, Buddy. When you need it, you're not going to have it.'

The street lit up from the lights of a car, and Buddy shifted his gaze from me for a second. 'I don't care what anybody says, the cops in this town are good!'

He stepped back into his living room and set his revolver under the cushion of the couch. I turned and walked off the step as the two policemen got out of their patrol car, their spotlight on me.

One of them told me to stop where I was and to put my hands on my head. He came toward me with his hand on his nightstick. His partner worked backup for him. When he got to me he asked me to step toward the house. I did. At his request, I placed my hands against the house and spread my legs. He patted me down, then let me stand up again. 'I'd like for you to come back to the patrol car with me, sir.'

I did as he asked. His partner went inside and talked to Buddy. 'You know the person in that house, do you, Mr Albo?' my officer asked me after he had checked my identification.

'Joe Elder. Buddy,' I said. 'He called me up a few minutes ago and told me to come over. I got here and he pulled a gun on me.'

'That's not quite how we heard it from our dispatcher.'

We batted it back and forth, our respective versions of the truth. By the time his partner returned from the house, I was fairly certain I would be going back to jail. The difference this time was my young friend had trapped himself with a lie. There would be a record of Buddy's call to me. His flank exposed, I was going to make him pay for his games this time. My cop pointed at me and said, 'He says he got a phone call, was invited over here to talk.'

The other cop nodded. 'I got the same story, plus a little more. Your name is Dr Albo, right?' I said it was. 'You and Mr Elder are having problems?'

I knew enough about the law not to suggest that Buddy had poisoned my dogs. Statements to the police amounted to public record. A groundless accusation would open me up to charges of slander. For all I knew, that was Buddy's plan.

'I don't like the guy,' I said, 'I'm not sure I'd say we have problems.'

'He tells me you were accusing him of sleeping with your wife.'

I expect I smiled. I hadn't seen that one coming. '*That* problem,' I said.

'I'm going to let you go with a warning this time, Dr Albo, but I'm also going to file a report on this incident. You come out here again, you'll be explaining yourself to a judge the next morning. Do I make myself clear?'

'Yes, sir.'

'Let me give you some free advice,' the senior partner added with a sigh. He had a dozen years on me, a look of perpetual misery that could only come from too much domestic bliss. 'You're going through a divorce, am I right?' I nodded. 'I see this kind of thing a lot more than you'd believe. Decent, clean-cut woman, all of a sudden she goes for something like that.' He pointed his thumb absently in the direction of Buddy Elder's house. 'Two reasons. First, it makes her feel young again. Maybe she's not sure if she's still desirable. She wants to find out. Second reason is she knows it's going to hurt you.

'Truth is mostly she wants to hurt you. Now when you come out to this fellow's house and make threats, maybe even get yourself arrested, she's going to know she won. You follow me?' I nodded. I followed. 'You seem like a bright enough guy, professor. You don't want to step into that kind of game.'

Once I was in the truck again and had started away, I began laughing. The son of a bitch was good!

Chapter 16

'I SAID I WANT to think about it,' Molly told me the following afternoon.

I paced nervously, my cell phone pressed to my ear. 'You said you *never* wanted to sell the farm.'

'We both said a lot of things, David. Look, I want to go down to Florida for a few weeks. Take a look at the situation. Doc says the housing market is getting stronger. I can flip a place in three-four months if I buy the right property.'

'You're quoting Doc on real estate, Molly. Listen to yourself.'

She laughed. 'That's why I need to go down there and take a look. You move back to the farm.'

'And Lucy moves in with the Sloans until you decide what you want to do. I know. I just don't know why you're doing this.'

'You're the one who wanted to move back to the farm. So move back. Make Walt happy.'

'I'll break Walt's heart. I didn't tell you but we've zipped our sleeping bags together.'

'That's sweet.'

'When are you going to take off?'

'Tomorrow.'

I hated the sound of that word. It meant she had already arranged everything. 'Am I going to see you again?'

Silence answered. When I didn't break it, she told me, 'Why don't you come out tomorrow around four-thirty? Lucy will be here. The two of you can see me off.'

MOLLY HAD THE CAP ON THE BACK of her truck, a few tools packed away in a trunk we had used over the years to keep the horse gear, and a couple of suitcases. She was travelling light, but not so light she couldn't stay for the winter if she decided to.

The weather was cold, the sky overcast. A brutal wind swept in from the north.

'People are crazy to live in this weather,' Molly announced happily. 'I called Olga this morning. It's eighty degrees today, blue skies, and just a light breeze.'

'I'll join you, if you want,' I said. 'Nothing holding me here.'

'You hear something from school?'

I shook my head, sorry I had broached the subject. 'It's not going to be good when I do.'

'I don't get it. Randy Winston's been screwing around with students since he got here, and everybody knows it.'

'And Walt can't open his mouth without offending someone. What don't you get?'

'Why you?'

'I refused to take my lawyer's advice.'

Molly looked out at the pasture. She shook her head and smiled, recalling our earlier conversation. 'Every time I start thinking that maybe you're telling the truth, I remember: this guy made a living by lying.'

'I never lied on the car lot. I told you that. That was the deal with Tubs.'

'It makes a good story, David. But I don't believe it for a minute. You can't help yourself. You open your mouth and a lie pops out. I think you're lying about Tubs, like everything else!'

'How many times have I lied to you, Molly? I mean about something important.'

'That's the point! I don't know. Last summer, you went into town for a couple of hours, you came back with whatever you went for and had a little smile on your face! Did you sleep with Denise? I don't know! How many times did you lie about her? I have no way of knowing. You won't even admit it!'

We heard Lucy's Toyota come off the pavement and climb the hill. A moment later she pulled her vehicle into the circle behind Molly's truck.

'You taking off?' she called.

'Not without a hug.'

They hugged. They talked about Lucy flying down for the week of Thanksgiving. Lucy had cleared it at school, pulling the divorce trump card to get them to give her the extra three days.

Molly said there was some good in it after all. Lucy glanced at me to see how I was handling the joke. I just smiled. I was thinking about an axe in Buddy Elder's skull, though I was more inclined to give him something along the lines of what he had fed Hawthorne & Co. I had heard that Liquid Plumber was an especially slow and unpleasant way to go, but naturally for an occasion like Buddy's imminent demise I would want to do my research. That's what Ph.D.s do.

'You're going to be all right?' Molly asked me.

'No,' I said. 'The minute you drive away from here half of my reason for living just disappears.'

'Don't do this to me.'

'You asked.'

She walked away, hugged Lucy one last time, and then to my surprise came back to me and threw her arms over my shoulders. 'You broke my heart, you bastard,' she whispered. 'I'll never forgive you for that.'

A moment later her truck started up and she drove away.

201

With Lucy's help I moved back into the house. The whole process took about ten minutes. I offered to fix her dinner, but Lucy said she'd told the Sloans she would have dinner with them.

'I'm going to have a talk with Mom when I go down for Thanksgiving, Dave. About the grass, I mean.'

'Sounds like you've got your mother figured out.'

With entirely innocent eyes she asked, 'What do you mean?

'Molly isn't going to want to let Olga know the two of you are having problems. Absolute best place to confess is with Olga in the next room. Your mother will just smile and say that's wonderful, Lucy! I hope you're only smoking good dope. Bad grass can be so irritating to your little throat.'

Lucy laughed. 'You think?'

As she was getting in her Toyota I said to her back, 'You going to tell her about the boyfriend?'

Lucy froze. It was a just a second, and then she turned. 'Nothing to tell. Not yet anyway.'

'The weekend's coming up. You never know.'

'That's right, Dave. You never know.'

'Be smart, Lucy. You want to get serious, fine, it's your choice, but don't assume a guy has been as careful about things as you would be. Some of these guys drink first and think later. Even *they* don't know where they've put it.'

I sounded like Tubs and I hated myself. At least I

hadn't mentioned genitalia turning into vegetable matter.

'Talking from experience, are we?'

'Say hi to your grandparents for me, kid.'

AFTER I FED THE HORSES and fixed my dinner, I settled into the guest bedroom across from the room Molly and I had shared. Then I went up to look at the work Molly had done on Lucy's apartment. The bathroom and kitchen appliances were in. She had the tile for the floor still in the boxes. I wasn't doing anything else, so I started tiling the kitchen floor.

Around midnight I had a good start and went downstairs. As long as I was working, everything was fine. Once I stopped the place felt enormous and empty. Not really frightening. Fear comes from the unknown. I knew who had killed the dogs, and a part of me yearned for him to show up and take his best shot. No, it wasn't frightening. Just empty and lonely and far too grand for a man on his own.

I spent a couple hours the next morning in my office. The latest short story I had been working on was in trouble. At least it had gone stale on me. I could not find the excitement I had felt at the beginning. On the first page a woman had gone off to meditate in silence at a Buddhist monastery for six weeks. Coming home refreshed and revitalized, she discovered her husband was living with another woman. The thing had seemed so rich at the beginning, so full of possibilities, but I had lost the momentum. I no longer had the distance and confidence I needed to write about love and relationships. My sense of humour had died.

I had eight weeks of paid leave, I told myself. I knew writers who could crank out a novel in that time, and I knew others who could produce a chapter and a full outline. For me a short story would be about right. The trouble was I could think of nothing but Buddy Elder, plot nothing but his murder. Pleasant as the fantasy was in the abstract, I did not dare think in practical terms about it. My greatest fear was that I would come up with something that might work.

So I went upstairs and threw myself into laying tile. In January my life at the university would resume or it would end and I would begin something else. If it came to starting over, I would probably get another teaching position. *Jinx* would get me something. I wasn't ready to learn another profession. The very idea of it at this late stage made me want to kill myself. I looked around my office and saw my shotguns in the gun case, a twelve-gauge and a four-ten. Definitely the twelve-gauge. Because if you're going to do a job, do it right.

Like murder, fantasies of suicide were a narcotic. I knew better than to indulge in them. New job, I thought, as if it were an accomplished fact. New city. Get busy and keep busy. When the time was right, think about meeting someone. That's what people did when they got divorced. They didn't kill the people responsible and go to prison or swallow a shotgun while they tried to slip their toes into the trigger guard. They smiled at a pretty face. They kissed strange lips and tried to forget how much they still loved the world they had lost.

At midnight, as I lay in bed, I began to think about murder again in a purely hypothetical way. A short story. I really couldn't help myself. It was the only thing that got me past the notion of suicide. Strange to say, but of all the sleepless nights I had spent since I learned of the complaints against me, this was the only one that afforded me some pleasure.

Chapter 17

LUCY CALLED THE NEXT AFTERNOON. The rain we had gotten the night before had turned the arena to mud. She asked me to throw some more water on because she wanted to practice running Jezebel.

'Want some competition?' I asked.

'Anytime you think you're up to it, old man.'

Barrel racing is a piece of Americana. It's simple, quick, and the wildest ride you can have on a horse short of bronco busting. The barrels themselves are set up in an isosceles triangle in one-half of the arena. The start and finish line is well below the bottom two barrels of the triangle. A rider runs the race alone, following a cloverleaf pattern around the triangle, turning three-hundred-sixty degrees at each barrel and finishing with a run from the top of the pattern back to the starting line. It is the sort of race that would leave the greatest thoroughbreds in racing history at the back of the pack, since only the American quarter horse has the ability to hit full speed in a single stride. Moreover it can stop and turn with the same efficiency. The trick of the race is to turn a tight circle on a reasonably fast horse. It doesn't have to be the fastest or the most athletic animal. Turn too soon and you take the barrel out, usually with the rider's shin taking a hit. Turn too late and the circle gets elongated. In a race measured to the tenth of a second a bad turn can cost you two or three full seconds on the clock.

In his best days Ahab was never the horse to beat. As he got older, he got the old warrior's applause whenever I got the itch to run him, but never the prize money, unless it happened to be raining. If it was raining, if the arena was soaking wet and getting worse instead of better, Ahab was the odds on favourite, assuming as they liked to say, Dave could stay on him to the end of the race.

When we bought Ahab, we didn't know about his talent. We thought all his first place victories came from his speed. We had never heard of the term mudder.

It was Lucy's belief that with patience any horse could be taught to negotiate adversity. I didn't try to disillusion her. Time would do that. She could practice all she wanted, Jezebel was Jezebel, and Jezebel only knew one way to run a race: wild-eyed, tail straight up in the air, and blowing exhaust all the way home.

Lucy praised me for the condition of the arena. It

was about six inches deep with mud. I told her to put her helmet on. She sneered but she wore the thing, and she strapped it down tight.

Since I was presumably smarter than a horse, the first time I ran the barrels I decided I should do the steering. Poor Ahab cracked *his* shin on the barrel. After that, I engaged the autopilot lever attached to all western saddles. It seemed to work fine. Ahab knew where he was going and when to turn. Besides, I soon found out two hands on the saddle horn were hardly enough. At the first turn in a barrel race it feels like the horse is falling down, you get that low to the ground. While you're still thinking about bailing out, the horse leaps into a full gallop toward the next barrel. Two more turns like that and most mortals over the age of eighteen are ready to call it a summer. Anyone lacking a proper sense of human mortality, of course, gets addicted.

In mud the whole thing gets dicey. We ran eleven races that evening with the floodlights on. Jezebel fell down six times. She won twice, the two times Ahab fell down. In defence of the old guy, Lucy said something about his rider throwing him off balance. I wasn't buying it though. In a barrel race I was always off balance. Ahab was used to it.

While we washed the animals down afterwards, I let my stepdaughter contemplate a hard truth: some of us are at our best in the sunshine, and some of us, like Ahab, only get tough in a cold rain. You don't train for that. It's in the soul. I didn't say that of course. What I said was, 'Maybe when you go off to college you might want to take both horses, Lucy.'

'Ahab's too old for serious competition,' she snapped testily.

'He looked pretty serious tonight beating your ass.'

'Jezebel can learn to run in mud.'

'You know in Texas nobody is going to know Ahab can win even with a novice on top.'

Lucy smiled at last. '*I'd* know.'

MOLLY CALLED THE FOLLOWING evening. She had gotten into an ice storm on the way down but had arrived safely at her parents' house. Did we catch any of the storm? Just rain, I told her. Then I said Lucy had come out to race. I got Molly laughing in no time. After that we talked about what I was doing with the apartment. I got off the phone in a good mood, but it didn't last. In fact I felt like crying. The intimacy between us had returned. The anger had cooled and settled and hardened. For the rest of our lives everything was going to be just like it had been before, without the romance. The romance wasn't coming back. I knew it now as certainly as anything I had ever known. It was over between us.

ON SATURDAY I DROVE LUCY to the airport and

got a big hug as she left. On the way home it occurred to me that I was going to be alone on Thanksgiving. Not especially relishing the prospect I called my former roommate when I got back and suggested he come out to the farm Thursday, but Walt told me he was spending the day with Barbara. 'Just the two of us,' he added cheerfully. 'Roger is going out of town with his new girlfriend.'

'Girlfriend!' I answered with a bit more surprise than I intended.

If Walt heard it, he didn't react. 'According to Barbara this could be the one.'

I said that was great, and I meant it, even if I didn't buy Barbara's optimism. From there we moved to more pleasant conversation, Walt's chances for a reconciliation. It came down to this: Barbara had said she was willing to talk about it. That was more than Molly was giving me, but I didn't happen to mention this. Instead, I wished my friend well.

It was good to hear Walt happy, but I got off the phone in a lousy mood. Having decided to make the effort not to be alone for the holidays, I was now virtually forced to make my next call. My mother was surprised to hear from me. We usually drove to DeKalb for the Fourth of July. But sure, she said, she could set another plate on the table. I could hear the question in her silence and began lying. I told her Molly and Lucy were in Florida. I was invited, naturally, but the last time I had gotten together with the McBrides, things had gotten a bit tense. My mother knew about tense. She had met Doc and Olga once, and didn't think it was at all unusual I could not get along with Doc. She wrote it off as class warfare. Doc McBride's only daughter had married the son of a car salesman. They could pretend it was fine, but it wasn't, and no harm as long as Molly and I got along. No problem there! I told her. After that my mother, suspicious woman that she was, always asked about Molly and me. She asked again this time. I laughed as usual and told her after my fashion: 'If it got any better you'd think we had died and gone to heaven.'

My mother told me not to blaspheme.

I MADE ARRANGEMENTS WITH Billy Wade to come across the road and feed the horses while I was gone. Wade wanted to know about the dogs. I told him we had packed them off to the pound. He was shocked, and I could tell he thought less of me for it. 'Hey!' I said, 'people drop their mutts off out here! What am I supposed to do, feed them all? Where does it stop?'

'I might've taken one if you'd asked me, Dave.'

'Next time,' I said.

I gave him twenty bucks so he would remember and said there was another forty in it for him when I got back. Turning to leave him, I stopped as if struck by a thought. Had he seen anyone around the farm lately?

Since I'd been gone, I added. Wade thought about it before shaking his head.

'An old burgundy Mercury Marquis maybe?' I prodded.

Wade smiled. 'I seen that!' I pushed for details, but the giant only smiled. 'Driving by kind of slow like. He parked down the road, in that lane.' Wade pointed toward an old service road out in the cornfields that was hard to spot and pretty much sheltered by weeds and brush. Kids sometimes pulled in there at night, but it wasn't the best place to go, just handy if you were desperate. On the two nights Lucy had been late getting back from dates I had checked down there first. Lucy's boyfriends hadn't been perfect fools.

'How long was it parked there?'

Wade scowled as if the process of thinking actually hurt him. 'He drove in around eleven o'clock, left a few minutes before midnight.'

Did he remember what night it was? We had another spell of pain. Sure didn't. Best guess? Wade grinned and told me that back in school he'd never guessed the right answer no matter how many times he tried.

'You see that car out there again and you let me know right away,' I said, 'I'll give you twenty bucks.'

The giant grinned happily. 'Every time?'

'Every blessed time,' I said.

I left Wade calculating his newfound fortune.

* * *

212

I HAD A MEETING SCHEDULED with Gail Etheridge before I drove to the airport Wednesday. For the first time since the diary had surfaced, Gail was showing a bit of lawyerly optimism. With my permission, she had brought suit in state court immediately after the hearing. Critical to our case, she thought, was the committee's refusal to let me finish my verbal defence. Additionally, she said that after the vice president adjourned the meeting he proceeded to instruct the committee as to the procedure they should follow. 'Major screw-up, David. First, you had walked out. Second, the meeting had been adjourned, meaning his instructions were never actually given. I've been sleeping with the university handbook, and the procedure is all spelled out. Any variance and they've violated their own policy.'

Due process was only part of it. According to Gail the state had set limitations on jury awards resulting from violations of due process. Defamation was another issue. There were no limits on defamation. 'Defamation makes them nervous. Right now, we're fast tracking the case, which will let me begin deposing key players as early as December. Once I do that, we're going to catch Dr Blackwell in some pretty embarrassing mistakes, like this thing with your bodacious ta-tas. The bad news is things are going to get expensive real fast. Depositions cost money.'

'I need to talk to Molly about the money,' I said.

Molly and I had set the bulk of our funds in an account requiring both of our signatures for withdrawal.

'I've got them on the run, but without the depositions to prove Blackwell screwed up the witness interviews, we can't push them as hard as we need to.'

'I can sign over my retirement funds to you, if you can carry me,' I said.

Gail seemed uneasy. She needed something. I asked her how deep I was into her. She said she would get a bill worked up. Roughly, I said. Roughly, I needed to get her about five thousand dollars for her to keep going. My truck was worth between three and four at auction, but I knew it would list retail at close to five. 'How about title to my truck?'

'How about cash? How much can you get me?'

'I'll get something lined out next week,' I said.

'I hate to do this to you, but I can't carry you on this, not with divorce proceedings going forward.'

Chapter 18

I SOUNDED LIKE A BOGUE. Bogues can always get you the money next week. I didn't blame Gail for worrying. We were bailing out of our property. My job was in jeopardy. With a divorce Molly was likely to get most of the cash, and that left the lawyer standing in line with the bankers and credit card companies.

I decided not to worry about it for the time being. I had enough worries on my mind just going home. Home always made me think about Tubs, because even dead the old bastard wasn't finished with me.

My mother hadn't collected on Chrysler stock, of course. That was just typical David Albo bullshit. The thing I told Buddy happened, though. Up to a point. Tubs had predicted a comeback. The salespeople had laughed their asses off, and he had called his broker ordering five thousand shares! The broker talked Tubs out of it.

Mom had a pension and a big old house in the

downtown that wasn't worth much more than what they paid for it forty years ago. She imagined herself a poor old widow, though she was mostly just afraid to spend her money. She had plenty, actually, but her fears let her miss out on the cruises her friends were taking. She drove an old car she was afraid to trade because Tubs always took care of the cars, and even with four sons, well, they didn't know cars like Tubs, did they?

When Mom wasn't worrying about her own finances, she liked to scold her prodigal sons for the debts we took on so blithely. We all lived in nice houses and drove nice cars, and charged whatever we liked on our nice credit cards, the typical American family. Suddenly, I wasn't in the mood to hear her scolding, because her dire predictions had come true for me. I was in trouble, and beginning to imagine everything I had juggled for years would come crashing down on me. But there was no way out of it once I'd called: Wednesday, Thursday, Friday, Saturday: the smothering embrace of home.

It wasn't quite as bad as I anticipated. A lot of TV, a lot of beer, a couple of late night escapes from the nieces and nephews down to our favourite watering hole, and, on the last night, a heart-to-heart with my oldest brother in which I suggested it was maybe time for me to change careers. If not now, I said, it was never going to happen. What was I looking at? The question hung between us until we both grinned: *Anything but cars!*

'The old man,' my brother told me with a shake of his head, 'stayed at it too long. With the money he made, Tubs could have bought his own dealership. Instead, he just kept trudging down to that Ford lot until it killed him.'

I shook my head. 'Tubs was a lousy manager. As a dealer he would have lost his shirt.'

I was the baby in the family, my brother reminded me. I didn't know how it was when Tubs was still fairly young. He remembered hearing Tubs talk about how much he hated the car lot. His comments sparked a memory: a long morning in the sun, Tubs making a rare offer to buy me lunch. He drove us out to a little restaurant at the edge of town famous for its pies. Tubs was not a serious drinker. He might hold a drink all night, then set it down untouched. He would drink a beer on the Fourth of July and talk about how good it tasted, but that was it. He never went back for a second bottle and might not even touch another until the next Fourth. Pie was different. The man lived for pie. Sometimes his lunch was a store-bought apple pie. Sometimes he would raid the vending machines with a stack of quarters and take every pie in sight. Given a choice, he naturally preferred freshly baked pies. He could talk about hot apple pie the way poets of old crooned about unrequited love.

On the afternoon that he took me to lunch, the air was rich with the odour of apple pie. The waitress knew Tubs just like bartenders know the alcoholics. 'Fresh out of the oven this morning, Tubs!'

Tubs ordered a whole pie for each of us without asking me what I wanted. As we walked toward an open booth, he said to me, 'The car business, Davey, is just too hard on a man. One of these days, I'm going to buy a little place like this and sell pies! You don't have to twist a man's arm to get him to take a piece of pie!'

I was still young. I hadn't finished my undergraduate degree. I could make more money in three months than some people made in a whole year, and all because of what I had learned at my father's knee. Tubs was, in my innocence, a man who could teach the world. He knew the truth about people. He knew the words that could move a person to action. He read the hearts of people even if their words masked their intentions. He could lead people to a crossroads and show them how to let go of their fear. In five minutes, sometimes in five seconds, Tubs could tell you who made the decisions in a marriage, the small ones and the big ones. He could wreck the tranquillity of the happiest couple without them understanding what he had done, if it would move them to a decision. He could neutralize the brother or cousin or meddling aunt if one or all of them were sitting in the closing booth and stopping a couple from making a decision. He could tell you a story and make you want to drive a brand-new Ford because of it, or even a used Chrysler if that was your heart's desire. He had that power, and the only thing Tubs wanted from it was to settle his fat ass in front of all the pie he could eat and not have to pay retail for it.

The man's fantasies broke my heart. I thought he didn't love his talent, and it *was* a talent. I never saw the like of it, but if it was only to keep his fat belly full, as if he thought he might really go hungry if someone walked away from him, it was a waste of genius.

It was against family policy to defend Tubs. We had it written in the family handbook. He had left the house early every morning and come home late every night. Saturday was a workday. Sunday he went to church to pray to God to keep the Bogues away. When he bothered to deal with any of us at the house, it was usually something that got us fighting among ourselves so we would leave him alone. What worked at the lot worked at home. All Tubs wanted was to have his own way.

Old habits kicked in. I couldn't tell my brother he was wrong about Tubs. I was not going to say Tubs did what he loved until the day he died, but I could disagree with the cause of death. 'It wasn't the car lot that killed the old bastard. It was the pie!'

The next day, Saturday, I wandered out to the Ford dealership. Milt was still the manager, the only face on the lot I knew. Though it had been a while, Milt recognized me at once and broke into a smile. 'You need a job,' he called out to me as I walked up, 'I've got one for you! All I've got here are order-takers!' A few heads turned, salespeople bristling at the insult or maybe just checking out the competition.

I shook his hand. Not today, I said. 'I just came by because I wanted to give you something.' I handed him an autographed copy of *Jinx*. Milt handled the book with the enthusiasm of a boy who has just received a pair of socks on Christmas morning. His words were kinder. 'Well that's... that's real thoughtful, David. I don't read much, but I'll give it a shot.'

'It's about us,' I said.

Milt looked at me without quite getting it.

'Life in the wastelands,' I said, gesturing toward the lot, using Milt's own phrase.

He flashed his big yellow horse teeth at me. 'You wrote a book about us? Is it X-rated?'

'You remember Debbie?'

'Debbie does DeKalb? You put that in?'

'Her name is Connie Q.'

'What's the page?'

'Start at the beginning.'

'Is Tubs in it?'

'Tubs is Jinx. You're Stitch, and Larry the Liar... well, he's Larry the Liar.'

'Hey! That lopsided set of duck nuts has himself a little church down in Peoria! Can you believe it? Preaching Jesus once a week and raising hell the rest of the time!'

I shook my head for Milt's sake, but I wasn't surprised. Larry had always had a soft spot for the Baptist girls.

We talked about the car business. Milt asked me about school. I expect we both lied. While we talked, different sales people approached with deals or troubles. Milt ran the place and never lost track of what he was telling me, but it was obvious he was busy. I said that I had better go. I had a plane to catch. Milt kicked the tire of one of the cars in the showroom. 'Ol' Tubs,' he said nostalgically, the first mention of my dad since I had handed him my novel. 'I mean but that man could sell cars!'

'Did he like it, you think?' I asked. I wanted to believe Tubs knew the gift he possessed. I wanted assurance that the thing with pie, that was just a moment of weakness.

Milt grinned at me with his horse teeth. 'You remember the first time you turned a hard case around, David? The very first tough sale you brought in with no one's help?'

'The first sale I made,' I answered.

Milt nodded. I knew he wasn't thinking about my first sale, though he had been there. He was thinking about his own. 'Every sale was like that for your dad.' He thought about it for a moment. 'The day he died he said to me, "I got some folks coming in tomorrow, Milt. If I'm not here, you take them yourself. They're buyers. I don't want them to get away!" So I asked him why he wouldn't be here. Tubs never missed a day of work in his life. He said he thought he had a touch of the flu. Hadn't felt good all day. David, your old man sold three cars for me thinking he had the flu. Turned out he'd had a heart attack that morning! Most people can't sell three cars on their best day. And all he could think about was making sure we got the next one. Did he *like* it? He lived it, brother! You had his talent, too. Tubs said so himself.' Milt shook his head with a bit of sadness. 'But I could see after the first couple of summers you weren't going to stay with it. Your skills got better but your heart wasn't in it!'

'I guess I just realized I was never going to be as good as the old man.'

Milt shook his head, but he wasn't disagreeing with me. 'Tubs used to say God calls the preachers, but the Devil calls the salesmen, and the worst of us peddle cars. You don't spend your life out here in the wastelands unless it's your calling. Not that I wouldn't trade places with you! You go into that classroom and even if you're not having a good day they hand you a pay check! Huh? Am I right? They ever cut your check back for a bad lecture?'

'It's a hell of a gig,' I said.

'Just don't let it turn you soft, friend. You lose the edge, you lose everything. Your dad taught me that!'

Chapter 19

I GOT HOME FROM DEKALB late Saturday afternoon. The horses were already in the barn. I walked down the hill and went across the road to the little house where Billy Wade lived. Wade was in a cheerful mood as usual. He got in a better mood after I handed him the money for taking care of Ahab and Jezebel. 'Any problems?' I asked. The giant shook his head. 'You see that Mercury Marquis drive by?'

'He came out every day!' I reached for my wallet. 'Naw, Dave. I'm funning you! He only came out one time!'

I handed Wade another twenty. 'What did he do?'

'It was after dark. I walked out to that service road way on out there. It was that Merc you was asking about, all right.'

'You write down the license plate number?'

Wade seemed embarrassed. 'I sure didn't. You didn't tell me to, did you?' I told him it was my mistake. I said to go on. 'Nothing more to tell. I went back to the house and watched. He drove away maybe an hour after that. Maybe an hour-and-a-half in all.'

'Next time, you come up to the house and let me know while he's still here. Can you do that?'

Wade slapped my shoulder. He told me not to worry.

The house was cold, and I nudged the thermostat up and surveyed the house for some evidence of a break-in. The windows and doors were all secure. My papers were all in place. Nothing had changed, but I had the feeling Buddy had been inside the house.

I glanced at the mail, flipped through the newspapers, then went to my office and checked my e-mail. In the kitchen I noticed the light on the answering machine blinking. I pushed the button. Eight messages. The first was a prof I knew in Sociology. He wanted to know if I had heard anything about Walt's suicide.

I didn't bothering listening to the rest. I went back to my office and got the papers out. I found the article in Saturday's paper. Hardly more than a note in Regional News, actually, it reported that the bodies of Walter and Barbara Beery had been discovered at their residence Friday evening by their son Roger. The sheriff's department was investigating the possibility of foul play.

I went online, hoping for more details, but there were no updates. I went back to the answering machine. Six calls from different people at the university, two hang-ups. I started calling until I got what I wanted. Randy Winston had the details. Walt had apparently visited Barbara on Thursday, Thanksgiving Day. I said I knew about that. What happened? Nobody knew. At some point during the afternoon Walt had walked up behind Barbara and drove a carving knife into her back. Walt had then hanged himself from a rafter in the garage.

I called the McBrides. Doc answered. He told me Molly was out for the evening. Did I want to talk to Lucy? I said no, but I needed to talk to Molly as soon as possible. Could he leave a message for her to call me the minute she got in? He could do that.

Because I didn't want to break off too abruptly, I thanked Doc for calling Judge Hollis.

'Glad I could help, David. I told Jimmy that wasn't like you at all.'

'No, sir, it wasn't,' I answered equably. 'I usually land the first punch, and that's the end of it.'

Doc McBride laughed as if I had made a joke.

Molly called me the following morning. 'Sorry I missed your call,' she told me when I answered, 'but I thought if he's going out I might as well too.'

The two hang-ups on the machine now made sense. 'I went to DeKalb,' I said.

'You tell them about us?'

'Molly,' I said, 'listen to me. I've got some bad news.'

* * *

AS SOON AS I TOLD HER about Walt and Barbara, Molly said she wanted to fly up for the funeral.

I didn't have the details just then, so I hung up and started calling around again. By the time I got the information and called back, Molly had switched Lucy's return flight. The two of them would be coming in that night. I said I would pick them up, but she told me not to bother. She had to rent a car anyway. Best just to get it at the airport, since she would be flying back the following Sunday. One week, I thought. One last chance.

THE TWO OF THEM GOT in late that evening. I had the master bedroom set up for Molly, and I took a little monk's cell on the third floor with a view to the back one-forty.

We got Lucy off to school the next morning and settled ourselves down so we could go through the tragedy of Walt and Barbara. The Sunday and Monday papers filled in some of the gaps, but I had found no one who knew more than Randy Winston. The paper was now calling it a murder-suicide, but that was all we knew. There was a nice summation of Walt's early career, however. It mentioned both of his books, *The Origins of Chivalry* and *On Courtly Love*, calling *Courtly Love* the definitive text in the field, even thirty years after its initial publication. There were several quotes included from various colleagues. The irony was even his most vitriolic detractors had sweet words for the man now. There were hints of course among these same people that the whole thing made sense. Words appeared in their remarks like stress, counselling, separation, difficulties. With a bit of imagination a reader could understand that Walt was a raging alcoholic with a bad marriage and troubles at work. Other than that it was a tasteful enough send off.

None of it, though, made sense to Molly or me. I suppose we knew Walt too well. Walt wasn't a violent drunk. Walt could be a laughing drunk or a sad drunk, even a bashful drunk, but never a violent one. The closest I had ever seen him to rage was the time another scholar quoted him out of context. Walt had slapped his hand on the table, rattling his bottles, and announced that the Inquisition had not been an entirely bad idea.

Pick up a knife? The man couldn't even carve a Thanksgiving turkey. I went through the last talk Walt and I had. Optimistic, I told Molly. 'He told me Barbara had agreed to talk about reconciliation.'

'That was it, then,' Molly answered simply. 'After they talked, she decided against it and Walt couldn't handle it.'

I didn't believe it, and told her so. It wasn't in his character to do something like that.

'I don't think any of us knows anyone else the way

we think we do,' Molly answered. There was a note of bitterness in this, and I knew we weren't talking about Walt anymore.

I WAS ALREADY PREPPING THE LARGEST room for paint in Lucy's apartment when Molly joined me. We had always worked without talking very much. When we needed to say something, we spoke in a kind of shorthand. We had been doing things like this our entire marriage, and that morning was no different.

Over lunch, we talked about our other properties. The apartment buildings were getting no lookers, I said. A couple of the renters had agreed to buy but wanted rent-to-own contracts. Molly swore sourly. If we wanted to wait thirty years we were better off keeping the property. I thought about making a pitch for keeping everything, including our marriage, but in the wastelands I had discovered the worst thing you can do is to try to close too soon, so I simply grumbled my agreement. To hell with them. If they wanted the property they could go to the bank. While we were on the subject of real estate I asked about Florida. Not as good as Doc had said, she answered, but there was money to be made, and Doc was ready to finance the venture if and when they found the right property. She was planning to stay in Florida then? I asked.

Still thinking about it. And me? I told her I had a decent chance of keeping my job if we could start deposing the university's witnesses, but Gail needed five thousand before she went any further. 'I told her I would ask you about signing off on that amount.'

'I'll drive into town this afternoon and take care of it,' Molly said. 'You can pay me back after the settlement.'

Molly's aunt had left her a fairly substantial pool of cash. It would be easier, Molly said, for her to write Gail a check. If she needed more, she could contact Molly directly. 'We can settle the debt later.'

'If you stay in Florida, what about Lucy? Senior year and all.'

'I told her she can move down with me in January and finish school in Ft. Meyers or stay with the Sloans and graduate here. It's up to her.'

'What do you think she'll do?'

Molly smiled. 'We drove out to a stable where she can keep Jezebel and Ahab. It was nice. The owner talked to her like he might be able to give her some work training a couple of racetrack Quarter horses for barrels, maybe teaching a class or two to kids. I think she was excited.'

I told Molly that was great. My tone said otherwise.

WE HAD TALKED TO LUCY about attending the funeral Tuesday, but it was scheduled for mid-afternoon. She had already missed three days of class the week before. She said if we didn't mind she would go to the visitation and miss the funeral.

After a spiritless dinner hour Monday evening, the three of us headed into town in Molly's rental. Walt and Barbara had made their arrangements a few years before, never dreaming they would be here together. Certainly Roger was not capable of handling something of this magnitude. He was twenty-five years old with the emotional maturity of an adolescent. There were no brothers or sisters on either side of the marriage, though quite a few cousins on Barbara's side showed up. It was apparently a tremendous imposition for them that Walt should end up at the same funeral as Barbara, but that much was Roger's call. I expect, as the lone beneficiary, Roger was counting his pennies. Five-point-five million, after all, just didn't go as far as it used to. One ceremony, one hall, one preacher: murderer and victim side-by-side. What was the problem?

The funeral home was divided into two distinct camps since Barbara had long ago broken ties with the faculty. A few too many secrets kept from her, I believe. The result was members of our department pitched in on one side with Randy Winston in the lead, and Barbara's clan, such as it was, on the other. It was like a wedding where the ushers ask, 'Bride or groom?' and seat you accordingly.

I had volunteered to do whatever was needed, hoping

at least I would be one of the pallbearers. Because Randy had not responded to my offer, I found him the moment we entered the funeral home. What did he want me to do? Randy told me it might be better for everyone concerned if I didn't participate. I was irritated naturally, but I said I understood.

When Johnna Masterson walked in, I thought about pointing her out to Molly, but decided there was no advantage in showing her the department's centrefold. I did, however, try to approach her. I was anxious to know what Buddy Elder had told her and just why she had ended up making her complaint *with* Denise instead of separately. When Johnna saw me moving toward her, she walked over to Randy Winston. Touching his arm, she whispered something. Randy's eyes locked on me at once.

I made no second attempt.

A while later I engaged in a clammy handshake with Roger Beery. He offered a few incoherent grunts when I talked about his parents, but that was the extent of our conversation. I could not decide if he was in shock or just didn't care. I didn't want to judge the kid on the basis of tears or a lack of them. I had not cried at Tubs's funeral. I recalled even that I had managed to laugh a few times with old friends. Lots of stories at that funeral, I can tell you. But Roger neither laughed nor wept. Someone quoted the newspaper to me. Roger had found the bodies. Could I imagine? I shook my head. No, I couldn't, I said. I swallowed my impulse to observe that in my researches about murder I had learned the killer was often the person who discovered the murder victim.

After a while I gravitated toward people I didn't know. I did quite well with these folks, especially when I got to talk about how Walt and Barbara had extended their friendship to Molly and me when I had first joined the faculty. I knew Barbara? That was always the question. My answer was always the same. A wonderful woman. This inspired remarks about Barbara's sainthood. Having never cared for any of the saints other than Jude, I agreed heartily. She sure as hell was.

The funeral home offered a large reception area at the front door, but the majority of people stood in the chapel where the two open caskets offered a last look. There was, finally, a small room for the family just off the chapel. In the thirty minutes or so I had been there, Roger had retreated to it a couple of times, coming back out after a minute or so. Smoking dope? Taking swigs? I didn't know, but I was curious. Three young women at different points had gone into that room. They stayed quite a bit longer than Roger, and since these girls looked a little ragged around the edges I began paying attention to the anteroom, wondering just what was going on in there. The last of them left the room when it was apparently empty and went over to Roger and said something. Roger reacted immediately, walking directly to the room. I followed him, stepping through the door only seconds behind him.

Denise Conway looked stricken at the sight of me. A moment later, she scanned the room for an exit. By a happy coincidence I happened to be standing at the only one. 'Denise,' I said, as if finding her at Walt's and Barbara's funeral was only to be expected, 'nice to see you again.' Denise retreated behind Roger's heavy shoulder without speaking. Actually, I think she swore. Her lips moved at any rate. I turned my attention to Roger, who was glaring at me angrily. 'I can see why you wanted to keep your love life secret, Roger.'

Roger told me to leave. His request was delivered a bit roughly, however, and to be contrary I didn't move. 'You might want to get a lawyer to explain to you what a deposition is, Denise. You're first on my lawyer's list to be deposed. You lie to her and you're lying under oath.'

Roger spoke for Denise. 'Go screw yourself, Dave.'

'Did Denise happen to tell you what was going on with her and your old man, Roger?'

It probably wasn't the nicest thing to say under the circumstances. Then again it's not real nice listening to a creep tell you to go screw yourself. Roger came at me fast, slamming me into the wall. While I was recovering, he opened the door and shoved me into the chapel. I got my feet under me and turned around, but he was on me again, pushing me back into a small clutch of mourners. Roger was not particularly athletic, but he got his weight behind his arms and rattled my bones. Trying not to fall down, I stumbled back and hit an old woman. We went down together. Several people stepped between Roger and me, ending the attack. The old woman was shaken, but it seemed to be the only damage. By the time I stood up several more individuals had stepped between us. Stabbing his finger in my direction for emphasis, Roger shouted, 'You're not welcome here, Dave!' To the men holding me he said, 'Get him out of here. If he comes back, call the police!'

Denise stepped cautiously out of the anteroom. She looked at me fearfully. 'It's called perjury,' I said to her. The men pushed me back angrily. 'People go to jail when they commit perjury, Denise!'

Randy Winston materialized in front of me as the men physically escorted me to the front door. 'Nice going, David. A real class act.'

Outside, the men let go of me. Including Randy, there were six of them. Their faces were tense, anxious. They did not want trouble, but they were committed: I was not coming back inside. I knew each one of them. What's more, they knew me. My sole pleasure at that moment was the fact that every one of them looked terrified when I feinted a charge at them.

I told Randy I needed my coat. He huddled with

his fellow bouncers briefly, but before they could decide on how to handle the matter, Molly and Lucy came outside, my coat in Molly's arms.

'Ready to go, dear?' she called to me cheerfully.

In the car, Lucy asked what had happened. Molly answered for me. 'You're stepfather just got eight-sixed from a funeral home.'

Lucy was quiet, afraid of a fight between us, I expect. Finally, I laughed. 'Walt would have loved it!'

While I still laughed, the tears came. Such is the nature of grief.

WE WENT OFF SEPARATELY when we got home. In my room, looking out the lone window into the darkness of the pasture, I tried to understand my friendship with Walt Beery. I knew there had been a time when he had been very proper, very brilliant, very young.

We were all young once, I suppose, but with people you meet in their late middle age it's hard to imagine sometimes just what they were like. With Walt, it was practically impossible. What I knew I had picked up in various places. Walt had never been one to dwell on the past. Partly, he didn't remember it very well, and partly, as with a number of people in their early sixties, the past was a mixed bag of fresh pain and stale laughter.

According to other Olympians, including Dean

Lintz, there had been a time when Walt rarely indulged in more than a single drink at faculty parties. In time it became two or three, then four or five. From the occasional happy hour at the faculty club, it started to be two or three nights a week at local bars, far from the observation of other university types. Then came his forays into campus bars. His classroom demeanour began to change, his interests to broaden.

There had been a serious affair with one of his grad students several years before I joined the faculty. I had heard about it from various sources. Walt himself referred to it as 'problems with Barbara,' but people who knew told me it was the real thing, the once-in-a-lifetime.

I never really understood how it had ended or how the marriage survived it. My impression was the student had taken the whole thing less seriously than Walt. Her thesis finished, she moved on. Maybe that isn't the way it was. I don't know. I do know that Walt began a radical descent from that point forward. He had flings, one night stands, barroom and classroom flirtations. He drank every night. His classes were nominally rigorous, but there were too many hangovers, then too many classes conducted after long liquid lunches.

By the time I met him, Walt was a dangerous commodity at the university. Just being in his company could get an untenured professor in trouble. He was also brilliant and funny and passionate about literature and, at the beginning, I paid no heed to the warning looks and Machiavellian whispers. Only later, as I became ambitious, did I learn to keep my distance. Such behaviour had seemed only sensible at the time. Now, at the hour of my friend's passing, it felt less than noble. Walt was a good soul, a great intellect, and certainly worth more than the limited friendship I had been willing to extend to him.

Or, as I told the black fields beyond my window that evening, '...worth more than the whole damn bunch of us.'

Chapter 20

I SERVED MOLLY BREAKFAST in bed the next morning. She was in good spirits, and the smell of her, the wild tangle of her blonde hair, the gentle outlines of her breasts stirred me.

We talked about Walt and Barbara. I thought about David and Molly. When she had finished her breakfast, I took the tray from her and sat down on the bed, our hips touching in casual intimacy. Taking her hands, I said, 'Do you know how long it's been since we've been on this bed together?'

'About a month,' she answered. Then thinking about it, she added, 'More like a couple, I guess.'

'If you want some help fixing up a house in Florida, all you have to do is ask. I'll resign and move down to join you. Whatever you want, Molly.'

Molly considered the offer without much seriousness. 'Strictly business?'

'If that's what it takes.'

239

'I can't do strictly business with you, David.'

'That must mean you're still in love with me.'

'That's why it hurts. I look at you, and I just start aching.'

'I didn't betray you, Molly.'

'Doc had a girlfriend,' she offered quietly, seemingly by way of explanation. 'I don't know when it started, but it went on for years. Maybe it's still going on. Who knows? Olga acts like she doesn't know about it, but I knew about it when I was twelve. You know what I hated the most? I hated that Olga put up with it, and I swore it would never happen to me.'

'It didn't happen, Molly!'

'Right. That's why we had a little lover's spat last night?'

'You saw Denise Conway? She's plain. Nothing about her is interesting.'

'I'm guessing she's more interesting when she's naked.'

'I wouldn't know.'

Molly smiled without affection. 'I read her diary, David. I read it so many times it makes me sick to think about you and her.'

'Makes me sick too.'

She pushed me away laughing as she did. 'You're a lying used car salesman! You can't help yourself. You'll lie about this until the day you die!'

'What if *she's* lying?'

240

'That doesn't make sense. *She* didn't give me the diary. Buddy did. He found it in her closet. She was hiding it from him.'

'Buddy told her what to write.'

'Please. This cost him his relationship. The two of them were going to get married until you came along.'

I shook my head, staying calm, pushing my case with the dispassion of a good salesman. 'Think about it, Molly. Last summer I was here all the time. We were working ten-hour days finishing the house. When did I have time to go into town and seduce this girl?'

'Denise looks like the kind of girl who doesn't take a lot of seducing. Besides, you weren't here *all* the time.'

'Talk to her today. Have her tell you something about me, something only a lover would know.'

Molly looked at me strangely. 'I'm not about to humiliate myself in front of that girl.'

'She won't answer you! I'll tell you right now: she won't say a damn thing because she doesn't even know me. Just talk to her, Molly. You'll see I'm telling the truth.'

'You should have stayed on the car lot, David. You're so earnest when you lie.'

From anger to amusement. Was I making progress or had I lost her so completely that I had become a joke?

*   *   *

241

I SPENT THE DAY PAINTING the largest room in
Lucy's new apartment. Molly called different people,
then left early, intending to visit the Sloans before she
went to the funeral at two o'clock. We caught snow
flurries late in the afternoon. Lucy rode Jezebel in the
pasture, working lead changes. I watched for a while,
then worked in the barn until she brought Jezebel back
to her stall.

After she had kicked down some hay for both horses,
she told me she had talked to her mother about the
grass. 'And?'

'She was glad I told her. I think she was proud of
me for being honest about it.'

'Get a lecture?'

'It wasn't as bad as I thought it would be.'

'Olga around?'

Lucy handed me a conspiratorial smile. 'Next room.'

Molly came back to the farm around seven o'clock.
I tried not to sound too curious about where she had
gone after the funeral, but Molly picked up on my
insecurities at once, and seemed almost to enjoy my
discomfort. 'After the funeral, quite a few of the faculty
adjourned to Friday's.'

She named some of the people who were there,
including the men who had participated in tossing me
out of the funeral home the night before. As an afterthought she mentioned Buddy Elder. 'Actually, Buddy
and Randy Winston talked me into leaving Friday's

and going to Caleb's.' Noting my exasperation, she explained, 'Everyone was dying to talk about you, David. As long as I was there, they couldn't.'

'So you went out with the two men I dislike more than anyone else on campus?'

'That was a plus, but mostly I did it because it was fun. I had a nice time.'

'Anyone make a pass?'

'Randy couldn't stop. When I didn't pick up on the subtle stuff he put his hand under my dress.'

'The son of a bitch.'

'I told him I'm staying at the farm until Sunday. If he wants to drive out and pick me up sometime for a real date, I'll be his love slave for the night.'

'If he shows up, I'll break his nose.'

'I think he knows that, David. He said he thought it might be a good idea if we met in town.'

'You're not going to go out with the guy?'

She shrugged indifferently. 'I haven't decided.'

'I feel like I'm the one who died. Damn vultures. So what about Buddy? Was he on his best behaviour as usual?'

'He thought I should give you another chance, considering the way Denise is.'

'Sweet guy,' I answered.

'He is. Sexy, too. I can't get enough of that southern accent. He makes whatever he's talking about sound like hot maple syrup has just been poured over it.'

'The guy pulled a gun on me, Molly. Twice!'

She laughed at me, imagining more lies, I expect. She had not heard about the gun, so *twice* was just typical David Albo hyperbole. 'I guess he and I have a lot more in common than I thought.'

THE PHONE RANG. LUCY answered it. A moment later she joined us, telling Molly, 'For you.'

Molly left the living room with the phone. I heard her laughing. Lucy rolled her eyes and said, '*Robert*.'

I snapped to attention. 'Who's Robert?'

'He's supposed to be showing her real estate, but I think he's been showing her something else.'

I felt the blood leave my chest. 'What does he look like?'

'I don't know. Old.'

I didn't know whether to be gratified or irritated. 'How old?'

'Your age... maybe.'

'Maybe?'

'Maybe younger.'

'Big gut, smelly, bad breath?'

She laughed. 'Noooo. Cute. Kind of. Nice ass.'

It was our general policy not to say the really bad words in front of Lucy, so I walked out on the front porch.

Molly finished her call fairly quickly and caught me as I was coming in.

'Robert?' I asked.

Molly glanced at Lucy, who simply shrugged. 'Not really your business anymore, David,' she said.

'Is this the guy you were out with the night I called?'

'The night you called I think I was entertaining the Miami Dolphins.'

With that, I made a fast exit for the den. An hour later the phone rang again. I had been reading without much concentration, thinking about getting ready for bed or making a drink or driving to Florida and finding Robert. Molly had already gone to bed, and I wondered if Robert had called back for some prearranged phone sex. Curiosity getting the better of me, I walked over and picked up the extension.

A young woman's voice said, 'Is Dr Albo there?'

Molly started to speak, but I interrupted. 'I have it, Molly.' Molly hung up.

'Dr Albo?' I thought it was Johnna Masterson's voice, but there was an edge of excitement or fear that made me uncertain. I asked who was calling. 'It's Johnna.'

'What do you want, Johnna?' I said this without the pretence of courtesy. If Johnna Masterson had wanted to talk she might have tried the funeral home the night before.

'I have to talk to you.' She spoke in near-panic tones, shuddering and gasping at the finish.

'Then talk.'

'Not on the phone. I'll meet you at the Denny's on Washington Avenue in an hour. Please!'

'Why would I want to drive into town? You won't even tell me—'

'It's about Buddy!' She sounded scared. It sounded like she was crying.

Was Buddy's game coming unravelled? If so, Johnna might have the information I needed.

'Please!'

'One hour,' I said.

I hung up, and went upstairs to see Molly. 'Johnna Masterson,' I said. 'She wants to talk.'

'Good for Johnna. Does she keep a diary too?'

'This could be important. I'm going into town.'

'Now?'

'Why not now?'

The phone rang again, cutting off Molly's response. Molly snatched the receiver up and spoke softly, her voice mellow. 'Hello? Yes. Just a minute.' She set the phone between her cheek and shoulder. 'Do you mind closing the door on your way out?'

Through the closed door of what was once *our* bedroom, I could hear Molly's voice, though not all of the words. She laughed the way she had once laughed with me.

I spent most of the drive into town contemplating just what I had lost and wondering if by some miracle

Johnna Masterson was about to offer me a way to get it back.

Over my third cup of coffee, watching the door and the sidewalk outside, I was still thinking about Johnna's motives and what it could mean for my marriage when the waitress came up to my booth. 'You Dr Albo?' I said I was. 'There's a call for you. Lady said it's an emergency.'

When I got to the telephone by the cash register, I heard Buddy Elder's voice. 'Hey, Dave. You looking for Johnna?'

'Where is she?'

'You're not stalking that poor girl, are you?'

'What do you want, Buddy?'

'I heard a rumour today at the funeral home. They're saying *letter of censure*. Good news, huh? Hope nothing happens to change their minds.'

'Do yourself a favour,' I said. 'Get out of my life before I decide to kill you!'

At just that moment Buddy Elder decided to disconnect. I looked up and saw the cashier staring at me. Why not? I had just threatened to take a life. I gave her a friendly smile, but I expect it looked like bad acting.

Chapter 21

I WENT TO THE HOUSE WHERE I KNEW Buddy was staying. His car was not there, nor did he answer the door when I knocked. I drove to his old apartment close to The Slipper after that. That too was dark, no sign of his Mercury. Finally, late, I checked Johnna Masterson's address in a telephone directory. There was only a rural route number, so I could not find her place. I tried her home number with my cell phone, but there was no answer. On a hunch, I went out to Walt's and Barbara's place. Roger and his girl-friend were out as well.

Tired and frustrated, I went back to the farm and crawled into bed around three-thirty. When I got up late the next morning the horses were already out in the pasture. I found Molly upstairs installing the base-boards. 'How was Johnna?' she asked cheerfully.

'She didn't show up.'

'Did you sleep with her too, David?'

'She told me last night on the phone she wanted to talk to me about Buddy.'

Molly's electric drill punctuated my answer. She stood up, walked to the next mark and set the screw. 'I keep trying to figure out why everyone but you is lying.' She gave me a pretty smile, and I could have sworn something had changed. 'How many were there over the years? Just so I know.'

'I've never cheated on you, Molly.'

'Now see?' She settled the drill on the makeshift worktable. 'You say that as if it's true, and we both know it isn't.'

IT HAD BEEN A SHORT NIGHT for us, though on that occasion Molly and I had spent it together. In fact, I had just started drifting off when I heard her tramping around the front room. I rolled over and saw this beautiful blonde wearing work boots and tight jeans, looking down at me in the gloomy first light of a Monday morning. This was how our third date ended.

'Make yourself at home, professor. There's food in the kitchen. The coffee just needs to be turned on. You want to see me again I'll be home when it's dark. You want to think about it for a few days like last time, that's okay too.' She bent over the bed and kissed my eyelids, something no one had ever done to me. 'Just don't think about it too long. You might hurt my feelings.'

I rolled out of bed and sat up. I told her I was just getting up myself. Molly laughed like one of her carpenter friends. She knew better than that! People with things to do got up at dawn. Poets and professors-in-training and used car salesmen could let the morning get away from them. I tried to pretend I was only a couple of minutes from sitting down to compose a little iambic pentameter while I drank my first cup of coffee, but all she did was laugh at me.

As she went toward the door I called to her impulsively: 'Will you marry me, Molly McBride?' Her step caught. Her shoulders froze. Then she looked back at me with a smile. 'Ask me like you mean it and I might.'

I was there that evening, and I asked her with a diamond ring.

I didn't have that kind of money on hand of course. I had called Tubs that morning and told him I'd found the woman I wanted to marry. I hated doing it like that, especially telling him I needed the money by that afternoon, but it was the only way to show Molly I meant it. Tubs didn't ask how long I'd known her. He didn't even ask her name. He told me to have the jewellery store give him a call when I found what I wanted. I could pay him back come summer.

Molly wasn't expecting a man on bended knee that evening, but she handled it well. She said she needed a couple of days to think about it, if I didn't mind. Nothing at all to think about, I told her. 'Just say yes and the three of us will live happily-ever-after.' That was the thing, she said. There were three of us. She wanted to talk to Lucy about it. A few days after that Molly said Lucy had told her it was all right. We set the wedding for early January in DeKalb. For various reasons we spent the rest of that fall, about six weeks in total, living separately. We would meet in the morning and usually late in the evening. On the rainy days, we would steal an afternoon in Molly's bed while the neighbour kept Lucy.

I finished the semester pretty much as I had started it. I would work most of the day, then drift over for beer and talk in the late afternoon at my favourite bar. A lot of times a whole group of us showed up. Sometimes only two or three of us were there. Beth Ruby was a regular and wouldn't let up with the carpenter jokes once she found out I was engaged. I didn't really care. My attraction to the woman had faded. Molly McBride was the centre of my life, and I was foolish enough to tell her that. That was when Beth started talking about 'a life sentence of monogamy.' I told her it sounded good, but even as I said it, I felt a little nervous, the way a man will when he puts a tie on for his first job and thinks that for the next forty-five years he's going to be doing the same thing. *Never* can sure seem like a long time when you're young.

A couple of weeks before the end of the semester,

about three or four weeks before the wedding, I was sitting across from Beth Ruby at the Pub, just the two of us. Monogamy was the topic of the afternoon again, and it was a long afternoon. After we had had enough, I said I was going, had to meet Molly later. Beth asked for a ride home. Beth usually walked because she only lived a few blocks away, but I had given her rides before. She made a show of her bare thighs inside the truck. They were very nice thighs, too. She laughed at me for looking. I wasn't ready to get married! I'd cheat on Molly with the first woman who came along. I said I was impervious. She opened her legs slowly and said, 'You would do me right here, right now if I let you.' I was still looking at her thighs, and I guess I forgot to tell her that I wouldn't. In fact, I didn't have a whole lot to say until I was pulling my pants up afterwards.

When I got home, I took a shower. I felt better after that but still guilty. Molly showed up as I was getting dressed. She asked me how my day had been. I told her it had been okay, nothing special. She saw the light on my answering machine and punched the button. Beth Ruby's voice was distinctive even on a cheap answering machine. 'Hey! I can't believe we did it in your pickup! Thanks for the first, Davey, and by the way, I was right and you were wrong. You're definitely not cut out for monogamy.'

Molly stood there for several seconds without speaking. Then she just turned and walked away.

I tried calling. I went by her house. For several days she wouldn't talk to me, but I finally wore her down. I said I could explain if she just gave me a chance.

Of course I couldn't, and I think Molly agreed to see me just to hear what I would come up with. We went to the best restaurant in town. We had a couple of mixed drinks and talked about our lives as if we had not seen each other for several years. In fact, it had only been a couple of weeks, the longest and most miserable of my life.

There was no explanation for what I had done, so I settled with saying I was sorry. I didn't think there was anything I could do to make up for it, but if Molly could forgive me I would do anything. It was stupid, irresponsible, the biggest mistake of my life.

Molly listened politely, but I wasn't sure I was making progress, so I fell back on an old standby: '...it didn't mean a thing.'

Very quietly but with a firmness I knew meant business, Molly answered me. Was she supposed to feel better because it didn't mean anything? I tried to explain that. Beth had wanted to prove to herself she could have me if she wanted.

'Well, she had you.'

What could I do to make things right? Molly looked at me for a long time without responding. Finally she said, 'Nothing. That's the thing. There's nothing you can do to ever make up for it.'

She wondered if I could I forgive her if I had heard something like that on her answering machine right after she had told me she had a boring day. I said I could. I wouldn't mind sounding like a joke between her and her lover? I tried to argue this, but Molly wouldn't give it to me. Beth Ruby had turned her into a joke.

I agreed that I would hesitate. But that didn't mean it would be over! If I thought it would never happen again, if I really believed it, nothing would keep us apart.

Molly considered this quietly. 'Easy to say, David.'

'I mean it!'

'Listen to me,' Molly said. 'No matter what you say, I know you believe there's a difference. Men are excused, women are stained.'

That wasn't true, I said. There was no difference. Things like that could happen to men or women!

'Do you want to marry the town tramp, David?'

'Of course not!'

'Neither do I.'

'It wasn't like that.'

'Be honest.'

'It was exactly like that.'

'And if I wanted one last fling, how would you handle that?'

'Molly...'

'It wouldn't mean a thing.'

She was smiling, baiting me with my own words.

'If that's what you want,' I said morosely.

'It's not what I want.'

I drew a deep, satisfied breath.

'You see? It's okay because you know it won't happen!'

What did she want me to do? She thought for moment and shook her head. 'Give me a couple of days to think about it.'

And that was it. Two, maybe three nights later I heard Molly's key in my door and looked at the clock by my bed. It was after three. I sat up, rubbing the sleep from my eyes. Molly appeared at the door to my bedroom backlit by the light in the front room. I could not see her face, but I could tell by the way she moved and by the stink of cigarettes on her clothes she had been out. When I spoke, she came toward me and pulled up the hem of her dress. Touching her thighs I understood at once what had happened.

'Who?' I muttered.

'I didn't get their names.'

Molly called me the next morning, about two hours later, actually. 'You still want to get married?' she asked cheerfully.

'More than anything,' I told her.

According to our custom, we never spoke about that night – never again mentioned the name of Beth Ruby.

Chapter 22

WE HEARD A CAR COMING OFF the pavement late the following afternoon. It was too soon for Lucy to be home from school, so I went to the window and looked down on the driveway from the third floor.

In summer you could not see who was coming until the car burst out of the heavy foliage and pulled into the circle before the house. In late fall, the leaves almost all gone, I got a glimpse of the vehicle as it crested the hill. Two men sat inside a brown and tan late model Jeep Wagoneer. I didn't know them. By their age and the clothing they wore, I was fairly sure they were not selling religion. In fact, I was fairly sure they weren't selling anything at all.

Molly and I went downstairs together and met them as they were getting out of their vehicle. I thought cops, though I could not have said why. Maybe it was the way both men locked in on me. Most men noticed

Molly first. I offered the standard country greeting, 'Help you?'

They reached into their jackets slowly at the same time and pulled out badges with picture IDs. I felt no satisfaction in being right. I looked at Molly for some kind of explanation, but she was looking at me. I think we both thought of Lucy at the same time. Supposed to be in school, out for a drive instead: a parent's worst nightmare.

'Is something wrong?' Molly asked, an unfamiliar tremor in her voice.

The older man shook his head, apparently understanding our fear. 'We'd just like to ask Professor Albo a couple of questions, if that's all right. I'm Detective Dalton. This is Detective Jacobs.'

As he said this, he extended his badge and ID for me to inspect.

I took a long hard look at his identification, trying as I did to figure out what they might want to talk to me about. Harassment? Stalking? An assault charge from the funeral home? What came next?

Kip Dalton was about average height, pleasantly thick through the middle, with neatly oiled black hair just starting to turn. In his late-forties, I guessed. He had the tranquil brown eyes of a preacher or a psychologist, a confidence I would have associated with a prosperous businessman.

Dalton's partner, whose identification I just glanced

257

at, was easier to comprehend and less interesting. He was so ramrod straight and uptight he might as well have been wearing a uniform. In his mid-thirties with thinning light brown hair, Detective Jacobs was a couple of inches over six feet and exceedingly thin. His eyes were deep set, small and quick. He had a jaw you could break your fist on.

Molly stepped forward aggressively the moment Kip Dalton announced their purpose. What did they want to talk about? Dalton was reluctant to explain himself in the driveway. It would just take a few minutes. Molly looked at me as she might have in the old days, reading my expression at a glance. Why not? She smiled at both men, the good country wife who has just remembered her manners. 'You care for some coffee?'

Dalton said that sounded like a mighty fine idea. We took them through the back porch and into our kitchen. Molly made coffee while Dalton complimented us on the restoration. He was especially interested in the enormous fireplace where the cooking had originally taken place when the house was newly built in the 1820s.

'Functional?' he asked.

I answered with the first lie that came to mind. 'Oh yeah! A couple of times a year we have people out and cook the meal right there, pioneer-style.' Dalton, who clearly enjoyed antiques smiled fondly at the notion. I said next time we would invite him. I glanced at Jacobs, who exuded all the warmth of an andiron. I included him in the invitation as well. Why not? It didn't cost me anything. As I spoke I was fairly sure Kip Dalton wasn't buying my line, but I didn't care. I continued talking about the old cookware we used and the flavour of coffee boiled on an open fire. I said it was quite a sight to see everyone standing around a fireplace like this all dressed up in early nineteenth century costumes.

Molly, who was used to my nonsense, didn't bother telling the men I was lying. Usually, she enjoyed it, what I could spin out on short notice, but I expect she thought it wasn't a very smart thing to do with a couple of detectives. After I had run down a little, Dalton moved about the kitchen, inspecting the old plank board table, the original brick floors and walls, the bric-a-brac on the various shelves.

'I was out here about ten years ago,' he said. 'Place didn't look anything like this.'

'It was all here,' Molly answered, 'but some fool thought he ought to modernize it.' She was talking about her father and his ill-conceived attempt to turn Bernard Place into an apartment building.

I asked what had brought him out to the house ten years ago. He had been on patrol, he said. He and his partner had found a party and had run the kids off after putting the fear of the law in them.

Jacobs spoke now, his first words since muttering

ma'am at the introductions. 'Seems like they had a lot of trouble selling this place. Sat empty for years.'

'That wasn't the reason. There were two owners, a brother and sister. One wanted to sell the place. The other didn't.'

Jacobs nodded at Molly's explanation. 'A squabble over the family inheritance?'

'Isn't it always?'

When she asked them their business with me Kip Dalton pretended it wasn't very urgent. 'We got a call from the university this morning. One of the graduate students up there in your department is teaching a couple of courses, and she didn't show up for her classes yesterday. Some people checked around. The usual. They went by her house, called her parents, contacted the hospitals. She just disappeared.'

Molly looked at me, as certain as I was, I think. 'Johnna Masterson?' I asked.

Dalton tried not to look surprised. 'One of her friends said she was going to talk to you about some kind of complaint she filed earlier this semester.'

'I haven't spoken to Johnna since early October.' I thought about leaving it there, but the instinct for self-preservation saved me. 'Two nights ago she called here and wanted to meet me in town. I drove in and she stood me up. You mind telling me who the friend was?'

Detective Jacobs stepped on my line. 'Where exactly were you supposed to meet her?'

I turned toward Dalton as I gave my answer. 'The Denny's on Washington Avenue,' I said. Jacobs had succeeded in upsetting me without doing very much besides staring at me with his arms folded across his skinny chest.

'What evening was this?' Jacobs asked.

'Tuesday,' I answered, 'the day of Walt and Barbara Beery's funeral.' I wondered what had moved me to tell them about a funeral I hadn't even attended.

Kip Dalton pulled a tiny notepad from his shirt pocket. Using a cheap ink pen, he wrote down the information. Jacobs asked about times. Molly said Johnna had called at about ten-fifteen. 'I remember because I was expecting a phone call, and I answered.'

Molly glanced at me. I took it from there.

'She sounded upset,' I told them.

From beyond our intimate triangle Detective Jacobs intruded again, 'Why would she be upset?'

'I don't know. She said she wanted to talk to me about a mutual acquaintance, one of the teaching assistants. Buddy Elder. He wasn't the friend who told you she wanted to talk to me, was he?'

Kip Dalton answered that in fact he wasn't. Someone else. He didn't offer any names. I knew how rumours could float in an environment like that. Pass a story to a couple of sources and it would come back to you as fact within the hour. Buddy Elder was the source of this information no matter where they had picked it up. I didn't think it was a good idea to press my cause too aggressively. Let them find Buddy on their own, I thought, and they'll believe he's involved in this.

'She didn't speak to you again?' Dalton asked.

'No.'

'What time did you get home?' Dalton asked.

'Around three-thirty.'

They pushed around the edges as if they were not really very interested. How well did I know Johnna? Was she the kind of young woman who might decide to disappear for a few days? Prone to depression? Flighty? What did I know about her friends? Boyfriends? I did not go into speculations. I told them the truth. She had impressed me as an extremely dedicated, level-headed student. She had dropped by my office a couple of times, presented one story in my class. 'When I first met her,' I said, 'she seemed a bit prudish, but the first short story she wrote was hilarious. It was called "Sexual Positions," a total knock-down-drag-out comedy.' Kip Dalton wanted to know if I thought she was promiscuous. I told him I thought she was talented. I got a look from Molly at this, but I didn't care.

As we walked both detectives back toward their Jeep Detective Dalton gave Molly and me a worldly smile: 'I'm inclined to think a young woman that age probably met the love of her life and just took off without telling anyone.' He shrugged indifferently. 'She'll probably get around to calling her friends in a day or two and wonder what all the fuss is about.'

'Not Johnna Masterson,' I said. Kip Dalton looked at me questioningly. He wanted to hear my theory. 'She was committed to her work,' I said. 'Taking off without saying anything would cost her too much: her teaching assistantship, her future prospects for a teaching position, and a semester of coursework with the grade of F. That kind of stuff happens with under-grads who haven't invested their own money in their education, but not with a graduate student, certainly not someone like Johnna Masterson. Even if she found the love of her life, they could wait a couple of weeks until the end of the semester.'

'That's pretty much what everyone told us,' Dalton said, apparently still not convinced.

The two men thanked us again for our help and climbed into their Jeep. After Dalton started the car, they sat for several seconds. Finally, Jacobs rolled down the passenger window. 'You care if I ask you some-thing, professor?'

He spoke softly and I walked toward him, so I could hear him better. No, I didn't care.

'Just now you were talking about Miss Masterson in the past tense. I was wondering, why you did that?'

I said I wasn't aware that I had. I smiled like the killer. I felt a twitch in my neck kick in. Detective

Jacobs assured me I had. 'I've been on leave the past few weeks,' I said finally. 'Johnna was in my class, but since I'm not teaching it now, I guess I was thinking back. She *was* committed.'

Jacobs smiled at me sceptically the way people do when they're standing in the front of a lying used car salesman. 'You think she still is? Committed, I mean?'

'Hard to say,' I offered. 'People change, don't they?' I heard myself talking without being able to stop. I was desperate for them to leave, and they just sat there listening while I told them Johnna could have had a secret life for all I knew. Call girl, drug addict, any damn thing!

Molly walked up. 'I think you've asked all the questions you need to.'

Jacobs, who apparently thought he was about to get a confession, was not really happy about Molly stepping into it, but he hunched his shoulders and grinned.

'Now I'll kindly ask you to get off our property,' Molly told him, 'and next time call us before you come driving out here.'

Detective Dalton leaned down so Molly could see his guileless eyes. 'We're not sure we need to see you again, either of you, Ms Albo, but we'll make sure to call ahead if we do. Thanks again for the coffee.'

Molly stood close to me as we watched them swing around the circle and drive down the hill.

Molly whispered to me as if they might actually hear her. 'They think you killed that girl, David.'

I couldn't answer her. Truth is I could barely breathe.

'DID YOU SEE JOHNNA Masterson the other night?' Molly asked when we were inside the house again.

'I told you what happened.'

'Yes, but we both know you have issues with the truth.'

I smiled as if Molly had missed the whole point, which I guess she had. 'Can't you see what's happening?'

'I can see you looked like hell when that Detective Jacobs started pushing you around.'

'I didn't care for his attitude.'

'Do you want me to stay?'

'Stay?'

'Cancel my flight. Until this gets resolved, I mean.'

'You do whatever you want, Molly. I'm not in trouble with these people.'

'David, those two aren't finished with you. If I leave now they're going to think it's because I know something.'

'There's nothing to know, nothing connecting me to that woman.'

'You went to see her.'

I shrugged indifferently. 'Other than that.'

'She charged you with sexual harassment.'

'She was misinformed about statements I had made. It wasn't her fault.'

'You think the cops will buy that?'

I thought about another lie, but stopped myself. 'No. Not after what happened at the funeral home.'

Molly stared me without speaking.

'It would mean a lot if you stayed,' I said finally.

'I'll make some calls.'

LUCY CAME HOME FROM school while I was in the barn. We talked for a while, and then she went into the house. She and Molly were upstairs in Lucy's bedroom when I found them.

'We're going out to dinner,' Molly said.

'Great,' I said.

'Just the two of us.'

I went upstairs to my third floor monk's cell to change clothes and watched from my window until they appeared. They took Lucy's Toyota. Later, I rummaged around in the pantry for something to eat. There was plenty of food. The trouble was I hadn't gotten a supply of beer, and I wanted something to drink. Food was optional, drink the staff of life.

The truck drove itself to my old haunts. I had the meatloaf special with a couple of beers, followed by three shots of whiskey at the next stop. Three bars, three more drinks. Everyone asked where I had been. I had a different answer at each bar. I said I'd had a consulting gig in Poland. That was at the first bar. At the second I said I'd been born again for a while, off booze entirely. At the next I said I had been in the Peace Corps in South America. At another, I said I had gone to Texas for a couple of years to work on a ranch busting broncos. The only story they called me on was the born again nonsense. They could believe the religion, nothing wrong with that, and I certainly needed it, but they knew I wasn't about to give up drinking!

A co-ed was curious about what had happened to me at school. She had fabulous breasts, almost in Johnna Masterson's league, and a bright-eyed innocence I found disconcerting so late into a good binge. I told her I just needed some time off. She answered, 'I heard you were fired.'

'I'm taking some time off until they fire me,' I said.

Having got what she wanted, and just a little accidental rub against my arm while she operated, she drifted off to join a younger drunk. I had persuaded myself she was interested in nailing a prof before the end of the semester and almost out of time. Of course, ex-profs don't really count. I left feeling old and foolish, like my friend and mentor Walt Beery. In my truck I considered the temptation: those wide innocent eyes, those great, round breasts. I swore at my folly. I had been playing her along with the cool indifference of a mature man, imagining it was just for fun, knowing I could resist if she wanted something more than a little flirtation. But if it hadn't been just the gossip she had wanted, I knew we would have ended up in the cab of my truck. Beth Ruby all over again.

I was faithful because I hadn't been tempted. All I wanted at that moment was a good excuse. In fact I wanted more than an excuse. I wanted to kick up a little dust. Fortunately, I knew where to find plenty of dust.

I WALKED INTO THE GLASS Slipper around midnight. Buddy Elder was not there. Neither was Denise. The doorman didn't remember my face, or he didn't care. I watched several dancers, picked my favourite and bought a lap dance. She was the very opposite of my wife, compact hips, hardly any breasts at all, dark hair, a small red mouth. I guessed her to be nineteen or twenty. She was just plain enough that she had to work to make a living, just proud enough that she substituted athleticism for sexual wiles. I liked that. Sexual wiles feel like an act if they're not done well. You can't fake a body slam. She made hard, repeated contact against my torso. She pressed her flat chest against my face with bony enthusiasm. Her eyes were distant, unfocused, completely at odds with the vitality of her young body, as if to say, nothing personal here. It was just the thing I needed, and I bought a second dance. I thought she might spot a sucker and play me a bit more skilfully, at least until she emptied my pockets, but I got the same thing. Slap, slide, breast-bone to nose bone, staring off into the distance, wagging her buttocks over my crotch.

As she was slipping her skimpy top over her prac-tically nonexistent breasts, I asked her if Denise Conway was still working here. The girl focused. 'How do you know Denise?'

I could see I had made a mistake, but I couldn't understand what it was. Old habits die hard. In a tight spot, I always conjured up a true statement. The ghost of Tubs. 'She was a student of mine this fall,' I said. 'She said if I came out here and saw her dancing it would embarrass the hell out of her.' I gave the dancer a nasty leer, 'So I thought I'd try it. Only I get here and I don't see her around.'

The girl relaxed. I had served up enough truth for her to buy it. Who knows, maybe she even thought I looked like a professor. Good diction, straight teeth, chalk dust under my fingernails, or maybe it was that I was a horny old goat. 'Denise don't dance under her real name is why I asked.' She laughed. 'I guess I should say she don't dance at all no more. She got married.'

'Married?' I expect I blinked. I know my mouth hung open Wade-style.

'Right before Thanksgiving. The guy she married used to come in here all the time, but now he don't want anyone looking at her no more. You know how it goes.'

'Buddy's friend? Roy, Ray? Something like that?' I asked.

'Roger. And he *used* to be Buddy's friend. Buddy and Denise broke up because of him. They had this big fight in here because of her. Everybody was like... *how*? Turns out Denise is like no dummy. Turns out, Roger is rich.'

'Lucky Denise.'

'Me? I'd rather have Buddy.'

I drove by Buddy's house. He was home. I drove by the Beery residence. The place was dark, the newly-weds apparently already in bed. At the farm I found Molly's rental and Lucy's Toyota parked side by side in the shed.

I showered and went to my room, but I couldn't sleep. Married, right before Thanksgiving. Walt had told me they were going out of town to meet friends of hers. An alibi? With five million-plus in play it was just was too neat for coincidence.

I lay awake working through the possibilities, but it always came down to Buddy Elder. I could imagine Roger falling under his spell, the three of them, Roger, Denise, and Buddy, working up a double homicide and making it look like domestic violence.

What still did not make sense was the disappearance of Johnna Masterson.

Chapter 23

I JOINED MOLLY FAIRLY LATE THE NEXT morning on the third floor. 'Guess what I found out?'

Molly looked at me, waiting but not guessing. Denise Conway and Roger Beery got married last week.' Molly didn't seem especially interested. When I tried to explain my theory that Buddy and Denise and Roger had conspired to murder Walt and Barbara, she laughed at me.

'Please, David.'

'I'm serious! He and Roger staged a fight at The Slipper.'

She smiled. 'Like you and Buddy staged one?'

I laughed and shook my head. 'I'm just telling you. Walt and Barbara were murdered. The three of them did it.'

'I suppose they're involved in Johnna Masterson's disappearance as well?'

'I expect an arrest any day now,' I said.

271

'Great. That means I can get back to Florida.'

'You and Lucy have a good talk?'

'Reasonably. I told her I needed to stick around for a while. I told her that you're in trouble. You know what she told me? She said you didn't sleep with Denise Conway. She said you're not lying.'

I considered a snappy comeback, but something in Molly's tone told me Lucy's faith in me was not the point.

'When we got home I showed her the diary.' Denise Conway's diary had become The Diary in our parlance. Molly met my stunned gaze with a degree of satisfaction I found cruel. 'She asked me how I could stand it, staying here in the same house.' The flesh around Molly's mouth quivered, almost a smile. Her martyrdom was now fully appreciated by her daughter.

'You didn't have to do that, Molly.' I said this without energy or bitterness. I was too tired to fight. A part of me had actually begun to accept the diary as fact. I carried the guilt of it at any rate.

'How many ways did you swear to her you were innocent, David?'

'I told her the truth. I told her it was none of her business.'

'You keep nothing from me, wasn't that it?'

I was not angry. My mood was closer to that of a man who has been told he has only a few weeks to live. I had no blood flowing through me. I had no reason to hope. I had nothing at all besides a madman who was determined to ruin my life one misery at a time. Devastation piecemeal.

'You're the one who got Lucy into the middle of this, David. Don't give me that look.'

I said it wasn't a look. 'I'm just afraid I've lost her too.'

Molly turned back to work without comment. Whatever I had lost, I had lost by my own doing.

'KIP DALTON,' MOLLY SAID, holding the phone receiver toward me. We had been working for close to an hour installing a tongue-and-groove floor. I blinked as I stood up and stretched. Dalton meant more questions about Johnna Masterson. I calculated the possibility of convincing him that Buddy Elder was behind it and decided I needed to go slowly. My credibility was in question. The first thing I needed to do was to sell Detective Kip Dalton on David Albo, The Honest Man.

I took the phone from her nervously because I had not been The Honest Man since I had walked out of the wastelands for the last time. Dalton apologized for bothering me. I tried to sound cheerful. It was the voice suicides use once their minds are made up, the enthusiasm thin, imaginary. 'Not at all! What can I do for you, Detective?'

Kip had a few questions. Could I come into the

sheriff's department around three o'clock? I told him I needed to check my day planner, then I laughed. 'What do you know? Free all afternoon.' Molly, who had been watching me intently through this exchange, whispered the word lawyer. I shook my head. Talking was my business! Dalton and Jacobs were just a couple of tire kickers I was going to turn into a sale!

The moment I was off the phone Molly told me to call Gail. I said I didn't need her. Besides Gail didn't understand what was going on. The best thing to do, I said, was to be upfront. 'If I go in there with a lawyer they're naturally going to assume I've got something to hide.'

'Dalton isn't buying a car, David. He's looking for someone who wanted to hurt Johnna Masterson.'

'Maybe I can help.'

I felt less confident when I walked into the brightly lit front offices of the sheriff's department and asked for Detective Dalton. I did not like the place. Men and women came and went wearing county brown uniforms, sleek compact handguns, and all manner of accessories strapped to their belts. These were serious folks with powers I had not fully reckoned with from the comforts of my ivory tower. The people they escorted all had the same hangdog look. They were rough people too, but at the moment all the mean had been squeezed out: they were at the mercy of others, and they knew it.

I was getting rabbity sitting there, and was thinking about walking away while I still had my freedom when Kip Dalton appeared. He was cheerful, courteous, and apologetic for keeping me waiting. I found myself liking him again. I would have bought a car from him. He was that kind of guy. At the same time it occurred to me I could never have sold Kip a car. He kept his defences up. He ran the show. It would take Tubs Albo to get this man to sign a contract. Even then Kip would have come out all right. Having come to this decision, I should have made for the door: pressing engagement, heart attack, business at the bank, anything!

For some reason I recalled an old woman who had appeared at the car lot one day. A veritable army of well-meaning children and in-laws surrounded her. Milt had asked me if they were buying a car or having a family reunion. I explained what had soon become quite obvious. They weren't going to let Mom get taken! The old lady had so much protection they couldn't all fit into the car for the demo drive. At the desk her two eldest sons sat to either side of her, while the younger ones took chairs in phalanxes behind them. When a buyer brought someone along to help negotiate a purchase we called that individual a third baseman. On that close, Milt said I didn't have a third baseman, I had the whole frigging baseball team.

They took most of the afternoon taking any semblance of profit from the deal. Milt fussed until he knew they were going to buy. Then he worked his way down slowly until that old woman's kids were sure we had nothing more to give.

As they drove off in Mom's new Ford Milt waxed philosophical about motherhood and loving children. The next day the old lady came back alone. Milt had explained to her kids after the deal was struck she just needed to sign off on some paperwork with our business office. Belaying their fears, he assured them that a purchase order was a contract. They had a copy! All she needed was to take delivery and that wasn't possible until tomorrow, since his business manager happened to be out.

With these assurances the old lady's sons and daughters went back to their lives. Having eluded a fox they had no idea the wolf was waiting. I could still remember leading that old woman, now perfectly alone, across the lot to the business office, where Tubs waited with his friendliest smile.

Milt told me later I had given the car away at the front door, but Tubs, God bless him, had skinned the old woman alive at the back! And not another word about mothers and the sons and daughters who loved them.

At that moment, entering an interrogation room, quite alone and defenceless, I realized I was that old lady, in way over my head and foolishly hoping for a happy ending. I was even treated to a friendly smile and a warm welcome. For the occasion they had ditched Detective Jacobs. In his place was a good-looking woman in uniform. For some reason, Lt. Gibbons seemed less intimidating because of the uniform. At the farm I had been treated to the good cop/bad cop routine. Now it was good cop/sexy cop. I should have been worried, but I managed to assure myself they had found out about Buddy Elder. The hard ass Jacobs wasn't necessary today.

I guessed Lt. Gibbons to be a couple of years past thirty, though I later learned she was in her forties. She was attractive, perhaps a bit heavy but in an extremely appealing fashion. Like Molly, she didn't appear to be someone who would back away from a physical confrontation. She could work with her hands, and she could hold her own in a room full of men. My kind of woman.

Naturally, she was serious about Johnna Masterson's disappearance. Unlike Detective Jacobs, who had kept his arms crossed over his bony chest, Lt. Gibbons did not appear to have any preconceived notions about my guilt. Dalton, too, treated me as a witness. I kept trying to assure myself that everything was fine. I was not the old woman naively seated before Tubs Albo. I was a witness. I was going to help put an end to Buddy Elder's game. Whatever it was.

'Lt. Gibbons works Sex Crimes,' Dalton explained casually. 'The sheriff thought it might be a good idea to get her into the case at this point.' Dalton was, he said, still convinced Johnna Masterson was going to turn up alive and well, but they had to work the case as if something had happened. A running start, he said, just in case. Gibbons reviewed my previous interview without a hint of suspicion. I answered as before with perfect honesty. 'You didn't call Masterson when she didn't show up?' she asked me.

'I called her house, but there wasn't any answer. There wasn't anything else I could do, so I went home.'

She asked about the times, and I had to explain that I had driven around some before I went back to the farm. Sometime after three-fifteen, in bed by three-thirty, I said.

'You didn't talk to her again after her call at ten o'clock? You're sure about that?'

'No, and it was ten-fifteen,' I told her, wanting to have everything correct and to the minute. 'We didn't talk. I'm quite sure about that.'

Detective Dalton sighed. 'That's where we have something of a problem, Dr Albo. You see, they tell us at Denny's a woman called you. She said, according to them, it was some kind of emergency. The waitress got you and you took the call.'

'Right,' I said, feeling some gratification in the fact that they had done their homework. 'But it wasn't a woman. The person who called me was Buddy Elder.'

Lt. Gibbons developed a slight frown, the only indication on her otherwise placid face that she was having trouble with my story as well. 'The call came from Johnna Masterson's cell phone, Dr Albo. It's the same phone she used to call your house at ten-fifteen.'

'Then you've got a suspect,' I told her without blinking or even considering the matter from their perspective. I knew Buddy was behind Johnna Masterson's disappearance, and it was about time they started looking in that direction.

'That's where we have another minor problem,' Dalton answered. 'We've only got your word that you talked to Buddy Elder on the phone that evening and not to Johnna Masterson.'

'The cashier heard the conversation,' I answered, and then I froze. The cashier had listened to me tell Buddy I was going to kill him. Only she had talked to a woman – and would naturally assume I had threatened to kill... Johnna. I had used Buddy's name, but I was betting in the all excitement of a death threat the cashier had forgotten that.

Lt. Gibbons tried to be sympathetic. They weren't suggesting I was lying. They were trying to understand what had happened, and, unfortunately, there were some discrepancies. That was all it was. It happened in every investigation.

How did I explain a woman calling Denny's? Gibbons asked.

It was a fair question, assuming the person who

answered the phone had not made a mistake. Dalton gave me this point with an expressive tip of his head. 'But assume it was a woman who called,' I said, already imagining Denise Conway in the role. 'The most likely explanation was Buddy either had one of his girlfriends call or he forced Johnna to do it.'

Lt. Gibbons gave me an incredulous look. Whether it was acting or not, I couldn't tell. 'You think Mr Elder abducted Johnna Masterson?'

'Johnna was agitated when she called me at the house. She told me she wanted to talk about Buddy. I got the feeling at the time Buddy had threatened her, but it's possible, given the way she talked, he had her even then. The woman was practically in tears.'

I expected curiosity at this point. This was the road I wanted them to take, but instead of responding, they changed the subject. Lt. Gibbons asked about my affair with Denise Conway. Didn't happen, I told her. Gibbons expressed mild surprise. I tossed my hands out, palms up. Bring her in. Ask her. Give her a lie detector test. New subject. What happened between Buddy and me at The Glass Slipper? Bad judgement. And the alter-cation at the funeral home? I wanted to talk to Denise, and her husband objected. Husband? I told them about Denise and Roger getting married. Kip Dalton asked me how I knew that. I got the feeling he thought he was the only one in the know. I gave a casual shrug of my shoulders. Denise had told some of her dancer friends about it. Kip was curious about this, I could tell, but he didn't press me on the details. 'You were telling Denise your lawyer was going to sue her for bringing charges against you?' Gibbons asked.

'I was talking about perjury in a deposition. I didn't mention filing a civil suit against her. Now that she's worth over five million I guess it's an option.'

Dalton asked, 'Some people tell us that when you tried to talk to Johnna Masterson that evening she was afraid of you.'

'She wasn't afraid of me. She just didn't want to talk.'

'Why do you think that is?'

Kip Dalton knew the reason. What he wanted was to know if I would try to conceal things. I also knew that his information came second-hand. Without a warrant the university would not hand over the evidence Blackwell had collected. That left me in the awkward position of explaining the charges. As these appeared to be frivolous without the diary, I had to bring that up too. I could see by their expressions they knew nothing about it.

'Is it possible for us to have a copy of the diary?' Gibbons asked.

What was the point? The whole thing was a lie.

'Why would she write about an affair that didn't exist?'

I explained my history with Buddy Elder. At the

time I would have described my demeanour as animated. In retrospect, I'm sure both Gibbons and Dalton imagined that I was coming unhinged. Like all madmen, I was intent upon proving myself sane and reasonable. The effect vacillates between paranoia and psychosis.

Lt. Gibbons listened patiently to my explanation, then asked about the material in the diary. I tried to make light of it. It was a complete fabrication after all. 'Nothing too serious, just graphic sexual encounters between the two of us in my office. Some abusiveness thrown in.'

'What kind of abusiveness?'

'It doesn't matter. It was all a lie. There was no affair!' She wanted to know anyway, and I told her. 'Fellatio. She didn't want to perform it in my office, and I forced her to do it.' I laughed, conscious of the inappropriateness of such a response but unable to stop myself. It was the abusiveness, I realized, that attracted Leslie Blackwell and Lt. Gibbons. Buddy Elder had understood his audience. A sexual encounter? It happens. Reluctance to co-operate? Understandable. Forcing it? That crossed the line. In Buddy Elder's script I was the pig all women hated.

Officer Gibbons said to Detective Dalton, 'I want to look at this diary.' To me Gibbons said, 'I'm still having trouble understanding how Johnna Masterson got involved in this.'

'So am I,' I said.

They kept nudging the inquiry forward, and I kept filling in the blanks. Nothing got better. As Lt. Gibbons quietly entered into the official record *bodacious ta-tas*, I realized I could delude myself no longer. I was not a friendly witness. I was The Man.

Still I pressed on. I had no choice. Buddy Elder had set this thing in motion, and my only chance was to describe the diabolical intricacies of it. It was a bit like explaining chess to a poker player. When I had finished, Dalton summarized for both of them. 'That's a fairly elaborate scheme, Dr Albo.'

I nodded enthusiastically. It was indeed.

'Why would he do that?'

I said I had no idea.

'Did you make a threat the other night on the telephone?' Lt. Gibbons asked.

I hesitated. They had the cashier's statement. 'Yes,' I said. 'I did.'

Lt. Gibbons pressed for a clarification. 'You threatened Mr Elder, not Johnna Masterson?'

'That's correct.'

'What did the two of you talk about, if you recall?' Dalton asked.

'Nothing, really. He said something about the university giving me a letter of censure instead of firing me. That was the rumour he had heard at the funeral home, anyway, and then he said he hoped nothing

283

happened to change their minds.' The detective didn't quite follow me, so I explained. 'The only thing that makes sense to me is he knew Johnna was going to be missing. He was telling me something was going to happen.'

'You think she was there during the conversation?' Gibbons asked.

'Buddy knew I was at Denny's. How could he have known that if he didn't set the whole thing up? I didn't even tell my wife where I was going.'

'So you're saying only you and Johnna Masterson knew you were planning to meet at Denny's that night?'

'And Buddy Elder.'

Dalton thanked me for coming in. I had sure given them a lot to think about. I nodded dumbly, trying to assure myself the interview had not gone as badly as it felt. Maybe they *did* understand. Maybe they were reluctant to let me know the real suspect was Buddy Elder. Such are the lies we tell ourselves after our worst moments.

As he walked me out of the building and over to my truck, Kip seemed almost sympathetic again. It was hard for a man to say anything these days without getting in trouble with someone. I grumbled my agreement, feeling vindicated – one man of the world talking to another. He shook his head and looked out across the city. He remembered the days when sex was just sex. Now, well if they could put the President of the

United States on a witness stand and grill him for eight hours on national TV about a blow job, no one was safe!

I measured that a couple different ways and decided the reference was to false testimony, not consensual sex. He might still be giving me the benefit of the doubt on the disappearance of Johnna Masterson, but he sure as hell believed I'd had myself a stripper from The Slipper. As far as I could see, that was a fact as unassailable as gravity.

I was already inside my truck, ready for the getaway when the second shoe dropped. 'You've given us a whole new perspective on this thing, Dr Albo. I mean to say, we could spend quite a bit of energy chasing down everything you've told us. Now I'm ready to do it, if that's what it takes, but I know the sheriff would feel a lot better if you gave us some assurance.'

'What are you talking about?'

'It would help the investigation if you'd agree to take a polygraph.'

'I need to talk to my lawyer about that,' I answered after a moment. I was feeling trapped, accused, and more than a little manipulated. On the other hand, I really didn't have anything to fear from a machine designed to uncover lies.

'Do that! I wouldn't want you to feel pressured.'

'No pressure,' I said. 'I'll call you next week and let you know.'

'I've got a better idea. Why don't you come in Monday afternoon, around three o'clock, if that's good for you, and we can take the test. If your lawyer thinks it's a bad idea, just give us a call Monday morning and we'll cancel the thing. Is that fair?'

'Sure. Plenty fair.' Kip Dalton slapped the side of my truck and smiled. For some reason I had made him a very happy man. I worried about that all the way home.

Chapter 24

WHEN I GOT BACK TO THE FARM Molly told me
I had a few calls to make. I was curious at her ironic
tone until she handed me seven messages: three from
the television stations, two newspapers, my agent and
Gail Etheridge. I called my agent first. Some folks in
Hollywood, he said, were looking at *Jinx* for a TV
series. Was I agreeable to the idea?

Sounded great, I said. We talked about things in
general. How was I doing? What was I writing? I lied,
as Walt had put it, like a villain.

When I finished with the call, I told Molly the good
news. Over the years we had had enough heartbreaks
and near misses to learn a bit of caution. I wasn't
about to start spending the big TV bucks, but neither
was I as pessimistic as Molly. 'Great. Does that mean
if the deal comes through you can afford a lawyer?'

On the subject of lawyers, I decided I should probably give Gail a call. 'You heard?' I asked when she

came on the line. I expect I evinced as much enthusiasm as a truant approaching his principal.

'Molly told me. The reason I called was to tell you the university lawyer is stonewalling us. His exact words: "See you in court, Counsellor."'

'Johnna Masterson's disappearance?'

'I don't think it helped.'

'Don't worry,' I said with a bit of strained confidence. 'As soon as they arrest Buddy Elder for it, they'll come crawling to us.'

'Molly told me you're practising law, David.'

'The sheriff's detectives just had some questions.'

'What did they want to know?'

I ran through the interview in detail. Her silence ominous, I found myself making excuses before I got around to mentioning Kip Dalton's request for a lie detector.

Once the excuses started, Gail lost her patience. 'You gave them motive, David. They don't care about your sexual harassment case. The flimsier the case against you the more sense it makes for you to be furious.'

'At the university! Not Johnna Masterson. And I made it clear to them Buddy Elder was behind this. If he turned up dead, that would be a different story!'

'Standard criminal behaviour, Professor. One slime ball points a finger at another slime ball. The more you tell them about Buddy, the more they like you for it.'

I tried to explain my strategy, but I didn't get far.

'I've got news for you, David. Even if I buy your theory that Buddy Elder is out to get you it doesn't make sense. What did you do to this guy? Murder his parents? Why in the hell would he go to all this trouble?'

'I insulted his short story.'

'And I thought it was something big like cutting in front of him in the lunch line!'

'It's a little more complicated than just an insult, Gail.'

'I'm going to tell you one thing, and then I'm going to shut up. Get an attorney.'

'You're my lawyer.'

'If I'm still your lawyer, why didn't you call me when they asked for a second interview?'

'I probably should have.'

'Probably?'

'All right. I screwed up. So shoot me.'

'How about I just sit in the audience while a penitentiary doctor sticks a needle in your arm?'

'It wasn't that bad.'

'I expect it was a lot worse than you think. Look, David, I'll represent you, if that's what you want, but you're going to have to think about hiring a trial lawyer at some point, and I'd say the sooner the better. This thing could get out of hand on us real fast.'

'What are you talking about? You're acting like they're going to arrest me!'

Gail sounded tired. 'Probably not until they find a body, but I wouldn't count on it.'

'They don't have anything, Gail!'

'You mean besides motive, means, and no alibi?'

'I didn't even see her!'

'The cops aren't going to believe Buddy Elder called you on Johnna's cell phone, David.'

'Why not?' I looked at Molly who had sat close through the entire conversation. She looked more worried than Gail sounded.

'They like their cases straightforward.'

'How's this for straightforward? Buddy kidnaps Johnna Masterson and forces her to call me on her cell phone. At midnight Buddy calls on the same phone and tells me the rumour is I'm about to get a letter of censure, and he sure as hell hopes nothing happens at the university to change their mind!'

'This guy kidnaps a young woman and quite possibly murders her, and he calls you up so you'll know he did it? That's insane!'

'Why not tell me? Nobody believes me!' I looked at Molly. 'Ever since that diary surfaced,' I said, my voice rising, 'no one has even considered I might be telling the truth!'

Gail answered with cool irony, 'I wonder why that is, David.'

'Dalton wants me to take a lie detector test on Monday. Maybe then—'

'Whoa! You didn't agree to take one? Tell me you didn't.'

'I said I needed to talk to my lawyer, but I think maybe I should!'

'Quit thinking, David. It's bad for your health! That thing about talking to your lawyer, that's the perfect answer. Believe me, you don't want to take a polygraph.'

'It looks to me like the only way.'

'You're representing yourself again, Dr Albo.'

'Okay. Point made. I'll cancel it.'

'Cancel what?'

I explained to Gail that Dalton wanted to schedule the exam, but I was free to call and cancel if she thought it was a bad idea.

'David, why don't you just confess?'

'Because I didn't do it!'

'So why are you trying to get yourself convicted?'

'We cancel the son of a bitch! What's the big deal?'

'Suspect refuses to take a lie detector.'

'That's what you want!'

'I'm not going to refuse a polygraph, David. I think it's a wonderful opportunity for you to demonstrate your innocence, assuming our conditions are met.'

'That's lawyer talk for refusing to take a polygraph.'

'Damn straight it is,' Gail snapped. 'Those exams don't measure truth or falsehood. They're machines! They measure how nervous you are. You've been framed for murder, if you're telling the truth. That's one hell of a scary situation. I mean, you could be going to death row if you don't convince the police you're telling the truth. Or look at it the other way. Say you're lying about *something*, some detail. Could be anything, something too embarrassing to admit – like a little sex in the office with your little stripper friend. You take the test and you're going to try to beat the machine on that one lie. The results come back and you end up looking like you're lying about a whole lot of things. Believe me, too much is riding on this for you to be calm!'

'I'll tell you what, *you're* starting to scare me.'

'That's good. That means I'm finally getting through to you.'

MOLLY WANTED TO KNOW ABOUT Tuesday evening the minute I got off the phone.

I ran through the thing in detail. When I had finished, I told her it was not as bad as Gail was making it out to be. 'Gail defends scumbags. The scumbags are guilty. The last thing you want to do with a guilty client is take a polygraph.'

Molly seemed hardly to hear me. 'You're going to listen to Gail?'

'I guess.'

'David – ?'

'I'll listen to her!'

292

That evening we had dinner in the kitchen with the TV on. As we weren't enthusiasts of the local broadcasts in the best of times, we didn't know where to go or whom to trust now that the stakes mattered. By chance, though, I found Patty Storm on Channel 3. Patty had been a student of mine during my first year at the university. Cute, ambitious, and possessing a remarkable degree of talent (in every sense of the word), Patty had quickly left English with an emphasis in creative writing and gravitated to journalism where, as she told me almost shamefully, she could make a living. I had seen her a couple times doing reports as I was surfing for something to watch, but I hadn't realized she had worked her way up to a co-anchor position.

'A former student of mine!' I told Lucy and Molly cheerfully. 'Let's watch this. Patty's all right!'

Johnna Masterson was still a second page story, but my name had come up as an individual sheriff's detectives were interviewing. Patty Storm did not use the word *suspect*. Mostly the report was about the search for Masterson continuing. There was a touching plea from her parents.

Lucy looked at me suspiciously when the report was over.

'Innocent,' I said.

'She's pretty,' Lucy rejoined.

'Johnna? She sure is. Smart, funny, totally likable.

Personally, when I commit murder I like to do it to someone who deserves it!'

'Don't make jokes, David,' Molly answered.

'How well did you know her?' Lucy asked.

I grimaced but I wouldn't back away. 'She was one of the women who filed charges against me at school.'

'So what happened? Or is this not my business either?'

'As long as we're all living in the same house it's our business,' I said. I glanced at Molly.

'Tell her,' Molly said. 'Tell her what you told me this afternoon.'

I went to the pantry and cracked open a bottle of bourbon. As I was pouring a couple of healthy shots over ice for Molly and me Lucy asked for one as well. I got Molly's nod of approval. Special occasion: her stepfather was coming clean.

'We got a call on Tuesday night,' I said. From there I went through the whole evening. I finished by explaining that I had something of a history with Buddy Elder because of some trouble at school, and I was fairly sure he was involved in this for no other reason than to hurt me.'

'How could he do that?' Lucy asked.

'I think he might be trying to frame me for this.'

Lucy seemed uneasy. Molly was scared.

'Don't worry about it,' I said. 'It will blow over.'

*   *   *

THERE WERE SOME CALLS after dinner. A number of people from the university who had avoided all contact with me for the past two months suddenly wanted to know how I was doing. As per Gail's instructions that afternoon before we got off the phone, I neither answered nor returned the calls.

At nine o'clock, Patty Storm, among others, left a message. She called me Dr Albo and reminded me of the class she had taken 'a couple of years ago.' She was working on a story and wondered if I could help her. Ten minutes later, she left another message. She had received information about Johnna Masterson's disappearance. For the sake of fairness, she wanted my response before she went on again. I was curious about her information, so much so that I thought about calling her, but I resisted the temptation.

Twenty minutes later we found out what she had. Johnna Masterson's disappearance now led all stories. The intro music was different, urgent, not the typical stuff. This was breaking news. I checked the other two local stations. The story was upgraded there as well. I went back to Patty Storm. She had the look of a reporter who knows she is on to something good, and I quickly realized I was the *something*.

'*Sources inside the sheriff's department are investigating allegations of an affair between Professor David Albo and an unidentified freshman co-ed, who, along*

with Johnna Masterson, filed charges of sexual harass-
ment against Dr Albo earlier this fall...'

'This is not good,' Molly offered quietly.

'...suspended from his teaching duties as the inves-
tigation continues...'

'Where did this woman get all this, David?'

'...the last person to talk to Johnna Masterson on
the night she disappeared...'

'Gail told Dalton we aren't going to play ball. This
is the payback.'

'...refusal to take a polygraph...'

They posted the university's public relations photo of
me. I had always liked the shot. It was about four years
out of date, a portrait of a thirty-three-year-old man
projecting confidence, training, scholarship, and just a
touch of sex appeal. On television, I came off looking
like an overbearing English prof with a hard-on.

'...what some witnesses are calling a brawl at a local
funeral home...'

Molly stared open mouthed at the screen. 'Nice
picture, huh?' I asked.

'...following Professor Albo's arrest on felony assault
charges stemming from an incident at The Glass Slipper,
a local establishment featuring topless dancing...'

I snapped Patty Storm off mid-sentence.

'I wanted to watch the rest of it.'

'This stuff is important if you make it important,'
I said.

'This stuff pushes prosecutors to try cases, David. You can't just ignore it!'

'Watch me.'

Lucy came down the stairs, her face red, her eyes wet. Shaking her head, Lucy looked at me as if I had just violated her.

'You saw it?' I asked.

'You liar!'

Molly and I both called out to her, but she headed for the back door and kept going.

As soon as she had driven off I looked at Molly. 'How about another bourbon on the rocks?'

'How about we forget the rocks?'

I got the good stuff out and our best crystal and poured us both three fingers' worth. 'To catastrophe!' I said cheerfully. It was how we used to celebrate the purchase of broken down houses we thought we could resurrect.

Molly smiled at me suddenly as if we hadn't a worry in the world. 'To catastrophe!'

Chapter 25

SATURDAY MORNING THE PHONE rang incessantly. At midday, a TV van pulled up into our driveway. Molly took her shotgun out and sent them off in a hurry.

In the evening Lucy, having not spoken to me all day, drove off again. Molly asked where she was going but didn't really get an answer. Alone for the evening, we talked about what happened after an arrest. That came down to money, I said. Like everything else, there were different prices for different people. A trial defence could be purchased at anything from bargain basement rates to a multimillion dollar media show. A public defender would get me the needle. Twenty thousand could probably keep me off death row. Fifty thousand would probably buy a retrial. A couple hundred thousand might get an acquittal on the second trial. Of course, if Buddy Elder decided to plant some evidence, which I thought he would do, there were only a handful of lawyers in the country who could get me off.

We could find the money, Molly said.

Of course we could, I answered, but that would stop all of our income. With my suspension continuing into the next semester, almost certainly now without pay, everything we had would go to the lawyers.

Doc and Olga could help.

I said it wasn't their problem. It wasn't Molly's either. Molly swore at this. This was our problem, and we were going to fight the bastards every step of the way!

'Move to Florida,' I said. 'Take everything. I'll get a public defender to advise me and defend myself.'

'We fight this together, David.'

With a coy smile I asked her, 'How do you know I'm innocent, Molly?'

'Because this isn't about your dick.'

'If Buddy Elder set this up,' I countered, 'wasn't it possible he had Denise keep a bogus diary?'

'Denise isn't on Buddy's team anymore, David.'

'Are you sure about that?'

THE SUNDAY MORNING PAPER featured Johnna Masterson with her beauty pageant smile on the front page, the headlines proclaiming, 'Search Continues for Missing Grad Student.'

My crimes and misdemeanours were listed mid-column. Unlike the article about Walt Beery, they didn't say a thing about my book.

The sheriff's spokesperson, Lt. Gibbons of sex

crimes, insisted there were no suspects. In fact, investigators were still trying to determine if a crime had been committed. Certain discrepancies in my statement to them, however, were troubling.

I hadn't even finished the story before the phone began to ring. The first two were death threats. One involved certain choice parts of my anatomy being fed to me. The other promised a handgun of a certain calibre rammed into a certain orifice before being discharged. The sincerity of cold rage from perfect strangers astonished me almost as much as their sexually deviant bloodlust.

It seemed to me only a matter of time before the sheriff came with a warrant for my arrest. When I heard Gail Etheridge on the answering machine I didn't bother picking up. Gail's message was supportive. This was what they did when they couldn't make an arrest. I just had to hang tough.

I decided to take Ahab around the property, though it was a cold, miserable day. I half-expected to find a grave out there somewhere, something easy to notice if you just went back and looked. What would I have done if I found a corpse? I thought about it without deciding. The right thing would be to call the sheriff. The smart thing would be to dig it up and drop it on Buddy's doorstep.

In fact, there was no grave. Nothing at all. I rode for nearly two hours before I took Ahab back to the barn.

Lucy was waiting for me. 'We have to talk,' she said.

I got the currycomb and brush from a shelf and began working over Ahab's flanks. 'I'm listening.'

'You have to change your story, Dave.'

I laughed at this. 'Why is that?' I walked to the other side of the horse, glancing over Ahab's back.

'Buddy wasn't with Johnna Masterson Tuesday night.' I looked up, frowning at her. 'He was with me,' she said.

I studied my stepdaughter's face. She was struggling with her confession. 'You were home Tuesday night, Lucy.'

'He called me.' She blinked as she tried to meet my gaze. 'He wanted to see me.'

'Is Buddy the guy you're interested in?'

Lucy rolled her eyes, an expression designed to convey adolescent opinion of adult intelligence. 'It's a little more than interest, Dave.'

I probably should have been angry. Giving the matter any thought at all, I should have realized the kind of trouble I was in, but at that moment all I felt was fear for Lucy.

I put the brush and currycomb away and got the shovel. I walked into Ahab's stall. 'Does your mother know about this?'

'I just told her. She's pissed.'

'You know how old this guy is?'

'Please, Dave.'

'Let me ask you something.'

'The answer is yes.'

I found myself holding a shovel full of dirty sawdust and unable to move. 'That wasn't the question,' I said finally, and dumped the load into the wheelbarrow. Back inside the stall I said, 'My question was if you actually saw him Tuesday night or just talked to him.'

'He was out here at midnight. We'd been on the phone for a couple of hours. He wanted me to come outside and, you know, drive around. I went out through my bedroom window.'

'What time did you get home?'

'A little before three.'

'You drove around with this guy for almost three hours?'

'We didn't drive the whole time.'

This came off too smart, too cute. 'This isn't a joke, Lucy!'

'I talked to Buddy last night. He says the two of you aren't getting along because of Denise.'

'How did you meet Buddy?'

Lucy gave me a look of exasperation. I was missing the point.

'Humour me,' I said.

'Kathy and I went to a college party. Her brother is in a fraternity. Buddy was there.'

'Buddy Elder was at a fraternity party?'

'Why not?'

'Why didn't you tell me you were seeing this guy?'

'He's only like ten years older!'

'That's the least of his problems!'

'He doesn't think you hurt Johnna.'

'He doesn't?'

'He told me last night you couldn't do something like that.'

I smiled. 'But you think I could?'

Lucy considered this for moment. I wasn't sure if she had made up her mind or not. 'I thought... when I saw the news...'

'That's not my style, Lucy. You know that.'

'They made it sound like—'

'It's what they're paid to do.'

I took Ahab into his stall and gave him a scoop of oats. Jezebel protested and Lucy took her a treat.

'Buddy thinks Johnna disappeared just to hurt you.'

'I want you to stay away from Buddy. I know it's not my business and I don't have any right to tell you what to do—'

'No problem. He ended it last night.'

'He ended it?' She nodded uncomfortably. 'Did he say why?'

'He asked me to marry him.'

I expect I swore, but I can't remember. I only recall looking at her as I tried to fathom my emotions.

'I told him I wasn't ready. I don't want to get married!'

'You said no?'

'He said you won't let me see him again if we're not married, so we might as well end things.'

LUCY WAS IN HER ROOM WHEN I went back to the house. Molly was upstairs sanding the new floor. I waited patiently until she stopped.

'You talk to Lucy?' I asked.

'She's grounded for life.'

'If Dalton gets hold of the phone records, Molly, he's going to find out about this.'

'If Buddy was with Lucy Tuesday he couldn't have done anything to Johnna Masterson, David.'

'He called me, Molly! He was laughing at me! He knew what was going on with Johnna!'

'Lucy says Buddy thinks Johnna is doing this to hurt you.'

I shook my head. 'Buddy has played us from the start. I don't care anymore if you believe me about Denise Conway, but this thing with Lucy was a setup. He spent the whole evening talking to her and driving around with her because he knew I would point my finger at him!'

'We don't know Johnna,' Molly persisted. 'She could have—'

'She had her revenge, Molly. She reported me to Affirmative Action.'

'How could Buddy kidnap her if he was out with Lucy?'

'Roger Beery did it. Tell me you don't think *he's* capable of something like that.'

'I thought you said it was Buddy. Now it's Roger. What's Roger—?'

'They're in this together, Molly! I told you, it's how they got away with killing Walt and Barbara!'

Molly looked at me as if stricken, and for the first time everything I had told her became possible. But then it faded and she shook her head. It didn't make sense. Walt and Barbara... for the money... maybe, but what did Johnna have to do with that? I told her I didn't know.

I CALLED GAIL THAT AFTERNOON and arranged a meeting for seven-thirty Monday morning. Big problem, I said.

Sunday evening passed in funereal silence. Molly had exercised a mother's prerogative. She had confiscated Lucy's television set, her keys, and both phones. Lucy thought she was being unfair. Molly told her she didn't know what unfair was.

Having walked the streets of Chicago without a place to lay her head at the age of fifteen, pregnant and alone, Molly knew about unfair. It was house policy never to ask about those days. When she was younger Lucy had made inquiries, of course. How had her mother survived? Molly had answered glibly. She got lucky and picked up a job as a waitress. The people at the restaurant gave her a little apartment to live in until she got on her feet. Later she got into a trade school and trained to be a carpenter. I was fairly sure that Lucy understood there was a bit more to coming off the streets than her mother admitted, but she never asked once she was of an age to understand such things. Molly said Lucy didn't know what unfair was, and Lucy retreated to silence. So did I, for that matter.

Around ten that evening, Molly came to me in my monk's cell on the third floor. 'You want to toss those books off the bed, Professor?' she asked.

I was reading Marcus Aurelius and holding the lesser Stoics in reserve. 'What did you have in mind?' I answered stoically.

'Clear your bed and I'll show you.'

We made love with the reverence and uncertainty of first times. Curiously, the weeks of celibacy had blunted the sense of urgency in both of us. We did not move quickly or work ourselves into a frenzy. We took our time, savouring the touch of flesh. We made it last, and even as it concluded we were quiet. The intimacy was more important than the rest.

And it seemed to me as we lay together afterwards that Molly had come to me because we were about to lose each other, that this was not a reunion but her goodbye before I went to jail.

* * *

WE DROPPED LUCY OFF AT SCHOOL shortly after seven-fifteen. She was humiliated by the door-to-door service, but Molly was adamant. Lucy had precious few rules to live by, but she had decided to break them. That was fine, she could do whatever she wanted, but if she wanted to live at home, she had better learn to deal with the consequences.

Alone with Molly finally I tried to talk to her about Lucy. 'Try to understand,' I said, 'what she's going through!' It was no use. Molly was doing what she thought was best. We got to Gail's office at exactly seven-thirty. Gail looked tired at the start of our meeting. As I related Lucy's confession her demeanour grew increasingly grim.

'You had no idea she was seeing this guy?' she asked Molly when I had finished the story.

Molly shook her head.

Gail broke her office's non-smoking rule and lit a cigarette. 'He asked her to marry him, and she turned him down?'

'I think things were happening a little too fast for her,' I answered.

Gail looked at Molly. 'If you want me to go to the prosecutor, we can bring criminal charges against this bastard. You know that?'

Molly shook her head. Lucy was almost eighteen. She knew what she was doing.

'Almost only counts in horseshoes and hand grenades.'

'I'm not going to put Lucy through something like that,' Molly answered.

Gail looked at me. 'I suppose you're ready to kill him?'

'Correct me if I'm wrong, but as an officer of the court aren't you obliged to tell the police if you know a client is about to commit a crime?'

'Tell me you're joking.'

I smiled good-naturedly, telling her nothing.

'What are the chances Johnna decided to disappear?' Molly asked. 'Lucy thinks, I mean Buddy told her *he* thinks Johnna did this to get at David.'

Gail considered the possibility for a moment, then shook her head. 'Have you seen her parents on TV? This thing is killing them. If Johnna Masterson disappeared to hurt David, I guarantee you one thing: she hates her parents a lot more than she hates him.'

'But it's possible?'

'Johnna Masterson is the victim,' I said.

'And you're the suspect,' Gail answered, her voice sharp with authority. Gail was tired of my Buddy Elder theories. It was time I faced up to the situation.

'No argument there. On the face of it, my story sounds incredible.'

'Then change your story before it's too late,' Gail answered.

'Even if it's true?'

Gail looked away from us, swallowing whatever

insult she intended. Finally, she said, 'A woman called Denny's. A woman, not a man. This was twelve, twelve-fifteen?'

'Just after Lucy gets off the phone and before she goes down the hill and gets in the car with the son of a bitch.'

Gail smiled at me condescendingly. 'The window of opportunity?'

'What would you call it?'

'Unless Lucy made the call to Denny's, you've still got a problem. You pick up the phone and it's Buddy Elder. The only way he knows you're at Denny's is if Johnna told him, but he's been on the phone with Lucy since ten-thirty.'

'He has a partner who snatches her.'

'While Buddy's on the phone?'

'The perfect alibi.'

Gail seemed dubious. 'Who was the woman who called Denny's, David? Another partner?'

'Denise Conway. Why not?'

'Why not? Well, for starters, Lucy comes out and gets in the car. Where's Denise – in the backseat?'

When I didn't answer her, Gail levelled her gaze at me as if she had caught me in a lie. 'I didn't like your story when it was possible. I'm sure as hell not buying it now.'

'What if I'm not lying, Gail? Can you just consider that for a minute?'

'It's a waste of time.'

'I know you don't like it. I don't like it, but I'm telling you what happened! What if she has a car parked out there, makes the call for Buddy, and then drives off before Lucy shows up?'

'Why go to all that trouble?'

'I don't know, Gail! Maybe because I'll look like a muddle-headed fool trying to explain how I got a phone call from Buddy Elder while he was seducing my step-daughter!'

Gail shook her head angrily. 'You're convicting your-self with this story, David. You can't stay with it!'

'You tell me what I did then! You're the attorney. Pick a story that will float, because I don't have a clue what you want to hear!'

Gail leaned back in her chair, looking exasperated. 'You need another lawyer. I can't handle this. I'll stick with you until you get someone, but I can't deal with you when you get like this.'

'Like what?'

'It's like you want to go to prison.'

'I want a lawyer who believes me.'

'They don't make lawyers that stupid.' Gail looked shocked by her own response, but she didn't back down. 'Sorry, but it's the truth.'

'If David says—'

'David says whatever he thinks people will believe. You know that, Molly. You of all people! Fine, that's

310

David. Part of his charm, once you get used to it. The trouble is we're not drinking cocktails and talking about cars and horses! We're fighting for his life here, and he's too stubborn to admit he's lying!'

'I guess you need to tell us what we owe you. For everything,' Molly answered. 'We're going to find another attorney.'

'I'll get a bill out to you this afternoon,' Gail answered with a touch of relief. She stood up, her eyes shifting between us. 'I can give you some names if you want.'

Molly would not look at her. She said that wouldn't be necessary.

In the truck, Molly said to me, 'What now?'

'Dalton,' I said.

Chapter 26

DETECTIVE DALTON, THE WOMAN in the sheriff's department told us, had the morning off. I told her to call him. We had information about the Johnna Masterson case. She said I could talk to Lt. Gibbons or Detective Jacobs. I shook my head. Dalton.

When she got the detective on the phone, she relayed what I had told her. Hanging up, she looked at us. 'One hour.'

I said we would be at the cafe down the street. 'When he gets in, call us,' I said, handing her my card with the cell phone number listed. 'We'll be here in five minutes.'

Forty minutes later Detective Dalton walked into the cafe where Molly and I were working on our third cup of coffee. We had been talking out our options again, the things we needed to do after the arrest.

'Are you going to confess?' Dalton asked cheerfully. He was alone, dressed casually, a man pulled in from his morning off.

'Only my innocence.'

He sat down and like a regular signalled the waitress for a cup of coffee. 'Does your lawyer know we're talking, Professor?'

I told him I no longer had an attorney representing me.

'Well, that must mean you wouldn't mind taking a polygraph.'

'Two conditions,' I said. 'First, I need to tell you a couple of things about last Tuesday night.'

Kip Dalton didn't really smile, but his expression seemed to relax. I knew then he already had the phone records and maybe a lot more. He expected me to recant. 'I'll listen.'

'Second, when you've got me hooked up to that machine, I want you to ask about Denise Conway. I don't care what you ask, but you cover the subject. When I pass this son of a bitch I want you *and* my wife to know that diary she wrote is a lie.'

Dalton smiled at this. 'You understand these tests aren't one hundred percent. What they do—'

'You're telling me I'm still going to be a suspect even if I pass.'

'I can't rule you out if the evidence says you did it. As far as what your wife thinks, I don't know a woman alive who would trust a machine over her own instincts.'

'Just ask the questions.'

Dalton gave me a grudging smile. 'I'll see that they're asked. Now why don't you tell me about last Tuesday night, the way it really happened.'

'My stepdaughter Lucy tells me she's been seeing Buddy Elder the past month or so without our knowledge.' Kip Dalton's eyes brightened momentarily. 'Tuesday night, according to her, she was on the telephone with Buddy from sometime after ten o'clock until midnight. At that point she left the house and was with him until about three o'clock in the morning.'

Dalton seemed to expect me to adjust my story. When I made no attempt to do so he seemed confused. 'You still believe the call at Denny's came from Buddy Elder?'

'No belief to it, Detective. I talked to Buddy.'

'And your statements to us are substantially accurate and complete?'

'No, sir,' I said. 'They were entirely accurate and complete. Except that we don't cook at the fireplace in the kitchen, and we never have folks out to the farm dressed up in costume.'

The detective stared at me for several seconds before he smiled. 'I thought that was stretching it.'

'Where did I go wrong?'

He shook his head. 'You folks didn't strike me as the kind of people who would throw a big fancy party.'

*   *   *

'YOU'RE STILL GOING TO BE a suspect if you pass?' Molly asked.

I shrugged my shoulders. We were in the truck driving back to the farm.

'So what's the point?'

'Right now Dalton is sure I'm guilty. Come four o'clock he's going to have to admit to himself that just maybe he's wrong.'

'You seem pretty confident.'

'I've got nothing left to lose.'

Molly smiled. 'You think they've got a setting on that machine for lying used car salesmen?'

'Everyone knows when a used car salesmen is lying, Molly. They're just like lawyers: their lips move. That's why Tubs was the best. Tubs never lied. The man didn't sell cars, he sold his own uncompromising honesty, and he taught me to do the same.'

'But you lie all the time, David!'

'Tubs made a big deal about keeping his word and never telling a lie, but it had nothing to do with honesty. He thought it did, but in the end it was just a sales technique. I got it up to here with never telling a lie.' I settled my fingers just below my jaw. 'I wanted to be honest without making a big deal out of it. I mean stories are fun! You make something up and people enjoy it! But I don't break my promises, Molly. I don't back away from admitting mistakes. I don't cheat people. I'm not perfect, I don't mean that, but when I tell a wild-ass story everyone knows it's a story!'

'But they don't, David. You're so sincere about things that people think what you're saying is the truth. Half of Lucy's friends think there was a mass murder at our house ten years ago.'

I smiled. 'Only half?'

'Randy Winston asked me if we had gotten the farm from Chrysler stock you inherited. I asked him where he heard that, and guess where he got it?'

'Okay. I get enthusiastic. But I don't lie to you or Lucy about the things that count. You know that.'

'You didn't lie about Denise Conway?'

'I broke your heart once, Molly. I swore to you I'd never do it again, and I never have.'

'Nothing happened?'

'Nothing at all. The whole thing was Buddy Elder's game, just like Johnna Masterson disappearing while he's driving Lucy around in the middle of the night. He decided to ruin us. The diary was the catalyst to everything, and that's all it was.'

When Molly didn't respond, I took my eyes off the road for a second. Her face was set and brittle. I thought she was about to tell me what a liar I was, but suddenly tears welled up in her eyes.

I pulled to the side of the road, and for a long time we just sat there holding each other.

*   *   *

AT THREE O'CLOCK I WAS back at the sheriff's office. The examination took about an hour-and-a-half. We went through a number of warm-up questions in which I lied and told the truth at the examiner's whim. By the time we got to matters relating to Buddy Elder, Johnna Masterson, and Denise Conway I was relaxed. Actually, I didn't care. I had finally passed the only test that mattered.

When it was finished, I found Molly and Lucy waiting for me in an interview room. Lucy was impatient to know the results. Molly was different. She already knew how I had done and simply wanted to go home and get on with our lives, if that was possible. When Kip Dalton walked in about thirty minutes later, he had the look of a man who just can't believe what he's seen. 'You ever take one of those things before, Professor?'

'Are you trying to tell me I passed?'

'You knocked it out of the ballpark.'

'We need to talk about anything else?'

Kip glanced at Lucy but shook his head. 'For now I've got what I need.'

Molly, Lucy, and I were already at the door when I stopped, as though remembering to ask something of no great importance. Tubs called it his Colombo Close, after the TV detective who always had just one more question. The pitch finished, the decisions all apparently made, he would come back at the point folks thought they were free of him. Detective Jacobs had worked it masterfully against me at the farm.

'I've got a question for you,' I said.

Kip Dalton appeared mildly curious, nothing more.

'The sheriff's department looked at the deaths of Walt and Barbara Beery?'

Dalton frowned slightly. 'We did. The case is closed. Why do you ask?'

'You were involved in the investigation?'

'I was lead investigator.'

'As I understand it, Walt used a knife. Is that correct?'

Dalton didn't react overtly, but tipped his head so slightly I might have imagined it. Yes.

'Did you have a problem with the blood splatter?'

Splatter, I knew from various researches into murder over the years, resulted when blood initially exited a wound. Police used it to determine the position of the victim and killer. Crime scenes without splatter frequently indicated staging. If Walt Beery had stabbed Barbara in the back there ought to have been distinctive streaks and droplets of blood on his clothing from the initial wound. I was betting no such splatter existed.

Kip Dalton said nothing. Even his eyes were inscrutable. 'You want to tell me what you're getting at, Dr Albo?'

'Just a question. You don't want to answer it, that's fine.'

'What kind of problem are you talking about?'

'Oh, I don't know. Like it wasn't there.'

'You were a friend of Walt Beery's, weren't you?' he said after a moment.

'I got drunk with Walt more times than I care to think about. The man didn't have a mean bone in his body, Detective. Suicide? Possible. But I'll tell you something. He'd have gone off alone to take care of it. He wouldn't have hurt Barbara for the world.'

'We never want to believe the worst in the people we know, Dr Albo.'

'Take another look at the blood splatter, Detective. That's all I'm saying.'

'Mrs Beery's blood was all over Dr Beery's shirt.'

'I don't doubt it for a minute, but splatter's something else altogether, isn't it? You can't fake splatter.'

Dalton was calculating my possible source, not even thinking about the splatter. 'Where did you get your information, if you don't mind my asking?'

'About blood splatter?'

Kip shook his head irritably. 'About there not being any.'

I smiled, my theory confirmed. 'I started from the premise that Walt didn't do it. From there, I just worked through it.'

I was fairly sure Dalton assumed I was lying to protect my source, but he didn't accuse me of it. What he said was this: 'The kid and his wife had a solid alibi.'

I gave the detective the look I used to deliver when it was time to sign a contract, followed by a glance toward my wayward stepdaughter. 'Sure is a lot of that going around these days.'

THAT EVENING LUCY HELPED me in the barn because I asked her to, but she wasn't comfortable being alone with me.

'Everything okay?' I asked her.

She answered without much enthusiasm. Everything was fine.

'You sorry you made the decision you did?'

Lucy slammed the lid of the feed barrel. 'Drop it, will you?'

'What's the matter with you?'

'Just drop it!'

In the house I told Molly, 'I'm not sure Lucy is happy with her decision.'

Molly asked me what I was talking about. I tried to describe her daughter's mood in the barn. Molly listened distractedly, not especially worried. 'She's seventeen, David. Anything could be bothering her.'

'I expect Doc and Olga had just about this same conversation eighteen years ago.'

'That was different.'

'No argument there. For one thing Luke didn't poison your dogs.'

'Lucy was with Buddy that night.'

'You're sure about that?'

'I asked her about it. They were at a party.'

'Then it was Roger. It doesn't really matter. First the dogs, then Johnna. Both times he had Lucy right beside him.'

'What's your point?'

'I'm not sure what Buddy intends to do next.'

'I thought that was obvious. He intends to watch you go to prison for a crime you didn't commit.'

'Buddy never quite does what I expect, Molly. What if there's more to it than that? What if he isn't finished with this thing until he hurts you and Lucy?'

'I can take care of myself.'

'And Lucy?'

Molly wasn't so quick to answer this.

'Lucy isn't with us on this, Molly. She's not afraid of the guy. Given the way she's acting tonight, I think it's possible she's having second thoughts.'

'She's not going to see Buddy again, David.'

'You sound pretty sure of yourself.'

'What does that mean?'

'She's seventeen. One phone call, one heartfelt apology and she goes to him and just maybe never comes back. Both times he's struck at us he was with Lucy. I don't think that's an accident. I think he's letting me know he can hurt my family anytime he likes.'

I finally had Molly's attention.

'The best thing is for the two of you to disappear. Go some place he doesn't know about.'

'I'm not leaving you. That's all the sheriff would need.'

'Then get Lucy somewhere safe.'

'She's got less than two weeks to go until Christmas break—'

'Forget school, Molly! This guy has decided to hurt us. So far he's done a hell of a job! I've lost a tenured position. You filed for divorce. Two of our friends are dead! And a young woman has disappeared, with me as the only suspect. This isn't a game you get to start over if things don't work out. There aren't any second chances if we're wrong. If you want to stay we can handle this together, but Lucy is vulnerable. As long as she stays vulnerable, he can hurt us, and there's nothing we can do to stop him.'

To her credit Molly said nothing more. She went upstairs to talk to Lucy. Half-an-hour later she was making reservations for a flight out the following morning.

MOLLY AND LUCY DROVE Molly's rental car to the airport at first light. I followed in my pickup. After Molly dropped her car off the three of us drove over to the terminal.

Lucy was quiet. Tense? Nervous? I couldn't really tell. I had even less feel for Molly's mood. It occurred to me that the two of them had probably enjoyed a long intimate discussion on the drive over. Things were settled now. No need to bring Dave into it. At the security gates Lucy gave her mother a perfunctory hug. When she looked at me I thought she was making an effort to remember my face. 'Take care,' she said and walked away.

When we went out and stood on the observatory deck to watch her plane take off, Molly seemed jittery.

'You think she'll try to contact Buddy?' I asked.

Molly shook her head. 'She understands that Buddy wants to hurt us.'

I thought about telling her that seventeen-year-olds are only rational if it will inconvenience adults, but there wasn't much point upsetting her.

'Did she tell Buddy about Doc and Olga? Can he follow her?'

Molly answered without a tremor of doubt. 'No.'

KIP DALTON left a message on our answering machine for me to call him. I knew it wasn't going to be good but I dutifully dialled his number. As usual the detective apologized for disturbing me. He said he would like to talk to me about a few things, if I wouldn't mind coming in.

'What's this about?' I asked.

'Some hunters found the body of a young woman this morning, Professor. We think it might be Johnna Masterson.'

I got into town a little after two o'clock and went directly to the county building. At the front desk I asked for Kip Dalton. A uniformed officer led me to an interview room and opened the door. Detective Jacobs greeted me with an icy smile. 'Thanks for coming in, Dave.'

'Where's Dalton?'

'He'll be along in a minute. Why don't you have a seat and we can get started.'

Jacobs's new partner stood up when I stepped into the room. He was a big man, six-and-a-half-feet tall, I thought, and almost certainly pushing three hundred pounds. He had a gut of marbled fat, a roll of pink flesh slopping over a crisp white collar, the same snarling smile Jacobs had offered. Jacobs introduced him as Tom Newsome with the State Police. We shook hands. Newsome tried to make me wince. I tried not to give him the satisfaction.

In his late forties or early fifties, Newsome was still mostly animal. That was the point today. I had Jacobs the jackal nipping at my ankles, Newsome the bull threatening with a direct assault. Jacobs made a show of reading me my rights. It was a sterling piece of intimidation and left me under the impression I had been arrested. Following this Detective Jacobs pushed a sheet of paper and a pen across the conference table. I held the ink pen while I read a benign statement indicating that I had been given the Miranda and had

waived my rights to an attorney. I pushed the paper
back and pocketed the ink pen. Jacobs had trouble
bullying me into a signature after the inconvenience
of asking for his ink pen back. I made a slight, insin-
cere attempt at apology and shot the pen back across
the table.

'I'm afraid we can't proceed with our interview until
you have signed that,' Jacobs told me.

I shrugged and stood up. 'I guess I'll take off then.'

Tom Newsome told me to sit down. I didn't care
for his tone and simply looked at him.

'Please.'

It still sounded like a command, but I obliged him
and took my seat. Jacobs asked me if I was familiar
with a certain woods. I wasn't, and said so. His eyes
appraised me suspiciously. 'You haven't been in that
area in the past few weeks?'

'I have no idea. I don't know the place.'

Tom Newsome stood up and walked behind me.
State Police officers had canvassed the area, he said.
They had a witness who had identified me. Jacobs
described the area by naming a couple of county roads.
I still didn't know what they were talking about. They
ran through my former statements. They called everything into question again. Jacobs slumped down in his
chair, his eyes locked on me. Newsome paced, sometimes in my view and sometimes behind me.

How was it possible people had seen me in the area

where they had found a body if I hadn't been there? I knew that police officers are permitted by law to lie to a suspect. The easy answer, however, would let them see I wasn't falling for their trick. I said I didn't know. They asked about my license plate. They had the number, so I played dumb. You tell me. One of the neighbours, Newsome said, had seen a Ford truck parked close to the woods the night Johnna Masterson disappeared. She had caught only three numbers on the license plate. The others were covered with mud. As it happened, three of the numbers matched my plates. How did I explain that? Couldn't. Did I drive a Ford truck? Sure, didn't everyone? Did I think this was a joke? I said I wasn't sure what to think.

Jacobs asked me if I still understood my rights. I said I didn't understand them the first time. Newsome informed me that a number of people at the university had heard me bragging about Masterson. '*All natural*, wasn't it, Dave? Isn't that how you described Johnna Masterson's tits?'

Jacobs pulled three photographs from the pocket of his sports jacket. I saw leaves, nothing more, but I knew she was there. Finally I understood. For a moment I struggled to breathe. Newsome leaned close, his breath at my ear. 'How's that for *all natural*?'

'Look at the next picture, Dave,' Jacobs told me. 'You like it all natural, don't you?'

When I didn't react Tom Newsome pushed the top

photograph away. The second photo featured a nude body ravaged by wildlife and decay. I looked away before I understood the full extent of damage. Newsome whispered. 'Come on, Dave. You like it, don't you?'

He shuffled the second photograph away, and treated me to a close-up of a face half-eaten away. I tried to stand, but Newsome took my shoulder and pushed me down into my chair. 'How many times did you rape her before you put her out of her misery, Dave?'

Jacobs smiled. 'The question is was he careful? Were you careful each time, Dave?'

'You know what I think? I think he meant to be careful, but he got excited.'

'Premature ejaculator?'

'Happens more than you think with these kinds. Vic starts begging, the next thing you know we've got trace. We going to find trace, Dave?'

I had had enough and stood up. Newsome's big hand took my shoulder again, but this time it didn't work.

'Sit down,' he snarled. 'We're not done with you yet.'

I ignored his order and walked to the door. Jacobs blocked my way. He raised his voice. Was he going to have to ask a judge for blood and hair samples or would I cooperate and give them whatever they asked for? I reached for the door. He took my arm. For a moment, we stood like that. 'Today,' he said finally, 'you walk. Next time, there's no way out but the needle.'

Outside the interview room, I thought someone would stop me or at least insist on escorting me out of the building, but I was on my own. Later I realized they had almost certainly monitored and recorded my every step.

'WHAT DID THEY WANT?' Molly asked.

I shook my head. Nothing. When she didn't buy that, I told her, 'They wanted to scare the hell out of me. They wanted me to think they were about to arrest me.'

She asked for details, but I didn't care to go through it. Intimidation, I said.

'I thought Dalton believed you.'

'I think Dalton does. To an extent at least.'

We watched the evening news while we ate dinner. The sheriff was still unwilling to make a formal identification, but he told a news conference the woman had been shot by a .38 calibre handgun. Suspects? The sheriff was a big old country boy somewhere in his late fifties or early sixties. He was pure politician: his face announced *yes* just by the way his smile flickered and died. His words told reporters something else: 'Not until we get a formal identification.'

'You think they'll come for you tonight?' Molly asked.

I shook my head. 'The difference between a viable

suspect and an arrest is physical evidence. My guess is their next move is a search warrant.'

Molly's smile curdled. 'One step at a time?'

I stood up. 'I need to go into town.'

Molly was surprised. 'You want some company?'

I shook my head. 'Not tonight.'

'What are you going to do?'

'It's about time I visit an old friend.'

BUDDY WAS HOME when I drove by. I could see him in his living room watching television. I parked my truck on a side street a block away and headed toward the back of his house along an alley. It was the kind of neighbourhood where a couple of security lights shined all night and a few dogs barked, but no one bothered with motion activated lights, or seemed especially concerned about the occasional pedestrian in the alley. I moved quietly and quickly, but made no effort to conceal myself in the shadows.

I had considered developing some kind of plan. A phone call to distract him, a sack of tin cans heaved up on his roof, even firecrackers. In the end I decided it wasn't necessary. Buddy had won too many confrontations with me to worry. He wouldn't be looking for a direct assault.

At the back door I used my shoulder and burst through the door and into the kitchen without trouble. I took a narrow hallway to his living room and got to him before he had completely come off his couch. I hit him once in the nose, driving him back to a sitting position and turning his face bloody. Then I pummelled him with body blows. He got a couple of swings in before I broke him and he curled into a foetal position.

'Are you having fun with my ass yet, Buddy?' Buddy was no more talkative than I had been outside The Slipper the night he pissed on me. I jammed my fist into his ribs. 'I asked you a question!'

'You're a dead man!'

I hit him again in the same spot. 'That's funny. I don't feel dead.' I struck the same rib a third time. 'The reason I came by,' I said, 'I wanted to borrow your .38. I think the sheriff would like to see it, especially if your fingerprints are on it.'

'I don't have it anymore, Dave.'

I pulled some baling twine from my hip pocket and tied off his wrists and feet so he couldn't move. 'You don't care if I check around and make sure, do you?'

'Take your time. Maybe the cops will show up.'

'Like I give a damn!'

After I had gagged him I started working through the room systematically checking his bookshelves and drawers. When I had finished with the house I took his car keys and searched the car. Back inside the house again, I cut the twine with my pocket-knife.

'Where is it?'

'To tell you the truth—'

I slammed my fist into his stomach. Buddy went down on his knees. 'Try again!'

Gasping, blood dripping from his nose again, Buddy still managed a smile. 'Why don't you try looking for it in your own house, Dave?'

'Is that the game?'

'It's all the sheriff needs to put you away. He finds the gun you used to kill Johnna and you're on death row.'

'The thing you want to think about is Roger Beery,' I said. 'How long do you think Roger can hold out once the cops take him in for questioning?'

'I don't know what you're talking about.'

'I think you do. I think we both know Roger's the weak link in your plan.'

I stood up and looked around for something else to hit. First, I took out the television set, then his DVD player. After that there wasn't much left of value, but I broke what I could and left in the same manner I arrived, walking calmly down the alley.

I got home around midnight and began searching the house. Molly came downstairs and stared at me. 'What happened?' She pointed at my eye, and I realized Buddy's punch had connected. I smiled at her. 'You should see the other guy.'

'Is he still alive?'

'For now.'

'What are you doing?'

'Looking for the gun that killed Johnna Masterson.'

'You think it's here?'

'Buddy didn't have it.'

'You looked?'

'With his permission, sure.'

'Need some help?'

'If you take the house, I'll take the barn, the shed, and the cellar. If we stay at it, I'd say we can probably be done by sun-up.'

Molly looked around my den in frustration. 'It could be anywhere.'

'If we check room-by-room and nook-by-cranny we'll find it if it's here. There wouldn't be much point in hiding it too well. The point is for us not to notice it and for the cops to find it on their first pass.'

We spent the rest of the night and early morning looking for the .38 Buddy had pulled on me outside The Slipper. From attic to basement, hayloft to grain barrels, we checked every conceivable recess, every dark hole, every shelf, every jar.

Exhausted we made ourselves a country breakfast of sausage and eggs and I finally told Molly what had transpired with Buddy.

Molly allowed herself half-a-smile. 'You hog-tied Buddy?'

'Only while I couldn't watch him.'

'So you think Roger has it?'

I shook my head. I wasn't sure. It wasn't at Buddy's house. That was all I knew. 'I thought he might be careless with it, but he's hidden it somewhere safe.'

'You going to check the Beery residence?'

I shook my head. I had lost the element of surprise.

Chapter 27

WE GOT MORE THAN OUR usual share of obscene threats with the phone calls that morning. The newspaper account had stirred a lot of bile.

At around two o'clock I walked down the hill to get the mail and found our mail carefully set between the flag and the box. The door was open and I could see someone had left a pile of reasonably fresh dog shit inside. I cleaned the thing out roughly with some advertisements, then climbed the hill and went to the barn and got some soap and water. Finished with that, I went up to Lucy's apartment and told Molly it was time for a beer. 'A little early, isn't it?' she asked.

'We might not have too many more afternoons together.'

She dropped her tools without comment and told me she needed a few minutes. I told her where I wanted to go and she laughed, brushing the sawdust from her shoulders. 'In that case, I'm ready.'

I pulled my truck into Billy Wade's driveway a couple of minutes later and walked up to the giant's front door. 'Hey, Dave!'

'You take care of the horses for us this evening?' I asked.

'Glad to do it.' I passed him a ten dollar bill. 'You ever see that Mercury around here again?'

'I've been looking! I see him, I'll come over and tell you.' I thanked him and wandered back to the truck.

We drove to a little village most maps didn't bother naming and settled into a booth as far from the regulars as we could get. An old waitress came across the floor, smiling at Molly and me, 'How are you folks this afternoon?'

We were fine. She commented on my eye, which really didn't look too bad, and I told her my stepdaughter's mare had popped me. When she asked what we wanted, I told her, 'Longnecks,' sounding, I expect, like Walt himself, 'and keep them coming.'

'We got plenty of those!'

'That's good,' I told her, 'because we're thirsty.'

'You okay?' Molly asked.

I shook my head, watching the old waitress at her business. 'Tired.'

'You didn't get any sleep last night.'

That wasn't it, and we both knew it. Our beers came, and after a toast to catastrophe that was half fun and half tradition, Molly said, 'You know what attracted me to you the first time we met?'

I swore. Then I laughed. 'I always figured it was the beer you had before I got there.'

'You weren't afraid.'

'Of what?'

She shrugged her shoulders. 'Of anything. What people thought, what they could do to you, the future, the past: you were doing what you wanted and you intended to keep on doing it.'

I considered telling her that graduate school is a peculiar time in a person's life. You're always broke, you're always chasing after something you can't quite catch, and you're young. You're not howling-at-the-moon-young. You're one step from respectability, and in that last mad dance of irresponsibility you are what you will never be again. Instead, I told her, 'It was a long time ago, those first nights, Molly.'

'And days. Remember the rainy afternoons? I never had such...'

'What?'

Molly blushed and laughed. 'Such orgasms.'

I howled, and every head and the bar turned to watch us. While I had everyone's attention, I called out to the bartender, 'You want to set everyone up with a fresh drink? He nodded and went to work. A couple of old codgers tipped their glasses at us, letting me know it was okay with them if I wanted to howl now and then.

'You know he's going to come for you now?' she said.

I lost my smile and nodded. I knew.

WE GOT HOME AFTER DARK, still reasonably coherent. We had thirteen messages, and I ran through them quickly. The seventh was Kip Dalton. I called his cell phone number.

'I'd like to ask you a favour,' Dalton said after I identified myself.

'I missed seeing you the other day, Detective.'

'Something came up.'

'I'm shooting straight with you, Detective. I expect the same in return.'

After a moment of uncomfortable silence Dalton told me, 'The sheriff wanted to try a different approach.'

It wasn't exactly an apology, but I let it pass. 'What's your favour?'

'We want to search your farm. I'd like to do it without asking for a search warrant.'

'Why is that?'

Kip Dalton chuckled pleasantly. 'For one thing because Newsome and Jacobs said you won't go for it.'

'I'll make you a deal. You bring everybody and their Aunt Mabel on out tomorrow. You can look anywhere you want as long as those two stay off the property.'

Kip Dalton laughed. 'Fair enough, but I think you ought to know their feelings are going to be hurt!'

What he meant by that was they would be the ones who arrested me when the time came.

Molly asked me about getting a lawyer once I told her what Kip wanted. I shook my head. 'They have enough evidence to get a search warrant. There's nothing a lawyer can do at this point.'

'And if they find something?'

'There's nothing here to find.'

Molly wasn't so confident. 'You're sure?' she asked.

I hesitated, then I smiled. 'I will be after tomorrow.'

They came early the next day and kicked around in our stuff using twenty officers and two dogs. They took a variety of items for testing with my permission, naturally, including my hair and blood and Molly's .22 Magnum, but they took nothing we did not recognize. When they were gone I think we both felt exhausted, though we had done practically nothing all day. I suggested a horseback ride, the fresh air would do us good, but Molly wanted to fix herself a drink and call Lucy. I kicked around in the office until she was off the phone. On something of a whim I called the university's lawyer, hoping I could stir something up. He played hard-to-get, and we didn't actually speak to each other until five o'clock, nearly two hours after my first attempt to call him. 'The reason I called,' I said, 'I'm interested in negotiating a severance package.'

'I'm listening.'

'I need three years' salary and benefits. In exchange for that, I'll agree not to bring suit against the university.'

The university lawyer didn't sound especially impressed, but he told me he would pass the offer on to the president.

I had been told to go to hell quite a few times in my life but never quite with such dispassionate sweetness. 'While you're passing things on to him,' I said, 'you might want to let him know Denise Conway is going to tell the court that her ex-boyfriend stole her diary and handed a copy of it over to the university as evidence without her permission.'

The lawyer's silence hadn't a bit of condescension about it.

'That's the bad news,' I said. 'The really bad news is she's prepared to declare under oath her diary was nothing more than a fantasy and that she never said it was anything else.'

'That's ridiculous.'

'Could be,' I said. 'Then again, you haven't asked her, have you? Seems to me you might want to interview Ms Conway yourself before you commit yourself to a litigation that could cost you a hell of a lot more than three years' salary.'

The lawyer told me he would get back with me.

*   *   *

ROGER BEERY SHOWED up the following evening. Once I recognized Walt's Volvo, I went to the den where I kept the shotguns in a locked case. Grabbing the twelve-gauge and slipping half-a-dozen shells into it as I went, I headed out the backdoor with Molly right behind me.

We got to the driveway just as Roger was getting out of his father's car. I put my shotgun to my shoulder and pointed it at him.

'What's that for, Dave?'

'Get off our property before I shoot you,' I shouted.

'Jeez, that's real friendly.'

I fired into his windshield, and Roger jumped away from his car in stark terror.

'Next one's for you, fat boy,' I said, keeping the gun trained on him. 'Now get out. I'm not going to ask you again.'

'I've got something you might want to look at. I just want to give it to you and then I'll take off.'

'Try the mail.'

Roger was holding a DVD in his gloved hand and stooped down gingerly to leave it on the ground for us. 'How about I put it here. You're going to want to see this.' He looked at Molly. 'Both of you.'

'What is it?' Molly asked.

'Just look at it. I'll call you tomorrow about what it's going to cost you to keep it off the internet.'

With that he backed away and got in his car. I kept

my gun trained on him as he circled us and drove away.

Molly went for the DVD case, swearing hotly as she picked it up. 'What do you think it is?' she asked.

'Let's go find out.'

Inside the house, we took our coats off and headed for the living room. Neither of us spoke. I still had the shotgun in my hand, but I wasn't looking for Buddy Elder when he stepped out of the den.

Buddy jacked a shell into the chamber of my four-ten and brought it to his shoulder. I had the better weapon, but Buddy was pointing his at Molly's head. His eyes blackened, his nose broken, Buddy hardly looked like the congenial grad student I had met at Caleb's eight months earlier. 'I'm going to have to ask you to put the gun down, Dave.'

I set the gun on the floor gently, hoping Buddy would point his weapon in my direction. In fact, he stepped closer to Molly just in case I wanted to try him.

Once I had let go of the gun and stood up again, he relaxed slightly, though he didn't take the gun off Molly. 'Hope you all don't mind,' he told us with his southern drawl, 'but I let myself in by the side door with a key.'

Molly started toward him. A single step. Buddy brought the four-ten around until it was aimed at my crotch. 'You want to see Dave without his balls?'

'Buddy, please!'

'Don't worry. Nobody's going to get hurt as long as you both cooperate.' He nodded toward the DVD case Molly still held and gave her a smile. 'You figure out what you've got there, hon?'

The blood left her face.

'Dave, you're going to love this,' he told me.

I didn't answer. At the moment, I couldn't.

'What I want you to do, Molly, is go into the living room there and turn the lights on and then off three times.' When she had done this he told her, 'Now turn the lights on and let's watch a movie.'

Molly turned the television on and inserted the disk into the DVD player. Meanwhile, Buddy gestured with the shotgun for me to have a seat. He had Molly sit in the chair beside mine, and then he hit the remote.

For a moment we waited in silence. Then Buddy told us, 'You know, I could just shoot myself for not bringing the popcorn.'

THERE WAS NO SOUND ON THE recording. The scene began with Buddy's face pulling back from the camera lens. He turned and walked away from the camera and sat down on a couch in a darkened living room, the same one I had wrecked a couple nights before. A single lamp illuminated him. For nearly a minute nothing happened. Then Molly appeared. She was absolutely naked and carried two drinks.

Molly swore. Buddy tipped his weapon into my crotch. 'You don't move,' Buddy told her. 'You come out of that chair and Dave here is going to hurt.'

On the video Molly handed Buddy his drink and set her own on the coffee table. Then she slid down between his legs and began pulling at his belt, laughing and telling him something.

I heard Roger's Volvo coming up the hill again.

In the video Buddy made no effort to help Molly undress him. He actually seemed to enjoy watching her struggle with his jeans. When she had freed his erection, Buddy said to me, 'This here is my favourite part, Dave.'

Molly took his sex into her mouth, and Buddy pushed her hair away so the camera caught her face in profile.

We watched this for a minute or so before Buddy broke the silence. 'It's just like I've always said, Dave. You can take the girl off the street, but you just can't get the street off the girl.'

Our front hallway clicked open and closed quietly. Roger Beery appeared and immediately went for the twelve-gauge on the floor in the hallway. 'Hey! You started without me!'

Buddy grinned. 'Dave couldn't wait.'

Roger walked behind Buddy and stepped up in front of Molly. 'You like that, don't you? You like giving head?'

Molly swore at him, but Roger grinned and put the

tip of his gun in front of Molly's mouth, 'I want you to kiss this and make it wet for me.'

Molly spat on the gun, then she spat at Roger.

Buddy walked behind her chair, positioning himself carefully between Molly and me. He was facing Roger. 'We need to set some ground rules here, Molly,' he said. 'First off, this is just payback for the other night. Nobody needs to get killed. All we're going to do is give Dave here a little sex show. Nothing you haven't done before. If you don't want to cooperate,' Buddy pushed the gun toward my ear, 'then we go to plan B. Up to you really.'

At just that moment someone knocked at the back door.

Buddy swore. Roger looked frightened.

'I'll see who it is,' Buddy said, and walked out of our living room. Then he stopped. 'And if either of them starts to move, shoot Dave's nuts off.'

Roger smiled. 'It'll be a pleasure.'

I said softly so that Molly could hear, 'Wade.'

That was when she cried.

I SAW MY OLD MAN work some amazing deals, but the only time he ever worked pure magic was one night at the fairgrounds.

We'd taken the cars down to this field with all the other dealers, and people had a chance to look at everything all in the same place. We'd been working the thing for three days, and I'd taken a Z in trade from a girl named Debbie, Connie Q. in *Jinx*. The Q. was for Quick. Debbie was my first, which made me one of a large fraternity.

In a small town like DeKalb it doesn't take much to get a reputation, of course, but Deb was way past that. Deb was a legend. There wasn't a man in the greater metro area under forty, maybe a straight man breathing, who didn't know her car on sight. It had been a nice car once, but like Deb it was beginning to show some wear.

I had a little trouble closing her on a new Mustang because she was buying with cash and she didn't have enough. It looked like I was going to lose the deal when Milt took the T.O. I'm not sure, but I think Milt might be the only manager in history of the cars to pull a customer out of the closing booth and insist on a second demo drive when the only issue was price. They came back a couple of hours later, the purchase order signed, and Milt gave me a full commission, instead of splitting it. He slapped me on the back and told me that was the kind of guy he was. When his people needed help, he was there for them.

The next day I saw some kid looking at that Z, and walked over and started talking to him. The way he was looking at that car you would have thought it was Deb herself. Milt had jacked the price up a couple thousand above the recommended retail on a mint condition piece, because, he said, it was the most famous car in DeKalb. Truth was he needed to get back everything he'd given away on the Mustang. We'd had lookers all day, but when they heard the price they started looking elsewhere. I figured this kid was there like the rest of them, a bit of nostalgia and then he would move on. But he was just a little different. I noticed it the minute he looked up at me with a gullible smile and said, 'I got my first blow job in a car like this!'

'You sure it wasn't this exact same car?' I asked him.

For a moment, the kid stared at me in disbelief, then he looked at the car again. 'I don't know,' he said. 'It was a long time ago.'

We talked a little more, and I found out he was planning on getting married. The fiancée was looking at a used sport utility vehicle at another dealership, but the car was for him, and he wanted a sports car.

I worked him without much enthusiasm, and he bounced in and out three different times. He wanted that car about as much as he wanted one more summer evening with Deb, but when his fiancée came by for a look it was all over. She wasn't letting him buy that car on a dare!

All the same he came back one last time, the fiancée sitting in their car with her arms crossed. It was the last hour of a three-day sale, and the kid just wanted to look at the Z one more time.

Sometimes you have to wear people down. A good manager knows that, and he's patient, but sometimes people need a new face before they can make a decision. I saw Larry the Liar in the bullpen. Milt was pacing and kicking tires and smoking. Larry had his eye on the fiancée. The only thing she needed was to feel good.

Milt was too smart to send the wrong salesperson in, though. There wasn't any lie on earth going to make that girl feel good about buying Deb's Z.

That left Tubs. Milt told me later he didn't think there was a chance in hell to make the sale, but he had to give it a shot before he turned the lights off and we all went home.

I made the T.O. by introducing Tubs as my dad. Tubs was worn down from three days of it. I think he had sold six or seven cars every day, and he looked like it. He was running on empty. Tubs could turn on a pretty good smile when he bothered, but at ten o'clock at night with the last customer at the fairgrounds getting ready to make his getaway, Tubs didn't shake hands, and his smile was about as friendly as a piece of rusty barbwire.

'You going to buy this car or look at it, son?' That was all he said. Not even a pleased-to-meet-you.

The kid pulled his eyes off his last memory of freedom and tipped his head toward the fiancée. 'She don't like it.'

Tubs shook his head in disgust and turned away. 'If a man's wife doesn't like a car, he better not like it either!'

Tubs actually got a couple of steps away before the kid said, 'She ain't my wife.' Tubs stopped and looked at him as if he hadn't heard right. 'She's my fiancée,' the kid explained.

'*Fiancée*?' Tubs sounded surprised.

The kid nodded his head in perfect misery. 'Yes, sir.'

'You're not *married* to that woman?' Tubs stepped in closer to the kid.

The kid grinned. 'No, sir. Not yet.'

Now he got inside the kid's space, lowering his voice as if passing a great truth along: 'Let me tell you something, son. I don't want you to quote me on this, Lord help me if you do, but if you let a woman push you around *before* you marry her, you ain't got a chance in hell *after*!'

That kid gave Tubs a hard look, but it wasn't half as hard as Tubs's glare. I thought the kid might pop him, but what he did was, he said, 'To hell with it. I'm buying the son of a bitch!'

Milt asked Tubs later that night over a beer that Tubs never touched how he got that kid to go full pop on a beat-to-hell Z. 'That one,' Tubs answered with a sly grin, 'was my Be a Man Close, because you either are or you aren't.'

Chapter 28

THE FIRST BLAST OF THE SHOTGUN sounded from within the house, taking me back to the present.

I looked up at Roger Beery. He was distracted by the sound but it wasn't possible to come out of my chair.

He had his finger on the trigger, and the weapon was pointed between Molly and me. I was ten feet away. Molly's position, seated in a deep chair like my own, put her nearly fifteen feet from Roger. There was no possibility of fighting him and no chance for any of us, Roger included, once Buddy returned.

I searched my failing imagination for a way to distract Roger, but what I needed was a miracle, Tubs-style. Not his Gun in the Face Close, either. I didn't care to feel righteous in my grave. I needed to make Roger Beery understand that they had come out to the farm that evening together, but Buddy planned on going home alone. It was that simple, if only I could make him see it.

How would Tubs have handled it? I considered the matter for a moment, my thoughts interrupted by the second blast from the four-ten just outside the house. Wade had somehow managed to elude Buddy's first shot. I wasn't so confident he had escaped the second. I gave myself forty-five-to-sixty seconds. Tubs had closed that kid in about twenty. The difference was the young man was primed to make a choice. I glanced at Roger, who was staring at Molly. Roger had his mind on something else altogether.

'You understand Buddy is going to kill you here tonight?'

I said this with a degree of calm and insight one uses when stating the obvious.

Roger's sneer had a certain amusement about it. 'Why would he do that, Dave?'

'That's easy,' I said, handing him my car salesman's grin. 'He marries your widow, and the two of them live happily ever after with *your* money.'

'You don't know anything. Do you know that? You don't have a clue!'

'You're a very intelligent young man, Roger.'

'I'm a genius, Dave! And you're a moron.' He rocked his head back toward the TV, where the picture showed Molly straddling Buddy on the couch. 'You didn't have a clue, did you?'

'Tell me something,' I said. 'When you watch that, is it Molly or Buddy that you want?'

Two muffled shots came from close to the barn. There was enough time between them for the first to be a takedown, the second to finish it. Wade had gotten as far as the barn. That bought us another full minute.

I glanced toward Molly. She still had tears in her eyes, but she knew I was working Roger. Her muscles had the look of coiled steel.

'I guess you read my novel a little better than I thought.'

'Buddy read it?'

'Every word.'

'He wanted to know how to work you.'

'You don't know what's going on, Dave. You don't understand anything.'

'I know we're looking at a triple homicide inside the house tonight. Only question is who's man enough to walk away, you or Buddy.'

'Nobody's going to get killed. Buddy told you what were going to do.'

'Tonight is about Buddy and Denise tying up loose ends, Roger. As long as you're around, they've got a prison sentence hanging over their heads. As soon as they kill you, they can move on. If you don't see that, I don't give you more than two or three minutes to live.'

I heard the kitchen door open.

'You've got the twelve-gauge,' I told him. 'As long as you're holding it, he won't try anything. But you can kiss your ass goodbye the minute you put that gun down.'

Buddy called from the hallway. 'Son of a bitch got away!'

Roger looked at me uncertainly.

'To him, you're just another sucker he can take advantage of. But you can turn the tables on him... and even keep Denise. The beauty is no cop in the world is going to look at you for this. They'll think Buddy was out here alone. You walk out clean, just like he will if you give him the chance.'

Buddy came into the room. 'What was he talking about, Roger?'

Before Roger could answer, I said, 'I was telling your friend here how easy it was to kick your ass the other night.'

Buddy laughed. 'Plenty easy when you're holding a gun!'

'You're the expert on that.'

Buddy walked toward Molly, and nodded toward the TV screen. 'You remember what night that was, Molly?'

'The night you killed our dogs,' I said.

'I didn't touch your dogs, Dave. That was Roger. Roger hates dogs.'

On screen, Molly laughed as she rocked her hips over Buddy while his hands squeezed her breasts.

'What do you think Roger? You want some of that sweet pussy or a little professional head?'

Roger's eyes darted from Buddy to me. 'I'm ready for a blow job.'

'You heard the man, Molly! Get down on your knees and show us how a pretty little pregnant girl makes her living on the streets.'

Molly slid out of the chair and knelt in front of Roger. 'Just don't hurt us,' she said.

'You've got my word on that,' Buddy answered. 'You cooperate and we all walk away good friends. Course, if you go to the sheriff or Dave comes after one of us, Lucy gets her own copy and we put another one on the internet for all your friends. That fair enough to keep the two of you honest?'

'Let's just get it over with.'

Buddy laughed. 'Damn, woman! This isn't your husband. Show some enthusiasm.'

'You know what?' Roger said as he stepped away from Molly and faced me, 'I think I'd rather have Dave do it.'

Buddy laughed. 'There you go!' Buddy pointed his gun at my head. 'You heard the man, Dave!'

With Buddy's four-ten close to my ear, I could see Roger lifting the twelve-gauge, the barrelling coming up level on Buddy. Buddy saw it too, but he couldn't respond in time. Roger's shot hit him in the chest. I felt the percussion of the blast, the blood splattering across my hair and cheek. The birdshot from Buddy's weapon hit our ceiling as he fell, showering me with plaster.

Molly came off her knees the moment Roger's gun discharged. Only a step away, she got hold of Roger's gun and struggled to hang on while Roger whipped the gun about, trying to throw her free. I got to them before Roger could turn the gun in my direction, and cracked his jaw with a right hook that felt better and purer than any punch I'd ever thrown.

Molly came away with the gun and rolled to a sitting position in time to see Buddy crawling up over the back of the chair I had been sitting in. His gun was already aiming in our direction when she pulled the trigger and blew his face away.

I GOT TO MY FEET AND WENT to Buddy. I checked his carotid artery for a pulse. He was still alive, but not for long. His legs twitched. His face was blackened, ruined. One eye had been ripped out. The other was open, blood pooling in it.

Picking up the four-ten, I aimed it at Roger as Molly searched him for a weapon. When she had finished I told her to call the sheriff's department.

I heard her on the phone. Two people shot, she said into the phone. She gave directions to the farm. She answered several questions with a yes or no. Roger tried to talk once, but I ordered him to shut up. He stared at me, his breathing ragged, his eyes wet. He thought I had lied to him, and now, because of it, he was going to jail.

I told Molly to hang up. She looked at me, frowning. Police agencies, I knew, liked to keep people on the line during an emergency. 'Hang up,' I said. This time, she did. 'Flash the lights just like last time.' She walked over to the light switch, three times off, three on. She didn't understand but she knew I was up to something. Our phone rang, but I told Molly not to answer.

I looked at Roger. 'You came in two cars?'

He shook his head. 'I drove us out.'

I smiled at him. 'Buddy needed a ride home, Roger. He couldn't very well drive your car away if he wanted the police to think you were out here by yourself.'

Roger stared at me, trying with his impressive IQ to comprehend what I was saying. I wasn't sure he did until we heard a car pull into our driveway and start up the hill.

'Sounds to me like a Mercury Marquis. That sound like a Merc to you?'

Roger blinked stupidly, but he finally got it.

'Now who's the dumb ass?' I snarled.

Buddy Elder's car idled in the circle in front of our house.

'If she drives away before the cops show up, she'll beat any indictment they throw at her. The thing to do is to get her inside the house and keep her here. That way she can't come up with some alibi. You get her involved in this and you can deal with the prosecutor. She drives off, you're looking at death row for Johnna's murder – with Denise as the state's star witness.'

Roger's eyes shifted nervously.

'Of course, if you're in love with the woman, the best thing you can do is tell her to run. Believe me, she will.' I kicked up one shoulder. 'At least one of you will be free to spend all that money.'

The car door slammed. I motioned to Molly to move back out of sight and pushed one of the chairs around a bit so I would have an unobstructed view to Roger as I retreated to cover. Roger started to stand up, but I told him, 'Stay down, like you're wounded, or I promise you will be.'

I listened for the sound of sirens, but the night was still silent. The door at the back porch screeched open and slammed shut.

'Buddy?' Denise called.

'In here!' Roger shouted. 'Buddy's been shot!'

We heard Denise running down the hallway. She burst into the room, eyes wide open in fright, her face bloodless. Seeing Buddy stretched out, his face broken apart, she ran to him and threw herself down over him with a shriek.

I went forward quickly, jerking her up by her coat. She made no resistance when I threw her over the back of the chair and searched her roughly for a weapon. While I did, Denise screamed profanities at Roger with a nastiness that surprised me. What happened? What had he done to Buddy? Roger answered in the same spirit. They had been planning to kill him!

I told them both to shut up. When they ignored me, I tossed her to the floor and stepped toward Roger, offering the butt of the four-ten as a threat. Roger shut up, but he continued staring at his newly-wed wife incredulously, and I couldn't resist.

'You didn't really believe she loved you?'

Roger didn't answer me. He did turn, however, and watched Buddy and Molly working themselves toward a mutual climax on our television. It was, under the circumstances, an eloquent rebuttal.

I heard the first sirens and left the room, intending to snap on the floodlights so they could find Wade. I got as far as the front hall when I heard the report of a handgun. I was down before I registered that I had been shot. My back on fire, my brain struggling to understand what had just occurred, I heard two more shots from a handgun, followed by the unmistakable blast of the twelve-gauge.

I tried to crawl across the parquet floor toward the four-ten I had dropped when I fell, but Molly came to me. As she held me, I tried to speak, but I couldn't. Turning, I saw Denise Conway lying across Buddy Elder's legs. The back of her head was broken apart, her peroxide blonde hair stained in blood. Roger Beery lay on his back, his arms and legs twitching oddly, blood on his face.

The front hallway lit up with whirling red and blue lights, the last thing I saw before I passed out.

Chapter 29

I WAS CONSCIOUS AGAIN when they settled me into the ambulance, but not for long. Later, when I woke up, I looked at the hospital room, did not especially like what I saw, and went back to sleep.

At ten I was fully awake and in a different room. Molly was in a chair close to my bed. From the number of magazines at her feet, I guessed she had been there quite a while. My voice cracked when I tried to speak. I felt dizzy, but I did not pass out.

'Wade?'

'He got out of surgery a couple of hours after you did. It was bad, but he's going to make it.'

'What happened?'

'Buddy had a revolver in his coat. Denise found it or knew it was there. After she shot you, she turned the gun on Roger. I don't think she even knew I was in the room.'

'They're both dead?'

'All three of them.' After a moment she said to me, 'I have the DVD, David.'

I closed my eyes, nodding, message received. When I woke up again Molly was gone. I talked to the nurse, then to the surgeon. That afternoon my mother showed up. She was the one who told me Molly wouldn't be back. 'She said to tell you she's closing the house up.'

I SAW KIP DALTON only after I had refused to talk to anyone else. I told him I had put together most of the pieces of the puzzle before Roger drove out to the farm, but not all of it.

Kip smiled at me. 'Anything you can give me will help, professor.'

'Buddy and Denise killed Walt and Barbara for the inheritance, but they needed to get rid of their new partner to get the money.'

'What did Johnna Masterson have to do with anything?'

I shook my head. 'Sport mostly, though it got blood on Roger's hands, which gave them a degree of control. I expect Buddy showed Roger how they could frame me for her murder and do whatever they wanted to her. That would have appealed to Roger, I think.'

'Well… they did.' Kip's face twitched as he said this, and I knew it was worse for Johnna than I could imagine.

'The night they came out to the farm, they said they were going to let us go if we cooperated.'

Dalton nodded. He understood how killers use false promises to control their victims.

'I think Buddy had convinced Roger they were going to terrorize us for a while and then stage another murder-suicide. Another bad marriage that ended badly. Truth was Buddy planned to kill Roger so Denise could inherit Roger's money. Given my history with Roger and Denise, the sheriff would not have been inclined to look any farther than the evidence right in front of him: Roger shows up at the farm and all three of us go down with gunshot wounds. No one would even think to ask Buddy Elder about an alibi.'

'According to your wife it would have worked if your neighbour hadn't stumbled into the middle of things.'

'When Buddy went out to take care of Wade, I had a chance to convince Roger he was the patsy unless he was man enough to make the first move.'

'You must have talked fast.'

'Have you tested the gun Denise used on Roger and me?'

Dalton nodded. 'It's the same gun that killed Johnna Masterson.'

'You know that night, I couldn't understand why Buddy took the gun with birdshot and let Roger grab the twelve-gauge. I figured he overlooked the difference in the guns, but I should have been known better. Buddy hadn't overlooked anything from the start. That was no different. The weapon he intended to use on Roger was the handgun they had used to kill Johnna. Once he eliminated Roger with it he could turn the birdshot on Molly and me, and no problem at all if he had to shoot us a few times before it took. The sloppier the work the more convincing the scene. The point was to make it look like we had a gun battle using *our* guns, as if Roger showed up to talk, and things got out of hand.

'That .38 is yours?'

I shook my head. 'Buddy told me one time it's cold. I expect it is, but once you matched it to the Masterson homicide and found my prints on it, you would have believed it was mine.'

'Closing out our investigation of that case as well,' Dalton muttered.

'At that point Buddy's only problem would have been controlling Denise Conway, who suddenly had five million all to herself, but somehow I don't think that would have been a problem.'

'I started doing some background on Mr Elder after you passed that polygraph, Professor. On paper he looked just fine, but when I called down to Louisiana I found out Denise Conway was his half-sister. They had the same mother, grew up together in the same house.

362

'According to the mother Denise got married about three years ago. Husband had some money. Eight months later, poor soul killed himself.'

'Police reopening that case?'

'I recommended they take another look at it. I'll tell you something else,' Dalton added with a sly grin. 'Your friend Mr Elder was plenty smart. He went to college just like his transcripts say, but their mother tells me Denise was the one in the family who tested off the charts. According to her, that girl was a genuine prodigy.'

'Denise was behind the whole thing?'

'Appears to be the case.'

GAIL ETHERIDGE DROPPED by one morning before I could get around much. She wanted to know if I intended to bring suit against the Beery estate. She wasn't drumming up business, just curious, I expect, but I suggested she find our neighbour before some shark got hold of him and have a little talk with him. If anyone deserved the mother lode, I said, it was Billy Wade. Gail said she would look in on him after she left me. 'Be sure you do,' I said, handing her a twenty, 'and give him this for me if you will.'

Gail waved the bill at me. 'What's this for?'

'He'll know.'

Pocketing the twenty she told me, 'I wanted to come by and apologize for not believing you, David.'

'I didn't have much of a track record,' I said. 'From your perspective it must have looked like pure self-destruction.'

'Well, you can be an unbelievably stubborn man sometimes.'

'No hard feelings, Gail.'

'How are things going at school?'

'They offered me three years' salary if I'd just go away.' Gail nodded at this with a vague look of satisfaction. She had probably calculated something like this and knew, too, as I did, that if I pushed I could get a lot more out of them and even keep my job. 'I told them to go to hell. I said I'd go away for nothing.'

Gail's satisfied smile curdled. 'I take it you're representing yourself?'

I laughed. 'What gave me away?'

She appeared to want to give me some advice, but as I wasn't paying for it she restrained herself admirably and changed the subject. 'Molly's going through with the divorce, I understand?'

My laughter caught in my throat. 'Looks that way.'

'I thought you two had worked things out.'

'I was in trouble, Gail. Molly wouldn't leave me until she got me out of it. That's just the way she is.'

'You're a fool to let a woman like that get away.'

'Molly's not the most forgiving woman in the world.'

'I guess I'm missing something.'

364

I didn't answer her. Gail could think what she wanted.

I SPENT A WEEK IN FLORIDA once I was up and moving around a little. Molly and Doc were already doing business together. She had a broken down house, a genuine catastrophe, she was living in and a second under contract that she intended to patch up for the snowbirds. She seemed happy to be starting over, a bit uncomfortable with me around but too polite to say so.

Lucy was doing well in school, working three nights a week giving private lessons on Ahab to rich kids and training a couple of wild-ass quarter horses fresh off the racetrack for the owner of the stable. We had a talk one evening on a horseback ride about the lie Lucy had told me, the affair that never was. Her idea, she confessed.

It might well have been Lucy's creation, or Lucy might have imagined it was, but we both knew her mother, if not in fact instigating it, had gone along with it. I didn't care to point this out because Molly wasn't really the one to blame. It was my fault.

'Do you have any idea,' I asked, 'what your mother went through those first couple of years after you were born, Lucy?'

Jezebel skittered because she felt Lucy's body stiffen. We were walking suddenly on forbidden ground.

'I can imagine,' she said carefully.

'You're way ahead of me then.'

'She never told you?'

'She never told me, and I never asked.'

Lucy considered this for a long time without offering a comment.

'I don't know who was more afraid of the truth, Lucy, your mother or me. I guess I was always afraid if I heard about how she got through it, I wouldn't be able to love her in quite the same way. I think she understood that or started believing it herself. We walked around your mother's finest moment, the choice to give you life, and ended up turning it into something she thought she should be ashamed of.'

Lucy blinked.

'What your mother did, coming off the streets and making a life for the two of you, not one girl in a thousand could have accomplished, and I made her think she had to keep it to herself.'

'I don't understand why she wants a divorce!'

'You remember when I told you that silence is the biggest lie of all?' Lucy nodded. 'Well, our lies caught up with us, kid.'

I MET ROBERT THE REALTOR, who wasn't an entirely offensive character. He and Molly were intimate. I could tell by the way he shook hands with me.

I had imagined something else for Molly and me

when I got down to see her, but it wasn't going to happen. A week into it and I knew the only thing Molly wanted was for me to take off. There were no words to erase our history together, and for a time it seemed there weren't even words to talk about it. The night before I left we had dinner together in Naples. Afterwards we walked along the beach. I think in the dark with the wind around us to carry our words off to sea we could finally speak about things that mattered.

She said she was sorry she had put Lucy into the middle of things. She should never have done that. She was the one who had left the farm for a drive with Buddy the night Johnna Masterson disappeared.

'It was my fault,' I answered. 'I should have said something. Instead, I just pretended to believe you both.'

'When did you know?'

I laughed and looked out at the dark mass of ocean. 'I knew from the start, Molly. I knew it from the moment Lucy told me she met Buddy at a frat party. The kid is a terrible liar. It's one of the things I love about her.'

Molly considered this for a moment. 'Would it have made any difference if you had said something?'

'You would have known upfront that whatever happened between you and Buddy doesn't change how I feel about you.'

Molly walked for a while without speaking, and I thought she might be ready to give me another chance. When she finally spoke, I knew all my chances were behind me. 'When I look at you, David, I see that night all over again.'

I wondered if she meant the deaths of Buddy and Roger and Denise or if she was talking about the humiliation of watching herself on Buddy's homemade video.

'We beat them, Molly.'

'We didn't beat anyone. We survived.'

'We survived together,' I said.

'I need to start over. I don't want to carry that night with me for the rest of my life.'

At the airport the next morning, Molly and Lucy were there to send me back into the winter. I got a hug from both of them, a daughter's kiss from Lucy.

I PICKED UP WORK AT THE FORD dealership in DeKalb a few days later. I told Milt, 'For a while.' Then I gave him a wink. 'And don't ask me to lie. I won't do it even if it costs me!'

Milt grinned with his big horse teeth. 'You're giving me shivers!'

'He was a good man, wasn't he?'

'Tubs? Tubs was golden, David. Look at the boys he raised if you don't believe it.'

'I never knew that until he saved my life,' I said.

Milt smiled but he didn't know what I was talking about. 'When was that?'

'The night I got shot.'

Milt tried to put it together, but he couldn't understand how a man already in the grave could save his son's life.

Back in the wastelands again, I got my wish and managed to put my name on the wall every month as the number one salesperson, but even stone-cold sober I wasn't any Tubs Albo.

I kept in touch with Molly by e-mail. It was all business, selling off property a piece at a time, moving the date of dissolution back a couple of different times so we could settle things financially and have the divorce as the last event of our relationship. Lucy kept me informed about the more intimate matters of their life. Oklahoma had offered her a full scholarship, and she accepted it. Molly sold the house they were living in and was shopping for another catastrophe she could resurrect. Robert bounced out of Molly's life, and now there was a man named Ted, who was a cabinetmaker. Fifty-something. Flat ass. Boring.

One day, in early June, I was working a couple in the closing booth when Milt called me out. 'Got a customer wants a pickup. Won't deal with anyone but you.'

I pointed at the desk where I had been working. 'I've got buyers here, Milt.'

'I'll take the T.O. myself, David, no split. You go take care of the pickup.'

I knew better than to hope for what I was hoping, but I couldn't help myself. Milt was conning me, and Milt didn't play games when it came to making money. There was no way he'd pull me off a close to go talk to some tire kicker about a pickup. So there was only one person it could be.

Two salesmen were keeping Molly company when I walked up. I doubt they were talking trucks.

'You looking for a pickup?' I asked.

Molly smiled at me the way she had the day I met her. 'Might be.'

The salesmen left us, and I walked over to be close, though not daring to touch her. 'What brings you north, Molly?'

'I got an offer on the farm a couple of days ago.'

'A good one?'

She smiled. 'Good enough.'

I waited.

'I thought before I took it I'd talk to you about it.'

'The farm is yours, Molly. You don't need to talk to me.'

'That's the thing. The minute I got the offer I knew we needed to talk. When I sell the farm that's it. It's all gone.'

'I thought that was the point.'

'So did I.'

'Well, if you're asking me my opinion, I'd say the only way to know is for the two of us to drive to the farm and take a look at it.'

She laughed. 'That's a long drive just for a look!'

I gave her a sly smile. 'They've got motels between here and there if we get sleepy.'

She grinned prettily at the idea. 'You can leave? Just like that?'

'I can do any damn thing I feel like, Molly. I'm fearless these days.'

'I knew a guy like that once.'

'Why'd you let him go?'

'He got careful. That was part of it. Mostly he knew too much about me.'

'Hard to forgive a man that, I expect.'

'We need to talk,' she said after a moment. 'About a lot of things.'

I took her hand and held it for a moment to be sure she wanted me as much as I wanted her, and then I said, 'What do you say we do that on the way home?'

Acknowledgements

I wrote this novel because I was fortunate enough to meet Martha Ineichen a quarter of a century ago. I hope you like this one, darling. I want to thank the people who offered their insights after reading an early draft of this story: Shirley Underwood, Rick Williams, Harriet McNeal, and Burdette Palmberg. You helped me more than you know. A special thank you goes to my brother Douglas, who introduced me to Tubs Albo when it mattered; to Matt Jockers I have real gratitude for teaching me the delicate art of patching drywall. It's a skill every novelist should possess. Much appreciation as well to Don Jennermann for a lifetime of encouragement in this hard, beautiful profession.

Finally I wanted to thank my agent Jeffrey Simmons and my editor Ed Handyside, the two men who brought this story to life.

CRAIG SMITH lives with his wife, Martha, in Lucerne, Switzerland. A former university professor, he holds a doctorate in philosophy from the University of Southern Illinois.

His first novel, published in the UK as *Silent She Sleeps* and in the US as *The Whisper of Leaves*, won bronze medal in the mystery category of ForeWord magazine's Book of the Year Awards.

The Painted Messiah and *The Blood Lance*, the first of his novels to chronicle the exploits of T.K. Malloy, have received international acclaim and been published across the globe in ten languages.

www.craigsmithnovels.ch

International Best-Selling Action
from Craig Smith

The Painted Messiah

A legend persists that, after the 'scourging', Pilate commanded that his victim be painted from life. Somewhere, the painting survives, the only true image of Christ, granting the gift of everlasting life to whoever possesses it.

Kate Kenyon, the wealthy young widow of an English aristocrat, has an addiction to mortal risk. She feeds it by engaging in the armed robbery of priceless artefacts with her accomplice and lover Ethan Brand. Their latest target is a priceless 'Byzantine' icon hidden in the tower of a chateau by Lake Lucerne. So far they have never had to shoot anyone. This time will be different.

Thomas Malloy is a retired CIA man looking for his first lucrative freelance assignment. His chance comes with a presidential favour to a rich but ailing televangelist. Malloy's task seems simple enough: pick up the preacher's newly acquired painting from a Zurich bank and get it to the airport. But, once in Switzerland, Malloy's old friend, the enigmatic Contessa Claudia de Medici tries to warn him off his mission.

Sir Julian Corbeau is an international criminal holed up in Switzerland to avoid US extradition proceedings. He is also the sadistic head of the modern Knights Templar. He *had* the painting and now he desperately wants it back and swears to wreak a bloody revenge upon those who stole it.

As the contenders vie for possession the bullets fly, the body count rises and the secrets of the portrait gradually unfold.

TRANSLATED INTO FRENCH, GERMAN, ITALIAN, SPANISH, RUSSIAN, CZECH, POLISH, GREEK AND TURKISH

OUT NOW   ISBN: 978-1-905802-15-9   Price: £7.99

Craig Smith's sizzling sequel to
The Painted Messiah

The Blood Lance

Kufstein, Austria, 1939
At the foot of a mountain known as *The Wilder Kaiser* lies the
body of an SS officer, his neck broken but his face a picture of
bliss and serenity. The dead man is known to history as Otto
Rahn, Himmler's own archaeologist. Rahn's pursuit of the
legendary Blood Lance of the Cathars has not only led to his
own downfall but set in motion a tragic chain of events reaching
far beyond the holocaust.

Switzerland 1997
Lord Robert Kenyon is a wealthy financier and a senior member
of a humanitarian order calling themselves The Knights of the
Holy Lance. Whilst climbing the North face of the Eiger with
his new bride, he is attacked and murdered and his young wife
Kate left for dead.

New York City 2008
When billionaire Jack Farrell, long suspected of connections to
European crime syndicates cuts loose after defrauding his own
company, ex CIA agent Thomas Malloy is assigned to track
him down. The trail leads to Germany and the Order of the
Holy Lance. With his friends, former art thieves Kate and Ethan
Brand, Malloy set out to unlock the secrets of the order: Malloy
seeks his man; Kate must find the truth about what happened
on the slopes of the Eiger eleven years before – and exact her
vengeance. Their first step is to kidnap a corrupt lawyer,
connected to the order, from his home in Hamburg. Things
don't quite run to plan – and all hell breaks loose.

OUT NOW   ISBN: 978-1-905802-29-6   Price: £7.99

Scotland has a new crime detective: a big man with a big heart... and very few scruples

The Stone Gallows
C. David Ingram

DC Cameron Stone spent three months in intensive care before he could recall what happened: the high speed pursuit of a vice baron through the night streets of Glasgow that took the life of a teenage mother and her child. Then the message from Audrey on the back of a 'get well soon' card announcing that she had left him and taken their young son, Mark, with her. Booze, anti-depressants and therapy have all failed to enable him to resume his old job.

So now Stone lives the worst part of town. He pays the rent by running errands for a private detective. His chores include tracking down a teenage runaway and surveillance for a woman who thinks her husband is sleeping with her sister. He's also paid by his former colleagues to do the work that's not quite clean enough for them to do themselves- putting the fear of God into any local scumbag who thinks he can't be touched.

It's been a bad week. Audrey has moved into the plush home of a plastic surgeon and is getting difficult about access to Mark. He finds his runaway in a brothel and just gets roughed-up for his trouble. There's the knife wielding kids on the stairs outside his flat and the daubing on his door: *Burn in Hell Baby Killer*. The only brightness on his horizon is his growing friendship with Liz, the sunny Irish nurse who lives on the next floor.

But things are about to get worse for Cameron Stone. Somebody is out to destroy him and everything he loves- unless he can get to them first.

'This great book makes me want to read the next instalment- Ingram having promised some interesting times ahead for Cameron Stone.' Paul Blackburn *Eurocrime*

'There were some stunning debuts last year but if we could only pick one it would be this world class Scottish thriller... With a cracking storyline and dialogue so authentic you can hear the neds speak, this Paisley author scored a massive hit with a debut that promises to be the start of something big.'
Shari Low *The Daily Record* January 2010

OUT NOW   ISBN: 978-1-905802-20-3   Price £7.99

The Spy Who Came for Christmas

David Morrell

On Christmas Eve in snow-covered Santa Fe, New Mexico, tens of thousands of pedestrians stroll through the festively decorated streets. Among them is Paul Kagan, a spy on the run trying desperately to protect a special package; a baby who just might be the key to a lasting peace in the Middle East. He is pursued closely by three extremely dangerous men, members of the Russian mafia whom he has just betrayed.

Attempting to elude his hunters, Kagan seeks refuge in a quiet house on the outskirts of the town. Once inside he discovers it is occupied by a woman and her 12-year-old son hiding from other evils and whom he has now put in mortal danger as his hunters manage to track him down. In the tense hours that follow, Kagan tries to calm the woman and the boy by telling them the spy's version of the traditional Nativity story as he prepares the house for the onslaught he knows to be coming...

'Master storyteller David Morrell gives us an amazing holiday classic that thrills us with heart-pounding suspense while tugging at our emotions.'

Tess Gerritson, best-selling author of *The Bone Garden*

OUT NOW   ISBN: 978-1-905802-18-0   Price £7.99